Adventures in Godhood

Arlene F. Marks

Milton, Ontario

This is a work of fiction. That means the people and many of the specific places described in this book do not actually exist, even though they may share a name and/or characteristics with ones that do. So, do not go looking for Carewe's in Yorkville, or the Crown and Ha'penny pub, or the blessed laundromat in the Cornerstone Plaza, or (Lord help you) Pussyjoy Enterprises on Eglinton Avenue. You will only be disappointed. There are several institutions of higher learning in Toronto, but none of them is named Upper Canada University; and if there ever was a Fun 'n' Feathers Strip Club in the city, it has long since closed. However, you can be assured that the view at night of Toronto Harbour does exist and is magnificent when seen from about ten storeys up.

Brain Lag Publishing
Milton, Ontario
http://www.brain-lag.com/

Cover design by Catherine Fitzsimmons

Library and Archives Canada Cataloguing in Publication

Title: Adventures in godhood / Arlene F. Marks.
Names: Marks, Arlene F., 1947- author.
Identifiers: Canadiana (print) 20210244429 | Canadiana (ebook) 20210244526 | ISBN 9781928011583
   (softcover) | ISBN 9781928011590 (ebook)
Classification: LCC PS8561.R2868 A78 2021 | DDC C813/.54—dc23

Acknowledgements

This baby has had a long gestation and many midwives, and I would like to thank some of them here.

Thank you to the friends, colleagues, and family members who have taken the time to read and comment on the manuscript at various stages of its development, in particular Clinton Cronk, Shelley Black, David Marks, Bette Walker, and the members of my writing group, the Collingwood Writers' Collective.

Thank you also to Marilyn Kleiber, a valued friend for many years, and to Ed Greenwood, my "Joe and Marge", who has never been too busy to read over my work.

And a special thank you to my publisher, Catherine Fitzsimmons, for loving the characters in this book as much as I do.

Chapter One

2019
May 27

The pigeon exploded on Detective Marty Breck's fifth-floor window ledge at 7:08 on a Monday morning. One second the bird was there, doing its little bobble-head strut, and the next it was gone—*pouf!*—leaving nothing behind but a crimson smear across the outside of the glass pane and a scattering of grey and white feathers on the sill.

His gaze having been inexplicably drawn to the window just a moment earlier, Marty flinched, nearly spilling his coffee as he slammed the mug down on the nearest flat surface and dived for cover behind the sofa. But there was no further gunfire, no shower of razor-sharp glass fragments. The window remained intact. There wasn't even a bullet hole.

Evidently, the pigeon had been the target.

Marty gloved up, raised the window sash, and conducted a careful inspection of the wooden outer frame. He found some peeling of paint, some wearing of edges—but no sign of a bullet, and no damage to the concrete ledge, either. The shot had gone straight past Marty's window. That meant the shooter must have been leaning out one of the other fifth-floor windows on this side of the building.

Grimly, Detective Breck lowered the sash again and removed his gloves. He had no love for pigeons. They were nothing more than rats with feathers. Nonetheless, a fired weapon was a serious matter in Toronto. A police matter. Snatching up his phone, Breck speed-dialed the station house.

"Dispatch," announced the voice at the other end.

Marty's heart dropped. Al Gerber, again? Just hearing the man's voice brought back unpleasant high school memories.

Bravely, he continued, "This is Detective Martin—"

"Right. What is it now, Breck? Someone's cat up a tree? A UFO sighting, maybe?" Gerber drawled.

Marty could practically hear his lip curl with disdain.

"Actually, I'm reporting a shooting death."

"You're—!" There was a sound like a crash. Marty smiled inwardly as he visualized Gerber falling off his chair in surprise. When the dispatcher came back on the line, he was all business. "What's your location, Detective, and what do you need?"

"I need a couple of uniformed constables to help me canvass the fifth floor of my apartment building and determine where the shot came from."

"And where is the body?"

"Part of it is still on my window ledge. The rest disintegrated when the bullet hit it."

Gerber paused. "You're saying the victim was a bird? Good one, Breck! I guess you suspect there's been *fowl play*. Hey, maybe it was a hit on a *stool pigeon* to keep it from *singing*!"

Now the dispatcher was falling off his chair for a different reason. Marty let out a long-suffering sigh. "Listen, what I suspect is that there's been a firearms violation," he tried to explain.

It was no use. Gerber couldn't hear him—he was still laughing uproariously at his own lame wit. And unfortunately, with no physical evidence to prove that a shot had in fact been fired, there really wasn't anything to report.

"To hell with it," Marty muttered. Ending the call, he poured the rest of his coffee into the sink and finished getting ready for work.

⸝⸝⸝

Later that day, Johnny and Flo were sitting on their customary bench in High Park, tossing chunks of stale bread onto an expanse of fresh-mown lawn. They watched in amusement as the pigeons they'd attracted raced back and forth after the free food, like tennis players chasing volleys. Abruptly, all the birds froze in place. For a moment there was total silence. Then a very unpigeonlike noise arose from the middle of the flock.

"Do you hear that?" whispered Flo.

Johnny nodded. "It sounds like a car with a weak battery."

In a tattoo of beating wings, the pigeons took flight. All but one. As Johnny and Flo stared in horrified fascination, the bird that was uttering the coughing, whining sound rocked in place for a second. Then it began ballooning in stages, as though someone were inflating it one breath at a time.

"It looks sick," Flo remarked uncertainly. "Maybe we should find another bench."

This time Johnny shook his head. "Maybe we should just get behind this one," he started to say. But before he could finish, there was a sudden *pouf!* and they were sprayed head to foot with gore and feathers.

"Did that bird just—?" sputtered Flo, her nose wrinkling with disgust as with thumb and forefinger she set about plucking bits of pigeon off her sleeves and pant legs.

"Spontaneous explosion," Johnny confirmed solemnly. "I've heard about this, but only in connection with antiquated mines and old mortar shells. Never thought I'd see it happen to a bird."

As he was reaching into his pants pocket for a tissue, they heard the sound of laughter. Johnny and Flo turned and saw a young man standing ten feet away from them. He was wearing jeans and a team windbreaker, and had obviously been using the smart phone in his hand to record their mishap.

Flo leaped to her feet. "Did you do this?" she demanded, pointing an outraged finger at him. "Just to have something to post on some video channel? You—you're a monster!"

Meanwhile, Johnny was doing something more practical. He'd pulled out his own phone and was taking a picture of the perpetrator to show the authorities. "The police are going to hear about this," he warned.

"Knock yourself out, old man," said the kid, grinning as he jogged away.

~~~

Every weekday morning for the past six weeks, Ellie O'Toole had descended into the gloomy bowels of the old medical building on the Upper Canada University campus to begin a seven-hour shift as Dr. Phinegal's lab assistant.

This structure was the first to be built when the university was established back in the 1880s. Med students commonly referred to the basement as "the dungeons", owing to its narrow, dimly-lit passageways, its tiny rooms with barred windows, and its heavy oaken doors with stout wrought iron fittings. However, there is an exception to every rule, and in this case it was Phinegal's spacious and well-lit lab. Though hardly cutting edge in terms of the technology it contained, it was an oasis of modernity by comparison with the rest of the rooms below ground.

Phinegal taught in the mornings, then lunched in the faculty dining hall, leaving Ellie alone with two dozen caged rats from nine a.m. until one in the afternoon. She didn't mind, though. In fact, by now she actually preferred their company to his, and felt relieved whenever he was late in arriving—which had been happening quite often lately, making her suspect that he might be feeling the same way
~~~

about her.

Phinegal's instructions had been clear enough for even a high school student to follow, as he'd made a point of informing her several times already. Rats in cages marked with a large red A were to receive twice-daily doses from the syringes with the red caps. Rats in the cages labelled with the large blue B got their shots from the syringes with the blue caps. One group was getting a placebo. The other was receiving something that Phinegal had concocted while working alone one night. He hadn't put a name to it yet, choosing instead to give it a numerical code.

Six weeks into the experiment, Ellie still had no idea which group was which, or what was in the solutions she was injecting. Obviously, Phinegal knew, since he prepared the syringes himself and put them into the fridge. And he'd made a convincing enough proposal to the university's allocation committee to secure funding for his work, so the committee members had to know the purpose of his research as well. Everyone else, including his lab assistant, was apparently being kept in the dark.

Phinegal had been hinting at some dramatic effect she should watch for—"a stunning development" were his exact words—but so far nothing of note had occurred. She had meticulously followed the schedule he'd laid out, and her recorded observations had all been the same: no change in any of the rats. Not in their appearance, or their behaviour, or their feeding habits. *Nada.* Ellie had certainly had more interesting summer jobs during her undergrad years at UCL, but none that paid as well as this one. So, hers not to reason why.

On this particular Wednesday morning, Ellie let herself into the lab and dropped her backpack onto the desk just inside the door. As she was shrugging off her jacket, she heard a noise that gave her pause. It seemed to be coming from the direction of the cages, but it was too low-pitched to be made by any of the animals. It sounded more like a machine that was having trouble starting. A car with a sick battery, perhaps. Or a gas-powered lawnmower clearing its throat.

Stepping gingerly, she followed the sound and found herself standing in front of one of the cages marked with an A. Something was wrong with the black hooded rat inside that cage. Its mass had apparently doubled overnight. Its albino cage-mate was frantically attempting to dig an escape tunnel, and even the animals in other cages were pressing themselves into corners, trying to put as much distance as possible between the hooded rat and themselves.

Ellie pulled out her phone and began shooting video. Was this the dramatic change Phinegal had been talking about earlier? As she was debating whether she ought to quarantine the still-expanding rat, all at once—*pouf!*—it exploded, launching bits of itself through the bars of its cage in every direction.

A considerable amount of rat ended up on Ellie's face and clothing. (Her phone had very sensibly leaped out of her hand at the moment of the blast and was now lying on the floor halfway across the room.)

That settled it, she thought, using both forefingers to squeegee rodent gore and clumps of black and white fur off her cheeks and forehead. B was definitely the control group.

When he arrived, Dr. Phinegal was less than pleased with the observations she had recorded. However, given the supporting evidence—which she had carefully preserved in plastic baggies after exhaustively photographing the scene of the phenomenon—he couldn't dispute them. Nor could he fire her for ruining the experiment, since she'd spent the next few hours injecting the remaining twenty-three rats on schedule, making her notes about each one, and then returning the lab to its previous orderly condition. He couldn't even scold her for making a lab coat dirty—the explosion had happened before she could put one on. Obviously frustrated and wanting her gone, Phinegal was left with just one option. He gave her the rest of the day off.

Ellie didn't wait around for him to change his mind. Throwing her jacket on over her blood-spattered clothing, she snatched up her backpack and headed for home.

Ellie lived alone in a small apartment just off-campus, two floors above a laundromat in a strip mall that had seen better days. The Greater Toronto Area was an expensive place to live. Normally, a full-time student wouldn't have been able to afford her own flat. However, the property was owned by someone who apparently owed her grandfather (a retired jurist) a large enough favour to warrant dropping the monthly rent by forty percent and throwing in the utilities and Internet access for free.

Being naturally independent, she'd thought about objecting to having strings pulled on her behalf. Then she'd reconsidered. After all, when still on the bench, Cormac 'Mack Truck' O'Toole had been a tough Superior Court judge. Even her parents thought twice about arguing with him once his mind was made up, and Ellie thought twice before arguing with *them*. So, there was nothing for it but to say, "Thank you", and move on.

As it happened, Ellie did her laundry every other Wednesday, generally in the evening. Today she didn't wait until after dinner. After scraping off the worst of the rodent gore, she let her clothing soak in cold water while she showered and washed her hair. Then, wearing a clean T-shirt and her last pair of jeans, she threw everything else into the laundry basket and took it downstairs.

The only other person in the laundromat was Rhoda, the manager. She asked Ellie to mind the store for a couple of hours while she ran some errands, and Ellie agreed. It was an easy favour to grant. At this hour of the day, the place was never busy. And, as a bonus, she would have the metal rack of celebrity gossip magazines near the front door all to herself. They were Ellie's drug of second choice.

About an hour later, she tossed her final load of washed clothes into the drum of the industrial-sized dryer, slipped her pay card in and out of the slot, then settled back onto her chair with last week's edition of *You Don't Say!*

The rumble of the dryer faded into the periphery of her thoughts as Ellie immersed herself in the alleged carryings-on of this issue's targeted couple. Cheating with an ex. Getting checked into rehab. Waging a custody battle over a pet. Seeing a UFO. She didn't believe a word of it, not for one second, but that didn't stop her from envying these people their fame. Nothing wrong with that, she told herself. As one of her profs had concluded in a lecture, humans were hardwired to desire attention. Everyone longed to be front page news somewhere, for at least a little while.

All at once, something was pinging off the margins of Ellie's awareness. A strange sound had begun beneath the noise of the dryer, as though a metallic object had found its way into the drum and was being tumbled along with the clothing. She listened intently. It was more than one object, she decided, and they were apparently bouncing around pretty hard in there.

Great. She stood up and checked her jeans pocket. It wouldn't be the first time that she'd accidentally washed and dried her keys. But no, they were exactly where she usually put them. So what could be making such a racket?

Her memory of that morning still painfully clear, Ellie crept up on the dryer, approaching it from the side. She stopped a foot away, turned her ear toward it, and heard the rhythmic mechanical sigh of the drum rotating, nothing more. Then she let out the breath she'd been holding and thought, *All right. If this isn't the source, then what is?*

The building was old. Maybe the pipes were rattling. Or maybe someone was trying to rattle *her.*

Ellie threw a glance in the direction of Rhoda's glassed-in

office. It was empty. Then she checked out the rear of the laundromat to see whether anyone could be hiding in the washrooms or the service corridor. They were all empty too, and the service door was locked from the inside.

For the second time today, she was alone and hearing things. What next? Was something else about to explode? Was she losing her mind?

As she was framing this thought, the strange sound abruptly stopped. Ellie counted the seconds. After fifteen had come and gone, she sank down warily onto her chair. After twenty-two, she dared to reopen her magazine. After thirty, she'd relaxed enough to focus her full attention on what was on its pages. Then:

"Ell-low," said a raspy voice behind her and to her left. It sliced through her concentration like a scalpel, dissecting her thoughts and instantly straightening her spine. No one had come through the front door. She would have seen them. If this was a flesh-and-blood intruder, then they must have had a key to the service entrance. And laryngitis, she added, considering how hard they had to work for each syllable.

"Are you—are you talking to me?"

"Esss," the voice replied.

Ellie leaped to her feet and spun around. She saw no one.

"Where are you?" she demanded unsteadily.

"I… ee-yer."

She cocked her head and let her gaze roam over the three rows of washing machines, searching for anything that was different or out of place. The top-loading machine in the corner snagged her attention. She'd noticed earlier that its lid was down, and there was an "out of order" sign taped to it. Could someone have climbed inside? Swallowing hard, Ellie crossed the room and carefully lifted the lid, just enough for a look.

It was more than enough. With a gasp, she jerked her hand away, letting the lid slam shut again.

Not someone. Some*thing* was inside the washer. A pale,

glowing mass of… of… ectoplasm. That had to be it. Like in that movie, *Ghostbusters*. There was a ghost inside the machine.

Her hands trembling, she fished her phone out of her pocket and called 9-1-1.

A man's voice answered on the second ring. "9-1-1. What is your emergency?"

"I need help. It's trapped inside the washing machine, but I don't know for how long," she replied breathlessly. "I'm at the laundromat in the Cornerstone Plaza near Steeles and Weston Road."

"Is it an animal, ma'am? Are you injured?"

"No, I'm not hurt. And I don't need Animal Control for this. I need—"

Who ya gonna call? teased the refrain at the back of her mind.

She knew who she needed. Ghostbusters. If only they existed!

"Ma'am? Stay with me, now. What's your name?"

"Ellie. Ellie O'Toole."

"Okay, Ellie. You're doing great. Now, can you tell me what you've trapped in the washing machine?"

"No." *Because you would never believe me.*

"Then can you describe it for me?"

Closing her eyes, she said in a rush, "It's glowing. And it's shaped like—like a mouth, a big blobby mouth, with a disgusting tongue and floppy lips."

Silence.

"It's a ghost, dammit!" Ellie shrilled at the phone. "It spoke to me! I heard it!"

More silence. Then a different man's voice came on the line.

"Ma'am? I'm dispatching a police officer to your location to assist you."

"You are? So you believe me?"

"Yes, and he will too. You might say he's our specialist in

this kind of emergency. Please remain as calm as possible and stay where you are. He'll be there shortly."

Hearing laughter in the background, she broke the connection.

Right, she thought bitterly. *A police officer with a butterfly net, no doubt, for me. Meanwhile, the damn ghost is probably sliming the inside of the machine.*

"Ell-lee?" rasped the voice again.

She whipped around, startled. Then a wave of horror broke over her, sending a chill the length of her body. " You know my name?" she whispered hoarsely.

"I… ee-yer. I… Demonai."

"The police are on their way," she informed the ghost in a voice half an octave higher than usual. "You can talk to them. I'm not saying another word to you."

Silence.

Twenty minutes later, an unmarked car pulled into the parking spot directly in front of the laundromat. Ellie watched through the window as a man wearing a well-tailored grey business suit stepped out of the vehicle. He was of medium height, with short, dark brown hair and a set of features that suggested his face had been assembled by a committee unable to reach consensus.

Not surprisingly for someone who was "an expert in this kind of emergency", his demeanour was friendly and open, she realized, the kind that might encourage distraught people to talk to him about what was troubling them. Whether or not he believed a word of it, he would hear them out, because that was his job. He would listen attentively, nodding in sympathy and eventually calming them down, so that he could kindly and pleasantly escort them to the nearest mental hospital.

Ellie was regretting having made that 9-1-1 call.

He stood in the parking lot for a long moment, visually surveying the area. Then he strode through the front doorway, paused, and gazed around the laundromat as well before making eye contact with her. His eyes were the colour of smoke. She swallowed hard, feeling as though they were pinning her in place. Like a butterfly he'd trapped in a net.

"Are you Ellie O'Toole?" he finally asked, pulling a small spiral-bound notepad out of his inner jacket pocket and flipping to a blank page. "I'm Detective Breck. You called 9-1-1 about trapping something dangerous inside a washing machine?"

"Yes. I—" Ellie couldn't bear the thought of saying it aloud again. Perhaps it would be best to let him see it for himself. Tiptoeing back into the corner, she beckoned to him. When he was standing next to her, she grabbed the lid of the out-of-order washer and flung it open, taking a reflexive step backward.

Nothing happened.

Tentatively, Breck leaned closer and stared inside. He made a show of looking all around the inside of the washer drum. Then he straightened up, cleared his throat, and asked, "Are you sure this is the right machine?"

"I'm positive!" she declared. "It even spoke to me. Told me its name: Demonai. And when I looked inside—" Ellie stuck her face over the aperture and repeated the detective's inspection. "It's gone," she murmured brokenly. "There isn't even a smear of slime to show that it was here. Damn!"

"I beg your pardon?" said Breck, his pencil poised to take notes. "Slime? Like what a slug leaves behind?"

"No. Like what a ghost leaves behind. Ectoplasm."

"Uh-huh." Breck put away his pad and pencil. "You reported a haunted washing machine? Tell me, did Al Gerber put you up to this?"

"No! Nobody put me up to anything. You must think I've lost my mind. But I know what I saw and I know what I heard," she said stubbornly.

All at once, a raspy voice said from somewhere behind them, "Hello, Detective Breck. And Ms. O'Toole. It's a pleasure to see you again."

Moving in tandem, they spun 180 degrees. Nothing had changed. They were still the only people in the laundromat. They exchanged wide-eyed looks. Hers had a *Now do you believe me?* tilt to it.

"Did it sound like that?" Breck asked her tightly.

"No. The ghost who spoke to me earlier could barely string two words together," she replied.

"That's true," said the voice. "But I've been practising since then."

"Since twenty minutes ago?" she challenged.

Breck motioned to her to keep the conversation going and began to prowl the room. Looking for microphones, most likely.

"Twenty minutes for you, a great deal longer for me," the voice replied. "Your kind travels a timeline at a constant speed and in only one direction. My kind is bound by no such limitations. I've had ample opportunity to learn how to communicate with you."

"With me?"

"With your kind. I find you... interesting. Definitely intelligent. Well worth studying. Fun to observe. Even more fun to play with. I'm over here, Detective Breck," said the voice. "In the dryer."

Ellie whipped her gaze to the left, where a faint glow was emanating from the circular glass pane of the machine that now contained a considerable portion of her wardrobe. "Oh, shit!" she muttered. She sidled over and risked a closer look. Her clothing was being tumbled by the rotation of the drum. In the middle of it all, hanging motionless, was a smallish, luminescent, roughly spherical object.

"Don't you dare slime my underwear, Demonai!" she warned.

"Demonai?" said Breck, coming now to stand beside her. He was scribbling fiercely in his little spiral-bound pad. "That's your name? And have you spoken to others of 'our kind', as you put it?"

The voice chuckled, sending an icy shiver across Ellie's shoulders.

"You should ask your grandfather about me, Ms. O'Toole. He'll have some stories to tell you. And you, Detective Breck, should look up a novel by an author named Claire Amory. I believe you'll find them both extremely informative."

"You say you can move back and forth in time," Breck persisted. "While practising your language skills, did you happen to blow up a pigeon on my window ledge two mornings ago? And one in the park yesterday afternoon?"

"Pigeons have been exploding?" Ellie echoed.

"Yes. Someone recorded the incident in High Park and posted the video online. The damned thing has gone viral."

"Your recent past is my long ago," said Demonai. "Those were crude attempts to speak through a living creature, and they failed. Now that I've learned how to make vibrations without disaggregating matter, you can expect to hear from me—or to have heard from me—fairly often. Check your memories from time to time. And be careful what you wish for from now on. Just saying."

And with that, the light inside the dryer winked out.

As it did, the two people in the laundromat let out the breaths they'd been holding.

"It's gone," Breck announced unnecessarily, slipping the little pad back into his pocket.

"I guess we have something in common, Detective," Ellie told him. "A laboratory rat exploded in its cage, right in front of me this morning."

He frowned. "Where was this?"

"Where I work, in the basement of the medical building at—"

"—Upper Canada University? That was *your* lab I visited?" He pulled out his pad again and flipped to a page. "I spoke to a Dr. Phinegal there. He claimed the rat had been stolen during a break-in. And he didn't mention you at all. You know, lying to a police detective—"

"He had no choice. Otherwise, he wouldn't even have called the police," she said. "He needs something credible to tell the university when they question the sudden disappearance of rat number 14 from his experiment, and the truth is just too weird to be believed. And for the record, he's only my boss for the summer. Once I decide between English Lit and Drama, I'll be a postgrad student at the university next year."

"Uh-huh." Breck made a brief notation on the pad before continuing, "So, we've got exploding pigeons, exploding rats, and now a haunted washer and dryer. It sounds like something from the tabloids, doesn't it?"

"Ye-es, it does," she said, struck by a sudden thought.

He cleared his throat. "Listen, I have to write up a report about this, and it needs to be as complete and truthful as possible, so I may need to contact you again. To ask you some further questions," he explained, stumbling a little over the last sentence.

She quashed the impulse to flirt. He was cute, in a lopsided way, but there were probably police regulations about fraternizing with witnesses in open cases or some such thing. "You want my phone number?"

"Yes, if you wouldn't—I mean—yes, I'll need it for my report," he said stiffly.

She told it to him, adding, "And just in case I think of anything else you should know, maybe you'd better give me your card."

"Oh, right!" he said, and dug into his breast pocket for one.

Before retracting his sensory pod through the fifth dimension, Demonai paused to observe the conclusion of this scene. If his kind had a mouth, he would be smiling. Instead, he felt a gentle warmth expand outward from the core of his essence. He knew exactly how Tillah would react when she met these beings: *Awww.*

In the Twelfth Dimension

Demonai wasn't actually a 'he', of course, any more than Tillah was a 'she'—their kind came in just one model—but the soft outline and gracefully undulating approach of his fellow being reminded him of the long flowing garments sometimes worn by threedee females. And the fact that he derived pleasure from observing the way she moved, just as many threedee males did when a female of their kind was in motion, had got Demonai thinking of himself as a 'he'.

The curiosity now rippling through her essence was all Tillah, just as the stern disapproval radiating in waves from the being following her was the natural state of Olla'set, their aggregator. (To Demonai's mind, that made Olla'set a 'he' as well.) Tillah and Demonai had each sparked to life inside one of his collection sacs and he never passed up an opportunity to remind them of it.

Olla'set extended a communication pod for melding. In teasing response to the other being's evident impatience, Demonai purposely delayed before extending one of his own.

What are you doing with that?

With what, Aggregator?

With that bubble of five-dimensional space you just submerged to the core of your essence. Did you remove it from my collection sac?

Not at all. I found it.

Of course, you did. In my collection sac.

Respectfully, Aggregator, you're mistaken. This bubble couldn't possibly be part of a matter collection, since it contains intelligent life.

Olla'set's shock, like everything he felt when communicating, was punishingly palpable. *In five-dimensional space? Impossible!*

I've been studying these creatures. They perceive three dimensions and can imagine the existence of those with higher numbers. They strive and question. They plan and make choices. What further proof do you need of their higher-order thinking skills?

They are my creations. Any truly intelligent being can create life in lower dimensions, Demonai, but only the Universe can bestow such a gift upon aggregated matter, and only beings of the highest order are worthy of receiving it.

As if simply claiming ownership and quoting doctrine would persuade Demonai of anything. The Universe had clearly been in a contrary mood when it ignited his aggregated essence.

Beings like us, you mean?

Of course, beings like us! Intelligence would never be wasted on creatures incapable of perceiving all the dimensions of reality, declared Olla'set. *These life forms—*

I call them threedees.

A fitting name for a plaything. These threedees cannot even perceive all the dimensions of their own limited reality. Therefore they cannot possibly be fully aware, regardless of how they behave, and I want you to stop wasting your energy on them.

I won't let you aggregate them, Olla'set.

I have no such plans for them. You misjudge me, Demonai.

Tillah finally joined her thoughts to the discussion. *Then what are your plans for them, Aggregator, if you wish Demonai to abandon them?*

Demonai knew from experience what the response to this question would be, what it always was when Olla'set perceived a challenge to his authority. The aggregator's essence sparked fiercely, then went ominously still.

So, you are together in opposing me?

It was a question, Aggregator, nothing more. I am curious to know how you plan to dispose of this five-dimensional bubble if Demonai is not allowed to keep it.

Tillah and Demonai had often cooperated to test Olla'set's patience in the past. But her demeanour at this moment was mild, even conciliatory, despite the provocative nature of her communication. Demonai couldn't help wondering whether she had plans of her own for the fascinating inhabitants of the matter inside the bubble. Had she known perhaps, even before Demonai did, that Olla'set had them in his collection?

All right, then, here is my decision. Since you are so enamoured of life forms in five-dimensional space, Demonai, you will compact yourself—all of yourself—and join your pet creatures inside the bubble. You will remain there for as long as it takes you to come to your senses and admit that our kind are the only truly intelligent beings in the universe.

Olla'set had returned to normal, for Olla'set: radiating self-righteousness as he issued edicts. *Tillah, you will keep the bubble for the duration of Demonai's captivity. You may insert a pod at intervals to check on his condition. When the threedees cease to amuse him, I am confident he will beg to return to fully dimensional space.*

It took a huge effort for Demonai to still his essence until after the meld was dissolved. Olla'set had no idea how much fun he had just sentenced the 'captive' to have.

Chapter Two

"Happy Saint Patrick's Day."

Yanked back to the moment by the voice of Stewart, his executive assistant, James Hollinger eyed the manila folder that had just landed on the desk in front of him.

"Don't tell me," he sighed. "It's the Harrington-Smythe account." This was getting to be a bad habit. "Whose idea was it this time? Theirs? Or did Elliot decide he'd had enough of them?"

"A little of both, I think," Stewart replied. "Problem is, there's no one left to hand them off to. They've burned their way through every partner in the firm. And it's too big an account to entrust to anyone less important than that. So, it's come back around to you. What do you want to do with them?"

Good question.

Euphonia and Iphigenia Harrington-Smythe were sisters in their 80s, and the most difficult clients Hollinger had ever had to deal with. They refused to do anything electronically. Everything had to be in person and face-to-face. That meant meeting with them in their home—which wouldn't have been so bad if they weren't also a couple of old maids on the prowl. The last time they'd cornered Hollinger in their parlour, they'd taken turns leering at him and giggling obscenely behind liver-spotted hands. Even after several years, the memory of being mentally undressed by a couple of oversexed octogenarians could still make his skin crawl.

If the sisters hadn't been old money, with solid-gold social connections, they would already have been referred to a competitor. In fact, now that every partner had had the opportunity to experience them, they still might be.

"What do I want to do? For the time being, not a thing, Stewart. This file can sit in my inbox until I get back from my annual retreat."

That was what he'd decided to call it, to avoid having to answer questions about it.

Each year, Hollinger spent three weeks ensconced in his penthouse apartment, giving pro bono financial advice and preparing tax returns for a select group of private clients. These individuals weren't the firm's usual class of clientele, but they'd been among his first walk-in customers back when Hollinger had opened his storefront office, next door to the Fun 'n' Feathers Strip Club. That had been twenty-five years ago. Hollinger had never forgotten the fact that exotic dancers had helped to launch the company that was now keeping him (and about twenty partners—he'd lost count) living in luxury. Some of those earliest clients were still making good money and filing annual returns, and they happily paid his "friends and family" fee to ensure that they got back every penny of rebate they had coming.

"Your retreat. Of course." Stewart's face pinched a little. "And it begins tomorrow? I'll make sure the other partners know." He looked about to say something more, but then apparently changed his mind.

As the door closed behind his assistant, Hollinger knew what Stewart must have been thinking—that having these women come to his apartment instead of his office probably meant he was being remunerated with sexual favours. In fact, nothing could have been further from the truth.

Twenty-five years earlier, it had been a different story. They'd all been a lot younger then. He'd received plenty of offers from girls wanting to pay him that way, but like a fool, he'd held out for cash or, in some cases, waived his fee altogether. He'd told them that he had goals. He'd told himself that he had integrity. But in truth, what he'd had was bad skin, thick glasses, and a lot of extra weight around his middle. He'd been utterly convinced that what he saw in the mirror was all that anyone would ever see, and he hated the thought of being laid by someone who was figuratively holding her nose while going through the motions, simply to cancel a debt.

As soon as he could afford the expense, he'd undergone dermabrasion and laser eye surgery and hired a personal trainer, and his resulting physical attractiveness to women seemed to confirm his earlier opinion of himself. But over the past few years, with his fiftieth birthday coming and going, and his hairline receding, and his waistline increasing, he had come to realize the truth. It wasn't his new and improved appearance that had begun turning women's eyes in his direction—it was the self-confidence that had come with it.

What he wouldn't give to be back in his twenties, knowing what he knew now! It didn't matter what shape his body was in. Despite the claims made by ads for workout equipment, what most appealed to women had much less to do with how the package was wrapped than it did with what lay inside.

Then, as now, he would focus his attentions on just one beautiful lady: Roxanne. From the beginning, she'd been his most loyal client, and he'd repaid her by helping her to become a successful businesswoman. Now, for the first two weeks of his retreat every year, they played house in Hollinger's penthouse suite while he did her tax return.

Her paperwork was always a disaster. Sometimes it took the entire first week just to organize her receipts. But her assets made it all worthwhile. Hollinger glanced at his watch. In just another few hours, Roxanne would be arriving for her annual financial consultation.

He could hardly wait.

～

Thankful that the threedees could not perceive the fifth dimension, Demonai withdrew his pod from the meld with Hollinger's essence. An idea had sparked in Demonai's capacious, clever, and very devious consciousness. In the resulting eddies of energy, an amusing game was taking shape. A puzzle, actually, for threedees to solve. A challenge that, if met, couldn't help but convince Olla'set that despite their dimensional limitations, these creatures were just as self-aware and intelligent as his own kind.

It would take more than one of them, though. Demonai anchored himself in the timeline, scanning for likely vibrations...

～

"Garry, I'm afraid I have bad news for you."

Of course he did.

Doctor Garrick Boehm shifted uneasily in his chair, and not just because it was entirely made of wood and paid pitiful lip service to the way the human body was shaped. He hated these post-meeting meetings. He was a scientist, but in today's world it wasn't enough to be curious about the workings of the universe and passionate about investigating them. These days, especially if the funding was coming from government sources, one had to be a canny politician as well. A negotiator. A media-savvy businessperson. Sometimes even a warrior. Boehm wasn't cut out to do any of those things, and for the past five years it had been costing him.

The theoretical physicist heading up the project, Dr. Edgar Dunberry, was apparently lacking in some of those areas as well, since he always returned from budget reviews with less than pleasing information to report—for Dr. Boehm, at least.

Boehm was acutely aware that his branch of the research was the most recently undertaken, and that in the event of a shortfall he would be the first to lose equipment and personnel. Dunberry was perpetually reminding him of this. As if constantly being starved for resources wasn't reminder enough.

"What do I have to give up this time?" Boehm asked, running a nervous hand through his shock of sand-coloured hair.

"All of it."

Boehm's jaw sagged. "What? You mean I'm off the project? Fired?"

Dunberry shook his head sadly. "I wish it were just one person. But our primary grant has been cancelled, so the whole project is being shut down. The federal government is trying to cut back its spending, and the provincial coffers can't cover the extra costs, and—Why am I even trying to explain this?" Dunberry demanded wearily. "Bottom line: we're done. Some short-sighted mandarin has pulled the plug, sending seven years of work down the tubes. They've given us seventy-two hours to turn over all our findings so far. Then we vacate the facility. Garry, I'm so sorry about this. Most of us were seconded from the private sector and have positions to return to, but you were recruited straight out of university."

It went against everything that he was feeling inside, but Boehm mustered an accepting smile. Money, he thought sourly. Everything in this world boiled down to money—the people who needed it and the people who had it. Somebody with money had decided not to share it, and now he was unemployed. Just once before he died, Boehm decided, he wanted to know what it felt like to have that kind of power over other people's lives.

"Listen, Garry, why don't you go to your office and clear out your things? We'll do all the data compiling and organizing for you. It will give you extra time for your job search. How about it?" There was a pleading expression in Dunberry's eyes. Boehm could almost believe that the old man was feeling genuinely sorry for him.

"Terrific, thanks," he murmured, getting to his feet.

As he made his way through the labyrinth of corridors to his closet-sized office, Boehm reflected on the years that he'd spent on the project. It would have been nice if he'd had a chance to reach some conclusions. Then at least he would have had something to publish in a paper, giving him an academic credential for his résumé. As it was, all he'd learned from Dunberry was how to act humble while being stabbed in the back, a skill that he sincerely hoped he wouldn't need in the future.

At last Boehm was able to close his door on the world and settle his rangy body into the hard wooden chair behind his desk. His desktop computer with the monitor perched atop it sat like a desert island in the middle of an ocean of paper. A random tumble of printouts, hand-scrawled notes, and carelessly dropped file folders, it was—appropriately, considering his current situation—a rather choppy and unfriendly sea. He was probably the only person in the building who could make sense of it. And Dunberry expected him to be packed up and gone by nine o'clock the next morning.

Uh-huh.

Boehm sifted through the clutter, discovering several broken-backed texts he'd used for reference and then forgotten to reclose. Many of the books on the battered metal shelf unit behind him had been borrowed from the university library. A few he'd brought from home. He would have to find and label a couple of boxes to pack them in. And what about the files on his computer? He would have to go through the hard drive, deleting anything personal, maybe e-mailing it to himself first or transferring it onto a memory stick.

There was a reason that moving house topped the list of stressful life experiences, he reflected glumly. It could take him all night to bring order to this chaos.

Well, what the hell? It wasn't as though he had to get up early to go to work.

~~~

A second wish. Congratulating himself, Demonai broke off the meld with Boehm's essence and continued the search. One more threedee and the challenge could begin…

~~~

Fingers poised over the keyboard of her laptop computer, Claire Amory scowled fiercely at the screen with its margins so precisely yet tactfully delineated in baby blue. Toolbar icons sat obediently awaiting her attention. The cursor pulsed patiently in the upper left corner of the page. And her mind, which should have been buzzing with story ideas, was just as empty of words as that clean white rectangle.

"Damn!"

She hadn't been able to write anything in over a week. It felt like an eternity. Bills were coming due and her savings were dangerously depleted. If Claire couldn't break through this infuriating block, she would have no choice but to accept one of Ralph Ignace's freelance editing assignments, just to meet the next rent payment.

Editing porn. This was definitely not going on her résumé. In fact, just thinking about some of the stuff Ignace's stable of authors regularly churned out made her want to take a shower.

Three years earlier, low on funds and desperate for any kind of writing-related work, Claire had answered an ad in the newspaper. She was from a small town. She was still learning how to get around the city on public transportation. How was she supposed to know that porn publishers placed want ads just like everyone else?

Claire leaned back in her folding bridge chair. As she did,

her gaze snagged on the file folder containing all the rejection slips she'd collected since arriving in Toronto. Some were form letters. Most had complimentary things to say about her writing. A few even praised it warmly. But all of them ended the same way: "Best of luck placing this elsewhere."

Three and a half years. Long enough for a scientist to make a Nobel Prize-winning breakthrough. Long enough for a computer nerd with marketing savvy to become a multimillionaire. Apparently not long enough for a small-town girl to rocket to writing fame in a city boasting at least twenty publishing houses. It hadn't been for lack of effort, either. There was probably sufficient paper in that rejections file folder to cover most of the wall space in her bachelorette apartment. Meanwhile, just enough money trickled in every month or two to keep her hopes up.

"Writing As a Masochistic Activity".

Nope. Too esoteric.

Every once in a while, she thought about getting a "real job", like the one she'd left back in Caverley Corners, minding the counter in Mr. Bowmeister's dry cleaning store. Then her stubborn side emerged to remind her: menial work was a trap. It would chew up her time and dull her creativity. She mustn't let that happen. She'd come to the city to be a writer, and that was what she would do.

Keeping in mind her mother's warning not to live like a hermit, Claire made a point of leaving the house at least three times a week. She'd signed up for general interest courses at the local community centre. She went shopping. She visited the library. And she'd taken out a free trial membership at a martial arts studio. That was where she'd met Sophie Hopper, her first and best friend in the city. Sophie was an activist and a feminist, and had introduced Claire to an organization she'd helped to start, Women for Professional Equality.

Then there was Ralph Ignace. He'd practically tried to

crawl into her pants the first time they'd met, but had switched gears without missing a beat or even raising an eyebrow when she'd told him she was a lesbian. Ralph always had work for her when she needed it, and never held back a payment on her. In a strange way, she considered him to be a friend as well.

"What to Do When Your Boss Is Hot for You".

Nope. Claire wasn't an expert in that area, thank goodness, and just thinking about what it would take to become one creeped her out.

Sophie Hopper and Ralph Ignace. Two more polar opposites Claire could not imagine. And if Sophie ever found out that Claire was cashing cheques from Pussyjoy Enterprises, there would probably be hell to pay.

"Small Town Memories".

Nope. She'd written something just like it shortly after missing her high school reunion. The piece had sold to one of the glossies for enough to support her for three months.

Maybe that was her problem, though. All the memories she had were of living in Caverley Corners, a safe little community in central Ontario where hardly anything ever happened. Nothing exciting, at any rate. You had to experience life before you could write about it. Go exploring. Take risks. Except there weren't any risks *to* take in Caverley Corners. That was why she'd decided to move to the city in the first place.

Unfortunately, she hadn't realized how expensive it was to live in Toronto. Everything she wanted to do cost money, and she didn't have any to spare. Living hand to mouth, Claire was missing out on what should have been the greatest adventure of her young life.

"Ten Ways to Get Excited Without Leaving Your Room".

No!

"Ten Ways to Get Excited Without Having to Pay For It".

Augh! Absolutely not!

Foolishly, Claire had believed that winning a couple of

regional short story contests would carry some weight with publishers in the city. Sadly, she'd been mistaken.

"Broken Dreams".

Now she was just being maudlin. It was time to pull up her socks, as her mother would say, and be proactive. Okay. Claire needed money. That meant she had to write and sell a really great story. One with heart. Preferably, one that she'd personally experienced. A unique real-life narrative could be slanted to several national publications to increase her chances of acceptance. So, this would be a story about— what? What was she qualified to write about besides growing up closeted in a tiny town and following her dreams to the big city?

When the answer came to her, she nearly gagged on it. Then she thought, *Well, why not?* She'd been editing the stuff for years. She knew all the tropes. Ralph loved her writing style. And Pussyjoy was making money hand over fist, so somebody had to be buying it, right?

Claire straightened in her chair and, gritting her teeth, began striking keys in ever faster rhythm.

Having found three suitable subjects for his challenge, Demonai set to work, teasing threads of their essence into the fifth dimension in order to create the necessary melds. He also transmitted gratitude to whatever force or entity had put these particular beings in his way. The fate of every living thing on the threedee world could hinge on the outcome of this experiment, but it wasn't the only test in progress, as Demonai was acutely aware.

Meanwhile, he was looking forward to seeing how the threedees reacted when they realized how each of their wishes had been granted.

In the Fifth Dimension

Tillah did not wait long to pay him a visit.

How can you bear it, Demonai, being confined to such a small space?

It's spacious enough for your entire essence to join me here, he invited.

Only in a severely compacted state. Thank you, but no. And what is that constant vibration?

That's the threedees communicating with one another. They generate wave patterns. I've learned to understand them. Would you like to know what they're communicating?

The location of food? The presence of danger?

Do you honestly believe I would have stood up to Olla'set on their behalf if that was all the threedees were about?

She paused, the essence in her pod shimmering. *You don't believe he actually created them, do you? You're certain he must have found them. You took a great risk, Demonai. He could have disaggregated you on the spot for stealing them from his collection sac.*

I never admitted to stealing them, he reminded her.

No, you just turned his attention away from your transgression by suggesting he'd been about to commit a worse one of his own. Tillah's amusement sparkled like tiny stars. *So, are these threedees meeting your expectations?*

If you mean are they mentally evolved, the answer is yes. And they became that way in spite of Olla'set's cruel games.

He had the bubble for only a short time, Demonai.

...that we know of. However long it was for us, it was hundreds of lifetimes for the threedees. I've sunk sense pods all along their timeline, not believing half of what I found. He made no effort to conceal his disgust. *They were worshipping him. Praying to him. And the worse he treated them, the harder they worked to please him. Tillah, he disaggregated them by the thousands and they made sacrifices of their own offspring to appease him. And their belief was so strong that when I began communicating with them in an effort to undo some of his damage, they called me an evil spirit and tried to drive me away.*

Wait. You found a way to communicate with them? Her pod glowed with excitement.

I had to, in order to study them. Monitoring is the easy part. Let me show you. First, you extend a pod and compact it down to three dimensions, then pick a spot and push—

Like this?

Her eagerness was explosive. Her first attempt flattened fifteen square miles of boreal forest. Her second displaced several million tons of ocean water, inundating fishing villages on multiple coastlines. Demonai took over then, showing her how to compact and refine her pod for precise transition through the interdimensional barrier, then decompact it for implantation into a three-dimensional space, all without causing so much as a ripple of disturbance.

There was more he wanted to teach her, about moving and changing coherent matter and infiltrating the containment membranes of the threedees, but it could wait. She'd made progress, and he knew that Tillah's curiosity would bring her back to learn more.

They spent a while monitoring the activities of the threedees. Demonai was confident that, like himself, she would eventually be able to communicate with them as well.

No wonder Olla'set was drawn to this bubble. There are bundles of coherent matter all through it, she observed.

Yes. The threedees are apparently collectors. (Like us, he nearly added, but stopped himself. Tillah wasn't the one he most needed to persuade.)

Collectors! How interesting! Of what?

Of all sorts of things. Things that they find and things that they make. Some of them even collect other threedees, constructing places to contain them.

And is there a goal to all this collecting? When the sac is filled, do they aggregate its contents to critical mass, then detach it and start over?

Some of them do. Threedee reproduction is the next thing I plan to investigate, once my current experiment is concluded.

Your experiment?

Everything was compacted in five-dimensional space. Positioned closer to Tillah's containment membrane than would normally be tolerated, Demonai could feel his essence quivering in sympathetic response to her sparkles of amusement.

Yes, my experiment. Observe.

Demonai! What have you done to these poor creatures?

I'm granting their wishes. Or rather, I'm letting them grant one another's wishes. This one has power but wishes for youth, this one has an uncertain future and wishes for power, and this one has youth and wishes for an uncertain future. I've created direct sensory-motor pathways between each wisher and the being who possesses what he or she wishes for.

Are you telling me that these threedees asked you to do this to them?

Not exactly. They all thought their wishes at about the same time. I simply chose the best way to answer them all at once.

And they can't feel the meld? It causes them no discomfort?

None at all. They have no idea they're linked. Shall we observe how they react when they discover what I've done?

Chapter Three

J ames Hollinger opened his eyes and knew instantly that something was terribly wrong. First of all, the room was purple. Not a pale, polite purple, like lavender or violet. This was a deep, angry purple, a shade that announced itself with a bullhorn, then stomped all over his retinas while wearing hobnailed boots. It practically made his eyes water just to look at it.

Second, this was not his bed. It was the size of a military-issue cot, with a mattress slightly thicker than a pad of writing paper. So, if it wasn't his room and it wasn't his bed, then where the hell was he? Had he been kidnapped during the night?

He was worth tens of millions. Kidnapping for ransom was a real possibility.

Shivering with trepidation, Hollinger raised his head and looked around. He was alone. The light filtering through the pale gauzy curtains cast no bar-shaped shadows on the wall above the bed. That was encouraging. And he could feel that his wrists and ankles weren't bound. Good. Unless there was muscle waiting to stop him just outside the door, all he had to do was find something to wear and get his ass out of there.

Hollinger flung aside the blanket, swung himself out of bed—and sat staring in bewilderment at a pair of legs that couldn't possibly belong to him and yet were clearly attached to his body. They were slender and hairless, and they emerged from the lacy hem of a short blue nightgown.

His heart was pounding—it sounded like drums in his ears—and he could swear an icy fist was jammed inside his chest, making it difficult to breathe. Desperately, he looked around the little purple room and saw a folding bridge table with matching chair, a battered chest of drawers with a cloudy mirror stuck to the wall above it, and a tea kettle resting on a hot plate in what appeared to be a kitchenette in the far corner. Once again, he asked himself: where was he? More to the point, *what* was he?

The mirror. The mirror would show him.

He should have closed his eyes while getting to his feet. Instead, he noticed the hand on the end of his right arm and fell back onto the bed, numb with shock. The hand was slim and graceful, and adorned with red nail polish. It went perfectly with his brand new legs.

Tentatively, he felt his cheeks. No whiskers. And not just smoothly shaven, but gone, totally!

"Oh, my God!"

With an apoplectic shudder, he clapped a hand to his crotch.

Nada.

His throat felt hot and tight. Tears were welling in his eyes. His stomach was doing flip-flops. There was a waste basket beside the bridge table. Reaching as far as he dared, he managed to hook the rim of the basket and pull it toward him, and not a moment too soon.

A while later, he lay back against the pillows, sniffling and hiccoughing.

Hollinger knew it would be traumatic, but it was even more important now that he look at himself in the mirror. Somehow, wobbly legs carried him across the room, where he stood for a long, silent moment, blinking hard and clinging with both hands to the dresser top.

The face he now wore wasn't unattractive. It was heart-shaped, with cupid's-bow lips, an uptilted nose, and wide blue eyes. And it was young—mid to late twenties. If he had to be the butt of some cosmic joke, things could have been much worse.

He could have ended up in Iphigenia's body. Or Roxanne's. Then he would have awakened to the sight of—

Oh, shit!

Hollinger went cold all over. What *would* Roxanne see when she woke up this morning? His corpse? Or would she find his body with this woman's mind inside it?

His imagination chose that moment to leap ahead, showing him the damage that could be done by two hysterical females to an expensively appointed penthouse apartment.

Dear Lord, he had to get over there!

~

Garry Boehm was having a very strange dream. He was sunbathing nude on a pale soft beach under the unreal brightness of a midday sky, and a beautiful naked girl with large breasts and dark flowing hair had just sliced off his left arm at the shoulder with a wicked little knife. But instead of blood, perfume was spilling from the wound and transforming into a thick, aromatic mist that billowed around him like smoke. Finally he coughed, sending the dream spinning off in thousands of tiny fragments and catapulting himself into another one much like it.

He was still nude, but lying on a huge bed. The blue sky had folded itself around him, becoming walls and a ceiling. The strong smell of perfume remained in his nostrils. And there was a voluptuous naked woman, with blonde hair this time, sleeping peacefully on a left arm that logic dictated must belong to him, but that he couldn't feel at all.

Dreaming or not, Boehm wanted that arm back. Sitting up, he held the woman still with his right hand and pulled himself free. And then she opened large brown eyes, gazed languorously up at him, and stretched. All at once a smooth hand was snaking across his shoulder to caress the nape of his neck.

He really had to marvel at the vividness of this dream. He was even experiencing the pain of returning circulation in his arm.

"Darling," came a silky voice beside his left ear, "I want you."

If he needed any further proof that he was dreaming, mused Boehm, this was it.

"I said, I want you," she repeated, her breath fairly melting his eardrum.

If she'd popped out of his subconscious, then she had to represent something. Perhaps she was symbolic of the resentment he'd felt when Dunberry told him the project was canned…?

The woman's hand had left his neck and was walking on fore- and middle fingers down his chest. He stopped it as it reached his navel. "I'm analyzing," he told her.

"So analyze," she cooed. "After all, it isn't your brain I m after."

He glanced downward.

So, it was *that* kind of dream!

Boehm sighed happily and leaned back against the pillows. "Oh, yeah, baby," he murmured.

〰

Claire Amory came soggily aware, conscious at first only of pain. She could feel that her body was unnaturally bert, which probably explained why every muscle in it was aching. Eyes shut, she took rapid inventory. Her head was pounding. And her mouth tasted like a swamp. And her breath smelled like one. And her tongue—

She didn't want to think about her tongue.

Claire hadn't felt this bad since she'd let Ralph talk her into a second glass of punch at last year's Pussyjoy office Christmas party. Was that where she was? Because she sure as hell wasn't in her own bed.

I will stay calm. I will stay calm. Even if I've been drugged and kidnapped and thrown into a steamer trunk, I will remain strong. I will NOT dissolve into tears like some stereotypical female victim, she told herself sternly.

Then she opened her eyes and had to clap a hand over her mouth to keep from screaming. And then she realized what she was feeling with her hand and yanked it away from her face.

Whiskers?!

Claire blinked hard several times and gazed around the tiny, windowless room. The overhead light was on, had probably been on all night. The place was furnished like an office, but it felt more like a cell. It did have a door, with a small window in it. And an old-fashioned keyhole, the kind they used to have in dungeons. The sight of it raised possibilities in her mind that made her stomach churn.

Carefully, she unfolded herself from behind the desk, ducking her head to avoid hitting the light fixture. Wherever this room was, it had a low ceiling. Claire's heart fluttered like a trapped bird as she stepped slowly toward the door and reached for the knob.

It wasn't locked. A little light-headed with relief, she pulled it open and leaned out, into a corridor with whitewashed cinder block walls punctuated by other doors identical to this one. Down the hall to her right, she saw a washroom sign. Good. Once her most pressing need was taken care of, there would be time to deal with the rest.

Or maybe not. Claire saw herself reflected in the mirror over the washbasin and nearly screamed again.

Gone was the heart-shaped face framed by straight dark hair. The one she now wore was indisputably masculine. It stared back at her from under a dishevelled dark blond mop, its lean, angular cheeks sporting a day's growth of beard. Its eyes were dark and deep-set, its expression twisted with horror.

Where was she? Who was she? Who was *he*? And where—?

Stupid question. Claire knew exactly where he was—waking up in her body, in her little bachelorette, and probably terrified out of his mind.

Frantically, she searched his pockets. Men didn't carry purses. They had wallets. If she was lucky, this man was carrying enough cash on him to pay for her cab ride home. It was an unaffordable luxury, but so was the time she would lose riding public transportation.

Aha! Found his ID! His name was Garrick Boehm. And… he had no driver's licence. Nothing with an address on it at all. Damn! If he'd already panicked and run home, she would have a hard time tracking him down.

Sophie, she thought grimly, *you'd better be wrong about men being the weaker sex.*

Claire jammed the wallet back into her pocket and hurried into a stall. Garrick Boehm's bladder was ready to burst. And she had a body to catch.

Boehm blinked, and the woman disappeared.

Okay. This was a dream, he reminded himself. Time could run backwards, things could materialize out of nowhere…

"Darling?" There she was, standing at the foot of the bed, fully dressed, holding a fan made out of credit cards—he loved the symbolism! "I just have to pick up a few things for Thursday night. Do you mind?"

"Go ahead, knock yourself out," he told her.

Her smile tripled in wattage. "I'll be back in a few hours," she promised, and was gone.

Feeling like Alice transported to Wonderland, Boehm

swung himself out of bed. There were doors in this place, leading to other rooms. What else would he find here? Solid gold bathroom fixtures? An old-fashioned ticker tape machine in the kitchen? A platoon of yes-men sitting around the dining room table?

His subconscious was having a field day. The bathtub looked like a marble shrine, surrounded by things on pedestals. Boehm glanced at himself in the bathroom mirror—set into the wall, not just attached to it—and found himself staring into the olive-complexioned face of a man he'd often envied, although not for his looks: James A. Hollinger.

The financial guru and media darling had recently turned fifty. He wasn't aging gracefully. There was creasing and puffiness around his eyes. His hair was still mostly dark, with patches of grey at the temples. The effect would have been distinguishing if only Hollinger's forehead weren't so high. In another couple of years he would be flat-out balding. And jowly. And nobody would care. They would still hang on his every word and fall at his feet in adulation, because the man was Filthy Rich.

Hollinger was constantly being interviewed and consulted. If there were a Money Olympics, he would give the colour commentary. No one would dare to fire *him* from a project— not without some sweetheart handshake that would pay the salaries of a hundred Garrick Boehms for several years.

Boehm opened a cabinet at random. Five shavers sat nestled in rechargers. Not one bore a brand name. Of course. Someone with Hollinger's money could get *everything* custom-made.

Feeling vaguely as though he were committing vandalism, Boehm used the facilities—all of them. Then, with rising anticipation, he went looking for the clothes closet.

It was a walk-in, almost as large as his entire apartment. Thirty suits if there was one. Real silk. Real wool. Tuxedos— plural! A different shirt for each day of the month. At least a dozen pairs of shoes, not counting golf cleats. And the accessories—! For a while, Boehm just stood in the middle of the room and turned a slow circle, devouring all those choices with his eyes. Maybe he wasn't dreaming after all. Maybe he'd died and gone to heaven.

He heard a peremptory knock at one of the doors. Boehm grinned at the face in the mirror and called out, "Come in." Then he snagged a monogrammed bathrobe off its hook and headed for the vestibule, shrugging the garment on as he went.

It was time to meet the next persona in this exceptiona ly long and vivid dream.

~~

Rifling through the purse he'd found in the closet, Hollinger had located Claire Amory's identification. Fortunately, he d also thought to count the money in her wallet before gettirg into the taxi. He knew it wouldn't be enough to get him all the way home from the Beaches, but there had been a credit card as well, tucked into a separate pocket of her handbag. With luck, she hadn't already maxed it out. It was a risk, but he was damned if he was going to take this body onto a bus or streetcar, or—the thought made him shudder—a subway train.

Hollinger spent the entire ride mentally rehearsing what he could say to a couple of hysterical women to calm them down. It wasn't much. By the time the driver had let him out in front of the condo building, Hollinger was certain of only one thing: the odds were stacked against him. In his own body, even outnumbered two to one, he might have been able to manage the situation. In Claire's petite frame, he was probably on a suicide mission.

Still, he had to try.

Nate, the uniformed guard at the entrance to Hollinger's building, was a former pro linebacker. To someone of Claire

Amory's stature, he looked like an impassable brick wall. As Hollinger paused, debating what he should do, the burly doorman gave him a slow, appraising look. "You're a new face, Missy. Are you one of Mr. Hollinger's private clients?"

Unwilling to trust his voice, James simply nodded.

"Well, your timing's perfect. Here, let me get that inside door for you." To Hollinger's combined astonishment and dismay, Nate not only let a perfect stranger into the building, he even tipped his hat to her.

"Thank you," said James, making a mental note to fire the doorman the moment he was back in his own body.

Hollinger entered the elevator car and keyed in the passcode to the penthouse floor. All the way up, he visualized himself walking in on a scene of chaos—two distraught women, one in a man's body, hurling insults and various breakable objects at each other. Not until he was actually standing at the entrance to his apartment did the chilling thought occur to him: how would Claire Amory react when she saw her own body walk through the door?

Hollinger paused, one fist poised to knock, as his stomach sank in sudden dread. Maybe it had been a mistake to come here alone in such a short, slight form. Maybe he should have brought someone with him. Someone like Nate.

All at once, Hollinger heard male laughter. It was faint, but definitely coming from the other side of the door. His door. And *his apartment*, he reminded himself sternly.

He knocked.

"Come in," sang out a very familiar-sounding voice.

Hollinger tried the knob. His stomach sank a second time. The door was unlocked. He nudged it open and peered cautiously around it before entering the suite.

The vestibule was in perfect order. So was the living room. Now he was confused. What the hell was going on here?

Just then, his body strode in and sat down at one end of the gold and grey divan. Hollinger watched in fascination as it crossed its legs, arranged the folds of its dressing gown—

his dressing gown, he thought savagely—and beamed expectantly at the new arrival. Ms. Amory was obviously feeling relaxed and well-rested and… well… *satisfied.*

Hollinger smiled with his lips and asked through gritted teeth, "Where is Roxanne?"

"The blonde? Is that her name? Lovely woman. She said she had to pick up a few things."

Of course. Nate had told him his timing was perfect. One woman leaves, and the next one arrives. "How many cards?" Hollinger demanded.

"Cards?"

"Credit cards, you—! How many did she take with her?"

"She was holding four or five, I guess. I didn't count them."

Hollinger cursed silently. Every year Roxanne went out to "pick up a few things". Every year she asked to take a couple of his platinum cards with her and he put a thousand dollars in cash into her hand instead. He didn't mind letting her shop with his money, but there had to be limits. If Roxanne maxed out even one of those cards, this would be the most expensive retreat James Hollinger had ever had.

With deliberate care, he placed Claire Amory's faux leather handbag on the rosewood console table beside a tray holding a leaded crystal decanter and several sherry glasses. Then, just as carefully, he composed his features and said, "You're probably wondering what is going on."

"Not really. This is pretty straightforward, as dreams go. The symbolism is very transparent."

No wonder she was sitting there so relaxed. Well, it was time to stress her out a little. "Listen, Claire—"

"Who's Claire?"

"You are, sweetie."

She shrugged. "If you say so. I've actually never thought of myself as that type, but I guess I can appreciate a metaphor as well as the next person. So if I'm a man with a woman's name, you must be a woman with a man's name. What is it?

George? Albert?"

She was infuriating. "Stop trying to turn this into some kind of party game," he snapped. "I'm James Hollinger, and you are in my body."

Grinning idiotically, the body in the dressing gown nodded its head. "This is wonderful," she said. "I hope I can remember all of it and write it down when I wake up."

"When you wake up?" he almost shouted. "You *are* awake, dammit!"

"That's impossible," said the woman in Hollinger's body, with maddening calm. "None of this is real."

"None of this?" He was stupefied. "What about Roxanne?"

"A metaphor. Like you, like this apartment. It's all symbolic of my innermost emotions and wishes. I always wanted to live a millionaire's life, and in this lucid dream, I'm finally getting my chance. I don't know whose body you have there, but you obviously represent something very negative about my subconscious, and I want you to leave now."

His gorge rising, Hollinger took a shuddering breath. "Now, see here, Miss Amory, or Ms. Amory, or whatever you want to call yourself—"

"I'd rather not call myself either one, actually."

"Listen to me, you goddamned—!" The sound of Claire Amory's voice rising in pitch hauled him up short. As long as he was in this female body, losing his temper wasn't going to accomplish a thing. He recomposed himself and started over. "You can deny it all you like, but this is your body that I'm trapped inside. You are Claire Amory. I am James A. Hollinger. Somehow, our minds were switched during the night. And no, doll-face, you are *not* dreaming, and neither am I, although I wish to hell I were."

The other person's face fell. "Oh, dear."

Finally! "That's putting it mildly."

"No, you don't understand. I'm not Claire Amory. I'm

Garry Boehm. I'm a man."

Hollinger felt the nausea returning. "You're a man?' he echoed weakly.

"Of course."

"Then where is Claire Amory's mind? And where is your body?"

"Probably together. We're a triangle. How exciting! The symbolism in this dream just keeps getting more and more complex."

The pounding in Hollinger's temples signalled a definite rise in blood pressure. "How many times do I have to tell you that this is not—!" He paused to compose himself, then continued in a more controlled voice, "We have to find them, Garry. Your body and her mind. This is serious."

"Why not just wait here?" came the infuriatingly serene reply. "My body, my dream. Anything's possible."

"You moron! What do I have to do to convince you that you're awake?"

Hollinger tried to recall the old tales he'd heard about dreams. A person who dreamed about falling would awaken before hitting bottom. No good—the penthouse was on the twelfth floor, and in any case, he wanted his body back in good condition. Should he have this Boehm fellow pack a suitcase? Not good either—if he finished packing and actually closed the valise, he would probably think he was dead.

"Slap my face," Boehm suggested quietly.

"What?"

"I've never had much tolerance for pain, and any time I've dreamt about being physically attacked I've always awakened at once. Slap me."

He'd been itching to do it anyway. Obediently, Hollinger delivered an openhanded blow that left his palm stinging. Boehm slowly raised a hand to cradle his bruised cheek as his jaw dropped in utter amazement.

"Good Lord! You're real!" He gazed wonderingly around

the living room, not one detail of which had changed. "It's all real!" he gasped. "And Roxanne?"

"Roxanne was real," James confirmed with a sigh. *Not to mention bloody expensive.*

"I've been deflowered," Boehm murmured in disbelief. Then his eyes rolled upward as he toppled sideways on the divan.

Claire's destination was a converted rooming house in the Beaches, a neighbourhood of older structures in the east end of the city close to the lakeshore. This building in particular was a sprawl of red bricks badly in need of pointing. It was joined to the sidewalk by several worn and pitted concrete steps. Its dark green front door could have done with a fresh coat of paint, and the dozen or so windows that faced the street hadn't been thoroughly cleaned in years. Nonetheless, she was humming as she bounded up the front steps and through the main entrance.

Claire took the three flights of stairs two at a time, pausing outside her apartment long enough for several deep, calming breaths. Care would be needed here. If she came on too strong, she might spook him. Spooked, he might panic and run. And the last thing she wanted was for him to fall down the stairs and break his neck, or race frantically into traffic and get hit by a car or something. If he died while inside her body, Claire wasn't sure she wanted to find out what would happen next, stronger sex or not.

She rapped gently on the door.

There was no answer.

Licking her lips nervously, she tapped a little harder. Still no response.

When a third, more aggressive knock failed to rouse anybody inside, Claire tried the knob. The room was locked.

There was only one thing left to do. Glancing around

furtively, she reached into her pants pocket and took out Garrick Boehm's wallet. He didn't have a credit card she could ruin, but his library card was plastic.

It worked. Silently the door swung open, on a space that looked as though a cyclone had torn through it. Drawers had been yanked open and their contents spilled out onto the bed and the floor. Her underwear had been all but tied in knots. Had Boehm done this? Claire hoped he had, because the only other explanation she could think of was that there had been a break-in.

As she looked around the room, her heart sank. Her laptop and printer were still on the bridge table where she'd left them last night, but she'd been robbed of something far more valuable than that. Her body was gone, and she had no idea where it was.

Sinking wearily onto the bed, Claire considered a depressing list of possibilities. If he'd run outside screaming, wearing only a nightgown, he could be in a psychiatric ward right now. On the other hand, if he'd retained sufficient presence of mind to get dressed, he could have taken refuge with a relative (who might or might not have the same last name as his), or with a good friend, in which case all she could do was—

A sudden knocking derailed Claire's train of thought. Mrs. Scotti, the landlady, called through the door, "*Bella*, I'm going to the grocery store. Is there anything you need?"

Without thinking, Claire replied, "No, thanks," then gasped as she realized what she had done. She'd answered in a masculine voice. Mrs. Scotti was the busiest busybody in the whole neighbourhood, and if she had heard Garrick Boehm making distressed noises in Claire's voice earlier—!

"What?" shouted Mrs. Scotti. "Claire, are you in there? Are you all right? Answer me!"

Claire groaned inwardly. There was no way she could reply. Even her silence was an indictment.

"Listen, you!" Mrs. Scotti's voice was painfully shrill. "I'm calling the police!"

Of course. And they'd have no problem at all believing that there was a body missing. The missing mind, on the other hand—that would be a much tougher sell. A peculiar whirlpool sensation had begun in the pit of Claire's stomach. She had to get away, preferably without letting Mrs. Scotti get a good look at her new face. The window was her only option. Out onto the fire escape, down to the alley, and along it to the main thoroughfare, where she could blend into the constant stream of pedestrian traffic.

It was a good plan, but it would have worked much better if Claire had been herself. Boehm wasn't just a man—he was a tall man, with large feet and rangy limbs. Manoeuvring his body through the window was like trying to push a grocery cart with two wonky wheels through a maze. His knees got caught in the window frame. His size twelves refused to clear the sill. Once outside, they got stuck in the wrought iron railing, nearly pitching her head-first down the stairs to the pavement below.

Aching all over—again—she finally limped out onto Queen Street, rubbing at several fresh bruises on her left arm.

For a long while, Claire walked, not sure where she might go, feeling only that for some reason it refused to divulge, the universe had decided to gang up on her. Who was this Garrick Boehm, anyway, and why didn't he have a driver's licence? You didn't have to own a car to have a driver's licence. Claire had a driver's licence, had even renewed it the previous year, and she hadn't driven anything since leaving Caverley Corners. How could he not be carrying his home address on him?

Stopped by a DO NOT WALK sign at an intersection, she looked across the road and found herself staring at the facade of Sophie Hopper's apartment building. Instantly, Claire's thoughts about the universe became more charitable. It might have taken away her body, but it had also directed her steps to the one person she could count on to help her.

Sophie had always been perceptive. If anyone could look beyond this rumpled white lab coat and recognize a friend in need of comforting, it would be her. Claire had absolutely no doubt of that. She glanced at the digital watch on Boehm's wrist and did some swift mental calculation. Sophie was an ER nurse at Toronto Mercy Hospital. Her duty shift began at noon. She might still be at home. Even if she weren't, the ride up to her apartment and back would be warming, at least. It was a little chilly to be strolling outside without a jacket.

Her timing was perfect. Sophie was on her way out, locking her apartment door behind her, just as Claire stepped off the elevator on the third floor.

Sophie Hopper was an impressively built woman—five-foot-ten in flat-heeled shoes and endowed with curves that announced themselves through even the shapeless all-weather coat she was currently wearing. Her perfect oval face was surrounded by a mass of flaming red hair, making her appearance even more striking.

Claire waited for her to turn around before calling out, "Sophie! Am I glad to see you!"

Taken by surprise, Sophie frowned at the dishevelled stranger for several seconds. "I don't know you," she said in a hard, flat voice. "Get away from me, you creep."

For the second time that day, Claire's heart sank.

"Sophie, please! You've got to help me! Look past the lab coat. I'm not that person inside. I'm really—"

"I don't give a damn! Listen, buster, you may think a nurse is an easy mark, but things have changed. I don't know how you know my name, but you'd better forget it fast and get the hell out of my way or I *will* deck you."

Common sense should have taken over at that moment. Claire should have remembered that self-defence was a compulsory subject at the Florence Nightingale School of Nursing Science, where Sophie had obtained her degree. It should have occurred to Claire that a woman nearly six feet tall who worked out four times a week and had a green belt in judo was probably a match for any man who accosted her under any circumstances. But it didn't.

"You've got to hear me out!" Claire declared. Then, recklessly, she grabbed Sophie by the arm.

There was no warning. "Ee-*yah*!" screamed the redhead, and all at once Claire was flying through the air.

She landed with a painful thud, rolled several times along the floor, and fetched up at the feet of a grey-haired woman in a blue cardigan and a blue and white printed dress. Focusing with great difficulty, Claire watched as the elevator door slid open and Sophie Hopper stepped into the car. There was a pause before the door closed again. Perhaps there was still time to—

"Get him, Mrs. Griesdorf!" Sophie called out stridently.

Then something hard hit Claire on the head and all the lights went out in her brain.

In the Fifth Dimension

Tillah's essence went utterly still. *So you're playing games with the threedees? Tricking and tormenting them? Tell me again how you and Olla'set are so very, very different from each other.*

I don't disaggregate them for my own amusement.

And you're certain Olla'set does?

Did. You may be its guardian, but the bubble belongs to me now, and I... grant... wishes.

But if, as you say, they believe you to be an evil spirit, why should any of them ask you for a favour?

Because they need help and can't find it anywhere else. But they've heard about something I did to help someone, like the female threedee in the gathering place, so they come to that place and they make a request.

And what makes them think you'll hear them?

Because I do. I return periodically to that point on the timeline and I listen to them. All of them. And I answer.

Tillah's essence was radiating curiosity. *Tell me about the threedee in the gathering place.*

It happened shortly after I learned how to communicate with them. I was in their distant past, monitoring the activities in a place containing a great many threedees, and I observed a lone female being attacked by four males in a passageway. When they were done, she shouted something at them, and one of the males picked up a piece of coherent matter and threw it at her, hard enough to cut through her outer membrane. He called her a name and spat on the ground. Then all four of them left her there. I was curious and melded with her essence. She was praying to any god who would listen, begging for her defilement to be avenged.

And you helped her. How? Did you disaggregate them?

I did something worse. I sank several compacted pods into the gathering place and captured the male who had thrown the matter at her. Then, in sight of all the other threedees, I lifted him into the fifth dimension, melded with his essence, and warned him that this female was never to be harmed again, and if anything happened to her, whoever caused it would be answering to Demonai. Then I put him back.

You told him your name?

Well, I couldn't let Olla'set take the credit for answering her prayer, could I?

And did many others come to that gathering place, with prayers and offerings?

Over time, yes. Females came, alone and in pairs. I couldn't ignore them, Tillah. The other threedees treated them so badly! If you had been there, I'm sure you would have protected them too.

So Demonai became a god by accident. Does it ever occur to you that perhaps the same thing might have happened to Olla'set?

Briefly. Then I remind myself about all the threedee offspring who have been dropped into the sea or thrown into volcanoes or left on mountaintops to die, in his name.

Are you sure about that? she persisted. *Do they actually use his name? Because, like you, if I wanted to take credit for something, I would make certain others knew what to call me.*

Demonai considered fiercely for a time, his essence sparking with the effort required, but he finally had to admit, *I have never heard Olla'set's name spoken aloud by any of the threedees I've monitored.*

As Tillah withdrew her pod, Demonai remained still, remembering. The abused female had called out to many gods for vengeance, not just one. In the restless whorl of dimensions that filled this bubble, all constantly rippling and eddying like excited essence, somewhere she was still calling out. Threedees were drowning and burning alive and being blasted to bits by the changes Olla'set had made to their world—the floods and tremors and exploding mountaintops. Demonai couldn't place a pod in the third dimension without sensing the threedees' terror and feeling them scream for mercy to a whole collection of strangely-named gods, none of them answering—and none of them Olla'set.

If he had communicated with them at all, they would have known what to call him. But they didn't, so he clearly hadn't. And why should he, if he truly believed they were inferior creatures?

Purpose began taking shape at the core of Demonai's essence. Having these creatures simply pass a practical test wouldn't be enough. Somehow, he had to get Olla'set inside this bubble and put him in communication with the threedees. Only then would he believe what Demonai already knew: that higher thinking skills *could* evolve in five dimensions, and that the threedees possessed them.

And for that, he was going to need more experimental subjects.

Chapter Four

The on-campus coffee shop at Upper Canada University was called Lazy Susan's Bistro. It had begun life as a book store back in the '70s, but had reinvented itself twice: first as a refectory when the original eating place in the basement of Tudor College had been forced to close in 1998; and again after being burned to the ground by an electrical fire in 2014. Now, rebuilt and conforming completely to code, the Bistro was an airy, cheerful place with patio seating, an antique wrought iron bicycle rack out front, and broadband Wi-Fi.

It also served hot chocolate with assorted flavours of marshmallows, Ellie's drug of first choice. When Detective Breck had called her to request a meeting after her work shift, she'd fully expected him to invite her to the police station. Instead, he'd asked her to suggest a location near the lab, immediately piquing her curiosity, and she'd given him the Bistro's address. Whether she paid for it or he did, she'd decided, Ellie was having chocolate today!

Breck arrived while she was perusing the marshmallow list. He stepped up beside her in line and leaned in to say quietly, "There are empty tables on the patio. We can talk out there."

"Okay," she replied. When she turned her head to ask whether he wanted anything to drink, he was gone.

Very strange.

Ellie carried her chocolate outside and sat down at the small round table he'd picked out, under a green and white striped umbrella at the far end of the patio. He'd taken off his jacket, she noted, and hung it over the back of the metal chair. Evidently off duty, he'd removed his tie as well.

"I was going to treat you to coffee, but you disappeared before I could ask how you like it," she told him.

"Thanks for the offer, Ms. O'Toole, but I'm fine. And thank you for agreeing to meet with me."

Now she was confused. Ellie hadn't thought she had a choice about that. And the formality of his manner made her wonder whether she could be mistaken about his being off duty as well.

Leaning across the table, he lowered his voice and continued, "Since our encounter with Demonai, I've been doing some research. I think he may be for real. About fifteen years ago, the Royal Ontario Museum hosted a selection of artifacts from an archaeological dig in Spain. According to the current curators, everything they put on display had been conclusively authenticated and dated back to the early Iron Age. One of those items was a figure representing a god named Dem-An-Noi. You'll never guess who he was the patron deity of."

Ellie paused in mid-sip and locked eyes with him. "Prostitutes and concubines. I looked him up too, at the university. A prof in the Archaeology Department told me that ancient scrolls and tablets from as far back as 700 B.C. mention Demonai—or some variation of that name—as a god-protector of sex workers."

Breck threw her a lopsided grin. "It kind of gives new meaning to the phrase 'trickster god', doesn't it?"

She groaned and shook her head.

"Sorry," he said. "I couldn't resist. Seriously, though, as a cop, I've had to deal with prostitutes. That might explain his interest in me. But what's your connection?"

She frowned. "Demonai mentioned my grandfather. He

used to be a Superior Court judge before he retired."

"Not many prostitution cases are heard that high up," Breck remarked.

"Then I haven't got a clue."

"Well, Demonai gave me one when he suggested I read a book by Claire Amory. I looked her up in Cyberpedia. Apparently, using the pen name Darienne d'Amore, she's churned out about two dozen paranormal romances, but her debut novel in 2005 was a fantasy written under her own name. I picked up a copy of it in a second-hand bookstore a few days ago and finished reading it last night." He reached down, pulled a paperback from his inner jacket pocket, and placed the book on the table between them.

Ellie cocked her head and read the title aloud. *"Three Heads Are Better.* What's it about?"

"Three people who are strangers to each other go to sleep one night, and when they wake up they're in one another's bodies, thanks to a playful deity named…?"

She gasped her next breath. "Demonai? She actually calls him that in the book?"

"She does. She's given the human characters fictitious names, but I'm pretty sure the young woman is based on Claire herself. You need to read this book," Breck advised her, "and then we need to speak with its author."

⸛

Two days later they were back at the Bistro, with Claire Amory's book sitting in front of them once more.

"I was up most of last night finishing it," was all Ellie could reply to Breck's inquiring stare.

"And?" he prompted her.

"And if we hadn't met Demonai ourselves, I'd call this a humorous fantasy. But knowing what we know about him… it's terrifying."

"I've located Ms. Amory," he told her. "She's living with

her partner in a speck on the map called Caverley Corners. It's a couple of hours northeast of the city. Are you up for a road trip tomorrow?"

"You've spoken to her?"

"Yes. When I told her I was investigating a series of unusual occurrences, she was hesitant about meeting with me. Then I mentioned Demonai's name, and she insisted we sit down for a chat."

Ellie cast a wary glance at the book. It hadn't moved.

"You're not a tagalong, Ellie. She knows we were together when it happened, and she's invited us both to have tea with her," he assured her, then added. "Have you told your grandfather yet?"

"Not yet. There's a big family dinner coming up. I was hoping to approach him then. Although, if I start talking about what I heard and saw in the laundromat and he shuts me down, all my relatives are going to think I'm delusional."

Breck leaned back in his chair with a quizzical expression on his face. "But you said he's retired. That should make him more accessible, shouldn't it? Available for a private meeting with you, maybe over lunch somewhere?"

"It's not that simple. When my grandmother passed away, it was like a part of him went with her. My aunt once said it was as though a light had been turned off inside him. After the funeral, he was always stern-faced. He never seemed to relax. He hardly even spoke. And in the courtroom…? Let's just say that he made a point of living up to his nickname: 'Mack Truck' O'Toole."

"Demonai wants you to hear your grandfather's stories about him. Let's go have tea with Claire Amory. Maybe she can give you what you need to get the judge talking about the past."

〜〜〜

According to the Historical Society plaque beside the front

entrance, Claire Amory's two-story brick home had been designed and built in 1853 by Elijah F. Dinsdale, to be the residence of Admiral William Caverley, of Her Majesty's Royal Navy (retired). Beautifully symmetrical in design, the Victorian structure was a celebration of woodworking artistry, with decorative gingerbread trim on its four gables and along the roof edges of its many porches, one of them on the second floor.

A heavy brass knocker in the shape of a lion's head hung on the front door. Breck used it to announce their arrival, and a moment later the door was opened by a smiling, dark-haired woman with bright blue eyes set in a heart-shaped face.

"Detective Breck?" she said.

He nodded.

"I'm Claire Amory. And you must be Ms. O'Toole. You're right on time," she told them in a voice that sounded on the edge of laughter. "I just took the scones out of the oven. By the time the tea is ready to pour, they'll be cool enough to eat. Please, come in and make yourselves comfortable."

She led them into a parlour that looked as though it had been transplanted from an early twentieth century English country home. "Cluttered elegance" was the phrase that came to mind as Ellie's gaze roamed around the room, pausing to admire the floor-to-ceiling fieldstone fireplace.

"How long have you lived here?" Breck asked.

Claire took a seat on the divan, facing her guests across a claw-footed low wooden table. On it sat a floral patterned teapot and three matching cups with saucers, all sporting graceful S-curved handles.

"We bought it about twelve years ago," she replied. "Sarah Jane and I were already a couple at that point. But I'd been imagining myself as mistress of the manor since childhood, when I kept passing this house on my way to school. I vowed that I'd live here one day. And now I do… thanks to Demonai."

"So that was the wish he was granting?" said Ellie.

Claire's lips quirked briefly. "With Demonai, it's hard to tell. We're all making wishes all the time, whether we express them or not, and he's a trickster, granting them at his pleasure in ways we don't expect. But I honestly believe that he has a soft spot for us, deep down, and wouldn't intentionally do us harm. Detective, you mentioned on the phone that you were investigating strange occurrences. Do you suspect Demonai might have been responsible?"

"We know he was," Ellie cut in, and she proceeded to describe the incident at the laundromat.

Claire's eyes were sparkling now. "And what were you doing just before he showed up?"

"My laundry. And I was reading one of Rhoda's gossip magazines while I waited for the dryer to finish up, and thinking—"

"—how nice it must be to be famous?" Claire supplied, one eyebrow raised.

"Ye-es," Ellie allowed uncomfortably. "You're saying Demonai read my mind?"

"And granted your unexpressed wish," said Claire. "One phone call to the media and you'd have been front page news—in a tabloid. You get what you asked for, but tilted ninety degrees. That's the way he operates." She leaned forward and poured the tea. Then she excused herself and went to the kitchen, returning a moment later with a bowl of citrus-fragrant scones and a small tub of margarine.

Meanwhile, "He did warn us to be careful what we wish for," Breck pointed out.

"Please, help yourselves," Claire urged them, handing out bread-and-butter plates that matched the rest of the tea set.

For the next few minutes, the conversation paused as scones were split and slathered, tasted and complimented. Then Breck said to Claire, "About your book, *Three Heads Are Better*: how much of it actually happened?"

She took a sip of her tea, then answered, "Confidentially,

all of it."

Ellie froze with her cup halfway to her mouth. "All of it? Really?"

"Really. It's a memoir, disguised as a fantasy because that was the only way it could be published. I'd wished for an adventure that I could write about and that people would want to read, and that's exactly what Demonai gave me. A best-selling comic fantasy novel. But he also gave me the kick in the rear that I needed to get out of my rut and get on with my life. He's the reason I moved back here to write instead of staying in the city. I spent the first year or so writing lesbian erotica for Ralph Ignace's various publications. The money was good, but it really wasn't the career I wanted. So, I drafted *Three Heads Are Better*, showed it to an editor I'd met while living in Toronto, and the rest I'm sure you know."

"Paranormal romance—that's the career you wanted all along?" said Ellie.

"Not at the beginning, but I came to realize it was the one that I was meant to have. Editors were always advising me to 'find my niche'. I never fully understood what they were talking about, until *Three Heads Are Better* suggested the plot of my first paranormal romance. It practically wrote itself, and while I was editing it, two more plots popped into my head. I wrote them one after the other, readers demanded a sequel to the first one… and next thing I knew, I was a branded romance writer, turning out two books a year and loving every minute of it.

"While accepting my first award from the Romance Authors of America, I thanked Demonai for setting my career in motion. Everyone laughed, thinking I was referring to a fictional character from my first novel. I wasn't. If it weren't for him, I might never have returned to Caverley Corners to meet Sarah Jane, the love of my life, buy the house of my dreams, and stir the emotions of readers all over the world with my stories. I wished for an adventure, but what I really wanted was to be happy, and in the end, that is what he's given me.

"Ms. O'Toole, if Demonai has taken an interest in you—and if he's acquainted with your grandfather, then I rather suspect he has—granting that idle wish for fame is probably just the beginning. He'll be paying close attention, trying to figure out what you actually want deep down. So, as much as possible, try to focus on that. The more clues you give him, the fewer detours you'll find yourself taking on the way to your ultimate goal."

"And how do I fit into all this?" Breck wondered.

"I don't know. There were three of us in my adventure, and we all came out of it changed for the better. If Demorai is multitasking, he may have plans for both of you, or even the two of you plus someone else you haven't met yet. Perhaps you should talk to James and Garry. We've stayed in touch over the years. I have your contact information, Detective. Would you like me to give it to them?"

"Yes, thank you, Ms. Amory," he replied. "Tell them we'll make time to meet with them whenever they're available."

In the Fifth Dimension

Demonai, your experiment is a failure, Tillah declared. *Your melded threedees are running around in mindless confusion.*

Confusion, yes, but not mindless. Their actions are purposeful. All three of them realized immediately that before they could begin addressing the unanswered questions regarding their current situation, they needed to gather in one location. This indicates intelligence.

Baffled intelligence. They lack information, and with their limited perceptual abilities they aren't likely to come across it anytime soon.

You need to give them more credit, Tillah. Threedees are natural problem-solvers, drawn to discrepancies and unanswered questions. That's the first thing I noticed about them. They're quite resourceful, and it's precisely to observe how they resolve the mystery of a predicament like this one that I'm running the experiment.

Really? I thought you just wanted to see how they would react to being toyed with.

Now you need to give me more credit. Everything I do in this time frame is intended to convince Olla'set that they're just as intelligent as we are.

He's much harder to persuade than you think, Demonai. Harder than I am, at any rate, and I have yet to observe anything about them that would demonstrate such a parity.

Be patient, Tillah. They've just begun to work on the

problem I've put to them. Are you able to understand their communications yet?

I've been listening carefully.

But can you understand the meaning of what they're expressing?

Most of it is still incomprehensible, but it is starting to make sense to me now.

That's because you have the ability to learn what you need to know, over a span of time. So do the threedees. Shall we position some pods and see how our three test subjects are progressing?

I think I'll leave that to you, Demonai. They're your obsession, not mine.

Hmm. That sounded more like Olla'set than like Tillah. Perhaps Demonai needed to focus on persuading her after all.

Chapter Five

After some lively discussion, Hollinger persuaded Boehm to call a taxi to carry them to Boehm's place, where his body would eventually have to turn up. At Hollinger's insistence, Boehm also instructed that the driver was to pick them up from the service entrance at the rear of the building rather than at the front.

"You've got a car," Boehm pointed out, leaning back against the service corridor wall while they waited for the cab to arrive. "Why not just take it and go?"

Hollinger thought they'd already settled that. "And where would you put it once we got there? Because I'm not leaving a Mercedes out in the open in any neighbourhood where you can afford to live."

Boehm said nothing. He didn't have to. The way his features contracted spoke volumes.

Hollinger knew he'd been right to be concerned as soon as the taxi pulled up in front of Garrick Boehm's medium-rise apartment building. The scientist lived in a section of the city that was ripe for urban renewal. Everything about it was old and tired and screamed 'working poor'. A Mercedes wouldn't just attract notice here—it would be stolen within half an hour.

They'd climbed all the way to the third floor landing before Boehm remembered that his keys were with his other body, leaving him no way to unlock his apartment door.

Unfortunately, the lock was a deadbolt, and neither of them knew how to pick a lock anyway. Their only option was to find the building superintendent and somehow convince him to let them inside.

"I know this guy. Let me do the talking," Boehm said. Despite his misgivings, Hollinger agreed.

The super had an apartment on the first floor. His door was ajar when they got there, as though he'd been expecting them. By now, it felt as though a three-ring circus was gearing up in Hollinger's stomach. Still, he remained silent.

"Mr. Rosseau?" Boehm called through the door.

It swung wide open, releasing a waft of something that made Hollinger want to wrinkle his nose. Evidently, the neighbourhood wasn't the only thing that was ripe around here.

"You know who I am? That's nice," said Rosseau, "because I know who you are too, Mr. Hollinger. Seen you on the tube. What can I do for ya?"

"My friend Garry Boehm was supposed to meet us here, but he's been delayed. We were wondering if you could let us into his apartment to wait for him."

"Garry's your friend? That's nice. Who's she?" he added, pointing with his chin.

"Oh, she's his cousin. From out of town."

Rosseau's eyes acquired a gleam that Hollinger recognized instantly. There might as well have been dollar signs printed on his eyeballs. "Really? That's nice. But Garry never mentioned anything about either one of you to me."

"What would it take to persuade you to unlock that door, Mr. Rosseau?" Hollinger asked.

"For you, sweetheart, a twenty. For him, a hundred." Seeing Boehm's jaw drop, he added, "Come on, Mr. Hollinger. You're worth millions. You gonna begrudge a measly hundred to an ordinary guy like me? Think of it as a security deposit, nonrefundable. And for an extra fifty, I'll even keep my mouth shut about you being here."

"That's extortion!" sputtered Boehm.

"Like you haven't done worse to get where you are?" Rosseau snapped back. "It's business, Hollinger. There's a price tag on the key to that apartment. Pay up or leave."

Reluctantly, Boehm opened Hollinger's wallet and began counting out bills onto the super's already-greasy palm. Hollinger bit his tongue to keep quiet, all the way back up the stairs. Finally, the two changelings were able to step inside Boehm's residence and shut the door behind them.

"Well," Hollinger remarked, letting his gaze roam around the living room, "it's a damn sight better than where I woke up this morning. At least the walls aren't purple."

Boehm flopped down onto the chocolate brown easy chair. Leaning his head back, he closed his eyes and said, "So, did you?"

Hollinger frowned. "Did I what?"

"What Rosseau said. Did you do worse things than extortion to get where you are now?"

"I guess that depends on your viewpoint."

Boehm opened one eye and figuratively shot a dagger out of it. "Forgive me for not seeing the humour in that remark."

"Fine, then." Hollinger dropped onto the brown and black striped sofa. "My firm exists for the sole purpose of helping clients to amass and protect their wealth. We advise them, and they can choose whether or not to act on that advice. In the early days, individuals came to me with small amounts of money, which could only grow through investment. I didn't do insider trading. Everything was on the up and up. And I lived hand to mouth, in a place not even as good as this.

"Then I began pursuing and landing corporate accounts. With larger amounts of money to work with, the menu of options expanded dramatically. Buyouts, takeovers, franchising… Were some of those takeovers hostile? Yes. And there were mergers that cost people their jobs, and some amazing technological innovations that ended up being bought and buried to preserve a big company's bottom line.

But nothing that I did, or counselled others to do, was against the law."

"The fact that it's legal doesn't make it morally right," Boehm countered. "And speaking as a scientist, I can assure you that just because you *can* do something, that doesn't mean you should. Did you know at the time how people lower down the food chain were being affected by your clients' business practices?"

"In an arm's-length, numbers-on-a-spreadsheet kind of way, yes, I did. But my legal and ethical responsibility was to my clients, just as Rosseau's legal and ethical responsibility was to prevent strangers from entering your apartment. So, he broke the law twice today, once when he extorted a bribe from me, and again when he let us in here without so much as asking to see our identification. Now you tell me, Garry: which of us is the bigger crook, me or Rosseau?"

A pause, then, "Your clients harm people on a much grander scale than Rosseau ever could. And you're their enabler, which makes you just as guilty as they are, as far as I'm concerned."

It was beyond disconcerting to hear his own stern voice taking him to task. "So, if I'm the bad guy, what does that make you? A victim?"

"Yes!" Boehm's hard gaze locked with his. Carefully enunciating every syllable, he said, "I lost my job yesterday because people like you hold the purse strings on government grants for scientific research."

"People like me?"

Now Boehm's eyes were flashing. "The entitled upper class. The one percent who don't give a damn about the rest of us."

As things finally came clear, Hollinger felt his own temper rising in response.

"Uh-huh. Well, difficult though this may be for you to accept, Garry, I didn't inherit what you saw back in the penthouse. I worked bloody hard to get it, starting at the bottom. Hard work creates opportunities, and courage takes advantage of them. So, if you don't happen to like the shape of your life so far, I suggest you channel some of that righteous indignation into finding a job, or making a discovery, or starting up a company of your own. Because I refuse to let you take it out on me!"

Boehm sprang to his feet, prompting Hollinger to stand up as well.

"How the hell am I supposed to do any of that while I'm in your body?" Boehm demanded, some of his anger already dissipating. "Or maybe I'd rather not. Maybe I'd prefer to remain James Hollinger and enjoy life as a multimillionaire."

If they'd simply switched bodies, Hollinger might even have considered making the trade. Instead, all he could do was laugh. "Wealth and fame, eh? You think that's all it's about? I guarantee, you'd soon discover what a headache they can be. For example: remind me again how much you had to bribe the super to let us in."

Boehm had to stop and think. "A hundred and seventy dollars."

"It could have been twenty if you hadn't been wearing my face. And, trust me, that's just the beginning."

≈

Lunchtime came and went, with no sign of Boehm's runaway body. Still, all they could do was wait. When the stomach rumblings became too loud to ignore, Boehm opened a tin of tomato soup and warmed up some leftover macaroni and cheese that they could share.

Hollinger half-expected to hear some kind of snide comment from his host—'Sorry, we seem to be out of filet mignon.'—but whatever Boehm might have been thinking, he kept to himself. In fact, he kept everything to himself, cleaning up the kitchen and moving around the apartment as though Hollinger weren't even there. Not only Boehm's silence but his very presence felt like a rebuke. Clearly, their earlier discussion was far from over.

With no one to talk to and no idea where Boehm kept the remote control for the TV, Hollinger had limited options. He found a couple of recent *Canadian Geographic* magazines and settled down on the sofa to read. Half an hour later, Boehm did the same, burying himself in a scientific journal.

Shortly before two o'clock they heard the unmistakable sound of footsteps on the stairs. Catching their breaths simultaneously, Boehm and Hollinger dropped their magazines onto the coffee table and froze. They listened hard. What had to be several pairs of feet were noisily making the turn on the second floor landing and on their way to the third.

Then came a deep male voice, carrying the ring of authority. "It's fortunate that we were able to talk those women out of pressing charges, Dr. Boehm. Are you sure you don't want to file an assault and battery complaint against them?"

"I'm certain," responded a second, much fainter voice.

As soon as he heard the scrape of a key finding the lock, Hollinger motioned to Boehm to move to the wall beside the door. They flattened themselves against it just in time. With a gentle creak, the door swung partway open.

"All right, sir," said a third man's voice from the hallway, "we'll leave you now. Remember what the paramedic said. If you begin to feel dizzy or sick to your stomach, or if your eyesight goes wonky, call 9-1-1 and request an ambulance. Just make sure you tell them to take you anywhere but Toronto Mercy Hospital. Okay?"

"I will. Thanks."

As two pairs of feet pounded their way back down the stairs, Boehm's body dragged itself wearily inside the apartment. The second the door closed, Boehm and Hollinger pounced. Hollinger grabbed the left arm, Boehm the right. They hustled this 'missing person' across the room, sitting him down with a fat *thud* in the middle of the sofa before moving in from both sides at once.

"Are you hurt? Where? How did it happen?" Boehm hollered into his own right ear.

At the same time, Hollinger was demanding shrilly into the other, "Charges? What charges?"

Claire's gaze swung from one scowling face to the other. One of them was her own, barely recognizable behind the outraged expression it was wearing. Just the sight of it made her feel queasy. She already had a throbbing headache, thanks to the old lady's purse. And the last thing she wanted right now was to pass out and end up on her way to the ER. So, she did the only thing that made sense under the circumstances.

She flung off their hands and roared in Boehm's deepest voice, "Back the hell off!" The headache backed off as well, but just for a moment. Then it returned with a vengeance. It was the final straw. This day had just been too much to bear. Claire gave herself permission to cry.

The man on her right got up and began pacing the living room, apparently made uncomfortable by the sight of tears flowing down male cheeks. Meanwhile, Claire's own body slid a consoling arm across her current broad shoulders.

"Claire?" ventured its occupant.

"Yes," she replied between sniffles. "Are you Garrick Boehm?"

"No, he is," came the response, with a finger pointed in the direction of the man still impatiently measuring off the carpet. "That's my body he's wearing. I'm James Hollinger, and I'm in yours."

"And I'm in his. So there were three of us switched around?"

"Yeah. It's a mess," Hollinger said. "But I suppose we ought to be grateful the number wasn't higher. I don't suppose you've got any idea why or how this has happened…?"

She gave him an apologetic shrug. "Sorry. I've been a little too busy to think about that."

"She certainly has—nearly getting my body arrested and apparently making it *persona non grata* at a major hospital," spat Boehm, no longer pacing. "Perhaps she'd like to explain how and why *that* happened."

Claire told them about the encounter in Sophie's apartment building.

"When I woke up, the police were on the scene and I was on a gurney, being put into the back of an ambulance. I couldn't let them take me to the hospital, not with a bump on my head and what would appear to be amnesia. They would have kept me under observation for who knew how long. So, I refused treatment on site, promising to visit my family doctor as soon as possible. I also had to promise to stay away from Toronto Mercy Hospital, because that's where Sophie works as an ER nurse."

"And the police brought you home?" Boehm said tightly. "I purposely keep nothing in my wallet that can lead anyone here if it's stolen. So, how did you know what address to give them?"

"I didn't," she snapped back. "There was paperwork to fill out at the police station, and when someone asked whether my address had changed, I knew it had to be on their system. So I asked what they had on file, and they told me. And if you think for one second that I had anything to do with—"

"Okay, enough!" said Hollinger. "We've all gotten off on the wrong foot, so let's start over by introducing ourselves. I'm James Hollinger, and for the next three weeks, no one at my office is expecting me to be available. As far as they know, I'm on a retreat."

"What about at your penthouse?" Boehm challenged. "What about Roxanne? She's out shopping with your credit cards, remember?"

"I made some calls before we left. That's all taken care of."

Boehm's borrowed jaw dropped. "How—?"

"Your turn, Claire," declared Hollinger, cutting him off.

"Okay. I'm Claire Amory, and I work from home as a freelance writer and editor. No one's going to miss me either. Except for Mrs. Scotti, my landlady. She keeps tabs on everyone in the building and could start asking questions, especially if I'm absent on the day the rent is due. First of the month. I think you'll agree that this would be a bad time to start skipping payments."

"With luck, we'll have everything sorted out by then," Hollinger assured her. "Garry, you're up."

"Who put you in charge?" Boehm wanted to know.

"I did," Hollinger returned. "Me and all the money that I'll probably end up throwing at the problems that are facing us right now. So, stop whining and tell us about yourself."

Wearing a sullen expression, Boehm replied, "I'm Dr. Garrick Boehm, a particle physicist, unemployed as of this morning. And as long as I'm inside this body, I'm also out a bunch of personal belongings, because entrance to the facility is restricted to those with the correct face and thumbprint. And a current ID pass. You left mine sitting on the desk, didn't you, Claire? Along with my office keys? And the thumb drive with all my personal emails on it?"

"Yes, but there must be a phone number I can call to instruct someone to hold your stuff for pickup," she replied reasonably. "When that's done, I'll go and get it for you. It's not the end of the world, Garry."

"In fact," Hollinger cut in harshly, "it's the least of our problems. We need to figure out what caused the three of us to trade bodies. In the meanwhile, we need to coordinate our activities in order not to draw attention to ourselves or arouse suspicion that anything is wrong. Fortunately, our day-to-day obligations are at a minimum right now, so we can all stay here for as long as necessary."

"Whoa!" said Boehm. "Why here? Why not at the huge and comfy penthouse?"

Hollinger levelled Claire's blue eyes at his face. "Because this is the last place anyone would think to look for me. At the penthouse, we've got Nate the doorman, we've got the news media—"

"—and we've got Roxanne," Boehm added dryly, "who's sure to get suspicious when she returns and you're not there."

"I doubt whether she'll be back, but yes, it could be awkward," said Hollinger. "I'll deal with that if it happens. Meanwhile, here we've got privacy."

"Think again. Here we've got Rosseau, the building superintendent," Boehm pointed out. "Or is paying off blackmailers and extortionists just a routine expense for you?"

Hollinger stared at him sadly and replied, "To get privacy? Yes. When you're James A. Hollinger, my friend, nothing comes free of charge."

In the Fifth Dimension

When Tillah next appeared, Demonai was ready for her.

I've decided you're right, Tillah. I have been too hard on Olla'set. But he's still mistaken about the threedees.

You must be enjoying your captivity, then. Olla'set won't even consider releasing you from this bubble until the two of you agree.

I'll prove to him that the threedees possess evolved intelligence. Then we'll agree.

Or, you could lie to him, tell him that you've come around to his way of thinking.

And then he would replace the bubble in his collection and go on tormenting these creatures without once trying to actually learn about them. And when his sac became full, he would aggregate the matter in it and wipe them all out of existence. I'm sorry, Tillah. I can't allow that to happen.

You care about them that much?

I understand them that well. In some ways, they're very similar to us.

For example?

Let me show you.

Demonai had anchored himself to several carefully selected locations, which they would be visiting in sequence.

What is this gathering place? Tillah asked once they were implanted at the first stop on the tour. *Or is it a collection container?*

The threedees call this a hospital. Beings come here to be repaired. Observe, Tillah. This female's collection sac has reached critical mass. She is about to expel a new threedee.

Interesting. She has a number of sacs inside her membrane, moving matter back and forth. But where is her essence?

Demonai had been waiting for that question. *Right there. It's coherent matter, like everything else in three-dimensional space. The threedees carry their essence in a special pod.*

But what happens when they retract the pod?

They don't. Threedees are expelled with all their pods already extended and that's the way they remain.

If their essence occupies such a small area inside their containment membrane, then perhaps Olla'set is right about these creatures.

He is wrong, Tillah. If you or I were that tightly compacted, we would occupy about the same amount of three-dimensional space.

And those other collection sacs? What do they do?

I'm not sure, but I do know that each one has a purpose, and they're all inside her for a reason.

Really? Observe how the female is struggling to expel the aggregated matter. This is not a very practical arrangement, Demonai, Tillah declared. *Collection sacs belong on the outside of the containment membrane.*

The threedees are made very differently from us, it's true. Observing them has made me wonder what a higher-order being might see if it were looking at us.

According to Olla'set, there are no higher-order beings than ourselves in the universe.

Olla'set also maintains that threedees can't possibly be mentally evolved, an opinion that I will shortly disprove.

Do you believe there is a higher dimension than our own, Demonai?

I do. Are you willing to accept that there could be? That it could even be inhabited by creatures we are unable to perceive, observing us? Studying us? Perhaps even amusing themselves by creating and playing with us?

Tillah's essence went still. *If that were true, it would be terrifying to contemplate. How can you even think of such things, Demonai?*

Their discussion was interrupted by a sudden high-pitched vibration.

And there is our brand new threedee, said Demonai, his essence warming with pride.

It's so small and feeble.

It will grow larger and stronger over time.

And it isn't sentient, Demonai. Observe its essence. Such a faint and sluggish little light.

That will grow and strengthen over time as well.

How do you know this, Demonai?

Let me show you.

Their next stop was also a gathering place, but not inside a structure. Demonai and Tillah implanted their pods and observed as a crowd of small and very excited threedees ineffectually pursued a spherical object. Larger threedees, both male and female, were lined up on the borders of the area where this was happening, witnessing the activity and making a great deal of noise.

This is a game, Tillah. There are actually two groups on the field, competing for possession of the sphere.

Then why do they keep repelling it with their pods? Why doesn't one of them just collect it?

Because possession is not the sole end of the game. Each group is working together as a team to accomplish a shared goal, and that is to move the object to a specific location in the opposing team's territory.

Wouldn't this goal be more speedily achieved if the larger threedees became involved?

Yes, but that would defeat the purpose of playing the game. The small threedees are the aggregated offspring of the larger ones, and this game is part of their education. You observed how weak the spark is in the essence of a newly expelled threedee. These creatures have a short lifespan, and it takes precious time for their essence to become fully functional. So the larger ones organize activities like this one to exercise the developing essence of their offspring. This way, everything inside the containment membrane reaches its full size and capacity at the same time.

So this game is meant to teach them how to collaborate effectively with other threedees? I imagine that would be a survival skill in a dimension as crowded with matter as this one is, Tillah commented. *However, not all threedees seem to be proficient at it. Observe, Demonai.*

One of the adults had left the sidelines and rushed into the middle of the game, waving his arms as he expressed dissatisfaction with the way it was being played. Tillah and Demonai watched him berate another adult and then take to task one of the smallest threedees, a male offspring who seemed to become even smaller as he was showered with abuse.

That offspring is the threedee we observed being expelled at the hospital.

Poor little creature! Is he making a wish that we could grant?

Tillah's readiness to become actively involved in the threedee world did not escape Demonai's notice.

No. He believes that he has failed and deserves to be treated like this, in the presence of other threedees. I know that he survives to full maturity, however. I've already made contact with him later in his life.

Tillah sparkled with amusement. *And played with him, no doubt. Do I get to meet him too?*

I don't think that would be wise. The knowledge that one being exists in a higher dimension than his own already makes him nervous. If he realizes there is more than one of us…

…he'll be terrified, Tillah supplied, *just as I would be if I thought—never mind. Tell me, Demonai, does he learn in spite of his aggregator to collaborate effectively with others?*

Too well, I'm afraid. Now he needs to separate himself from the group and achieve things that the others cannot. And I am helping him.

Show me!

Chapter Six

1967
March 26

"**S**lattery, you are *such* a loser!"

With a sigh of agreement, Rick Slattery slid over on the sofa as his friend and roommate Cormac O'Toole dropped down beside him. Mac exhaled noisily, then gazed around the living room, grinning with bleary satisfaction. "Some bitchin' happening we had, eh?"

Rick did not respond. They had hosted a pre-exam party the previous night for nearly fifty people, and he had been awake for an hour already, glumly assessing the damage.

Snack food littered the apartment like bomb shrapnel in a war zone. Someone had overturned a full bowl of popcorn on the coffee table, then walked away with the bowl. Peanut shells, pretzel sticks and cheese twists had landed and stuck in puddles of spilled beer that had been left to dry, turning the hardwood floor into a minefield for bare feet.

Not all the guests had been total slobs. The engineering students had thoughtfully erected pyramids of empty beer cans on nearly every horizontal surface. Someone had left a leaning tower of pizza cartons beside the front door. And the faint aroma of weed hung in the air, no doubt as a friendly reminder to mellow out.

"That chick was so hot for you, man! How did you manage not to score? No, never mind, I already know the answer." O'Toole shook his shaggy head in disgust. "I worry about you, man. This is supposed to be the best time of your life, and instead you walk around as if the weight of the world is on your shoulders. Do you have any idea how good you've got it? Your uncle is the dean of the law faculty, all the profs know it and give you chance after chance, and time after time you keep blowing it. Don't you *want* to be a lawyer? 'Cause if you don't, you need to point yourself in a different direction, *ay-sap*. I'm serious, man. You need to learn how to have fun. I'm your best friend, and hanging out with you lately feels like I'm watching a slow motion train wreck."

"Are you done?" Slattery inquired wearily.

"That depends. Are you listening?"

"Yes. Are you? If I don't get my law degree and pass the bar, I'll be breaking a tradition that's been part of my family for ten generations. Nobody cares whether I actually practise law. I just have to graduate from this faculty at this university. So that's what I'll do, whatever it takes."

"Does your family realize that you're struggling just to pass your first year courses? Or don't they care about that either?"

Slattery simply shrugged.

"Well then," said O'Toole, getting to his feet, "here's my suggestion to you, my friend. You take that antique lamp or gravy boat or whatever the hell it is that you found at the flea market in Wasaga Beach last weekend and rub it a few times, and hope that there's a genie inside who can help you get through the next four or five years of your life with both your health and your sanity intact. Meanwhile, exams are looming, so if anyone is looking for me, I'll be working my ass off to qualify for another fun-filled year at this prestigious institution of higher learning." He paused and sniffed the air. "Higher being the operative word in this case," he added. "I'd open a window if I were you. You know what they say about the effects of second-hand toke."

"So you're leaving me to clean up? Again?"

Mac surveyed the living room and made a sour face. "You're right. Call in the groupies, man. This place is too disgusting for either of us to touch."

Mac was the one with groupies, the one with the Gibson guitar and the semi-famous folk rock band. Mac had also been blessed with broad shoulders and easy charm and beer-ad good looks. Rick was the sidekick, the one with the forgettable face and fade-into-the-woodwork nature and nothing better to do than be a sounding board for other people's brilliant ideas—when he wasn't busy keeping the apartment habitable, that is, and worrying about flunking out of school. Living proof that opposites did attract, Mac and Rick had been close friends since high school, the force of nature and his shadow.

Sometimes Rick got depressed enough to wonder why someone like Mac would even associate with him. Sometimes Rick's father even wondered about it, aloud. At those times, Rick and his mother would lock eyes in silent commiseration.

That was why he had bought her the lamp for her birthday. Antiques were her secret pleasure. Even though the one he'd picked up at the flea market was probably just a mass-produced replica, he knew she would appreciate the thought.

Richard Slattery Senior, meanwhile, had taken his wife on a European tour for her birthday, so the gift from their son would have to be sent to their hotel in Paris. Rick went to his bedroom to prepare the lamp for mailing. As he unwrapped it from its cocoon of white tissue paper, however, his heart dropped. He'd forgotten about the tarnish. Or maybe it was just dirt. Whatever it was, it lay in dark blotches all over the spout of his mother's birthday present. Rick cradled the lamp in the crook of his left elbow and rubbed experimentally at one of the spots with his other shirt sleeve.

Hey, Ricky, let's have some fun.

Slattery froze in mid-wipe. Hardly daring to breathe, he stared uncertainly at the lamp. Had he really heard that?

Come on, the voice coaxed, *you know it's what you really want.*

"Mac, that isn't funny, man," he called out.

There was no reply. Slattery dropped the lamp back onto the tissue paper on his bed and went to find his friend, but Mac had gone out. Slattery was alone in the apartment with the owner of the voice. No, he amended, his heart racing after a rapid and thorough search of every closet in every room, he was just alone in the apartment, period. And hearing a voice as clearly as if someone were standing right beside him.

"I'm going bonkers," he murmured.

No, Rick, you're not. I'm Demonai. I live in this lamp. And if you seriously want to have the best time of your life, don't tell Mac about me.

"Trust me, I won't be telling anyone about this, because you're not real."

The voice chuckled, raising gooseflesh all up and down Slattery's arms.

Test me. Make a wish.

"You're kidding." Rick's voice came out an octave higher than usual. He hadn't paid much for the lamp. Perhaps he ought to drop it in the nearest dumpster and just send his mother a card for her birthday this year.

I'm serious, Rick. You can wish for anything except lasting harm to another living being.

Professor Lindhurst had wrapped up his final lecture on ethics with those words. Hearing them now brought Slattery's stampeding imagination to a halt. He'd been right the first time. Mac was playing an early April Fool's joke on him. If he looked carefully enough, Rick would probably find a camera and a speaker hidden in his bedroom. And hadn't Mac made a point earlier of telling him to rub the lamp and hope for a genie?

All right, my friend, Rick decided. You want to play? Let's play.

"Okay, Demonai. The apartment is a sty. Clean it up."

Done. Walk into the living room.

Slattery strode through the doorway of his bedroom and found himself standing, speechless, in the middle of a scene straight out of a Disney animated film. Every room of the apartment had been invaded by glowing white orbs about six inches across. They darted and spun in all directions, like a pillaging army of overweight Tinkerbells. Wherever they paused, something disappeared in a bright flash of light. The pyramids of beer cans, the pile of pizza cartons, the peanut shells and cheese twists that had been sat on and stepped on and trodden into the area rug, even the butts in the ash tray, all blew up and vanished before his astonished eyes. When the orbs had finished their work, they shrank to points of light that all winked out in unison, leaving the apartment cleaner than Rick had ever seen it.

This was impossible.

"Holy shit...!" he breathed, suddenly finding breathing itself difficult.

Is that real enough for you, Ricky boy?

The voice was directly behind him. Slattery spun around and found himself staring at a pale, pulsating ball of light hovering just a couple of feet away. His heart nearly stopped. The orb was blocking the path to his bedroom—an ominous sign—but it also didn't seem to be making any move toward him. For at least thirty seconds he stood as though frozen, never taking his eyes off the thing. Then he blinked, and it was gone.

"How—? How did you—?" he gasped.

Not important. What you need to keep in mind is that I'm on your side. Hey, man, I'm offering you the opportunity to have fun. To have groupies, if that's what you want. You can be the main attraction. Mac can be your sidekick for a change. What do you say to that?

It sounded wonderful, which meant there had to be a catch. Slattery had grown up reading stories about supernatural beings who offered to grant wishes, and none of those tales had had happy endings. Willing his voice to remain steady, he replied carefully, "I like it, Demonai. It's just—This is a lot for an ordinary human to take in all at once."

Listen, I understand. You need time to digest what's just happened. That's cool. When you've figured out what you want me to do next, just rub the lamp. Oh, and next time…? No more parlour tricks, okay? Make a real wish. Revenge is my specialty, by the way. Tell me who's pissed you off lately and I'll help you get even. It'll be fun.

Yes, it would be fun, he suddenly realized.

"One question, Demonai. What did you do with all the garbage you removed from the apartment? Is it vaporized or something?"

Nope, just collected. I can put it back if you like. Or I can disaggregate it. Whatever you wish.

"Actually, there is somewhere I'd like you to put it."

Sitting on his bed, his legs outstretched, with the lamp perched on the pillow beside him, Slattery waited, gleeful anticipation growing like a bubble inside his chest. Shortly after one o'clock, he heard the apartment door open and close.

"Hey, those groupies did a great job!" exclaimed Mac's voice from the living room. "They worked fast, too. What did you promise them? Whatever it is, I'm up for it, man."

Slattery said nothing, just glanced at the lamp and grinned. He heard Mac's footsteps travel from the living room to the kitchen, and then to the hallway outside Rick's door. He imagined Mac reaching for the knob of his own bedroom door and had to clap a hand over his mouth to avoid spoiling the surprise.

"Rick, are you hungry, man? I have to grab a clean shirt and get back to the stacks, but I brought you something from the hamburger joi—Hey! What the hell?!"

With that, Rick's merriment could no longer be contained. It blew his hand off his mouth and poured out of him in howls of uncontrollable laughter. A moment later his door flew open and Mac stalked in, struggling to keep a stern expression on his face.

"Rick Slattery!" he scolded in mock indignation from the foot of the bed, sending his friend into even more spasms of hilarity. After a pause, Mac joined him in laughter. "This was brilliant, man! Did you do it all by yourself?"

"I must confess," Rick managed to reply between guffaws, "I did have a little bit of help."

"Uh-huh. Well, I'm glad you finally decided to have some fun, my friend. It looks good on you. By the way," he added on his way out the door, "your lunch is somewhere in my bedroom. Happy hunting."

Once Mac had left the apartment again and Slattery's laughter had subsided, Demonai commented, *Let me guess—you want me to find that hamburger?*

"No, thanks. Just take out the garbage. Vaporize it this time, please. Or whatever it is you do to get rid of stuff permanently."

Your wish is my command.

Recalling the expression on Mac's face as he entered the room, Rick burst out laughing again.

You really enjoyed playing this joke on your friend, didn't you?

"I did. I haven't had that much fun since…" He fell silent, instantly sober.

…since before your father sat you down to have a serious talk about your future?

Rick stiffened. "How do you know about that?"

I sort of eavesdropped on your conversation with Mac earlier. It was a logical guess. Besides, I have some personal experience in this area.

"The Slatterys are a special breed, son," said Rick, quoting from memory in a poor imitation of his father's baritone voice. "You have greatness in your genes, and some very large footsteps in which to follow. We're confident that you'll do something memorable with your life."

Memorable, Demonai repeated. *There's some wiggle room there. Did he say* how *he expected you to be memorable?*

"I've always assumed he was talking about changing the world. Becoming a political leader, or a captain of industry, or a Supreme Court Justice. Something lofty. Something impossible," he added wistfully.

Why would that be impossible?

"Because in order to change the world Slattery-style I first have to graduate from law school, and right now I'm not sure I'll even be able to do that."

All right, then, let's forget about doing it Slattery-style. How would you like to be the most memorable law student ever to walk the halls of this venerable institution?

"And how would I do that exactly with a grade point average of 2.4?"

How long do you think it will take Mac to forget about the joke you played on him today?

"I don't know. A long time, I guess. Wait, Demonai, are you suggesting—?"

Not suggesting, Ricky. Recommending. Urging. Prescribing.

"But how is playing pranks on people going to make me memorable, except to the people I play the pranks on?"

These pranks won't just be played on people. They'll target the institution itself. The administration. The professors. All the self-important beings who reside on the pompous plane of existence. You aren't the only one whose life they delight in making difficult. Trust me, your classmates will adore you. Even your victims will secretly admire you.

"Right. How about the police? Will they secretly admire me too?"

The police won't be able to touch you, because you will have an ironclad alibi every single time.

"Then how will anyone know that it was me?"

Oh, they'll know, Ricky. They just won't be able to prove anything.

Slattery grew thoughtful.

"Keep talking, Demonai."

In the Fifth Dimension

Their next stop was outdoors.

We are near the gathering place where he continues his education, Demonai explained. *Observe.* Compacting several pods, he used them to grasp and lift an object, reorient it, then return the object to a different location.

What did you just do? Tillah wanted to know.

The object I moved is a transportation device. This one belongs to a being who has been creating obstacles to our little friend's success. At his request, I have placed it atop another object, making it difficult for that being to access, so that she will experience the same level of frustration as she has been imposing on others.

Could he not simply communicate his dissatisfaction to her by making sound waves?

He could. But then he would be no different from the many other threedees at this place of learning. Only he is capable of making this particular statement in this particular way.

Because you are helping him?

Yes. I am his sidekick.

I sense that you enjoy playing this role among the threedees.

Yes. The more I learn about these creatures, the more I want to find out about them.

That is very interesting, Demonai, because I have observed that the more you find out about them, the more like them you seem to become. This may be a negative consequence of being compacted and confined for so long in five dimensions. I'm trying to decide whether to ask Olla'set to release you as an act of mercy.

No, Tillah, I don't need to be rescued. What I need is for Olla'set to join me here so he can learn about the threedees. Surely he must be curious about what I'm doing inside this bubble.

Actually, he isn't. After each visit with you, I meld with him and share information. He knows everything that you and I have observed about these creatures.

He may know what we have observed, but he doesn't know what we know about them.

And what do we know, Demonai? That they are born small and weak but grow and develop into adults. That the adults teach their aggregated offspring how to be members of a society. That they communicate with one another by generating sound waves. That the strong threedees tend to abuse the weak. I'm sorry, Demonai, but we know nothing about them that would convince Olla'set to change his mind about them, or even to come and take a closer look at them.

Then let me show you something that might.

Demonai had been saving this, hoping he wouldn't have to use it. He guided Tillah to the final stop on the tour.

What is this gathering place? It's certainly full of material objects. There is hardly room for the threedees to move around inside it.

Some of the threedees choose to spend their lives trying to understand the universe. They have an overwhelming desire to acquire knowledge about the nature of reality, and they do much of their investigating in places like this.

Aren't we going to implant our pods?

No. You are going to meld with one of the threedees, and see what she is seeing at this moment.

Gently, carefully, Demonai coaxed a thread of the threedee's essence into fifth dimensional space and showed Tillah how to connect with it.

At once, Tillah's essence began to spark. *Demonai! She sees a living creature, one that is as differently made from the threedees as they are from us. How is this possible?*

The third dimension is filled with life, Tillah, both sentient and nonsentient, from extremely large to extremely small, made in many different ways. The beings we have been studying are aware of all the other creatures that surround them and thirst to know more about them. So, they have invented this device to assist with their observations by making the tiniest life forms appear much larger. What do you observe about the creature under the microscope?

Its shape keeps changing. Its essence is quite visible and it appears to be contained in a flexible membrane… Tillah's essence went still again. *It's made the same way we are. Is it sentient, Demonai?*

It might be. You are melded with the threedee who is studying it. What does she believe?

Tillah paused to sample the threedee's thoughts before replying, *She considers it to be an extremely primitive form of life. She has no plans to attempt to communicate with it. Demonai, is that how our kind would look to a higher-order being? Just a sac full of essence, drifting through its corner of the universe, ingesting whatever matter it comes across, and occasionally reproducing by breaking in two?*

I'm sorry I had to upset you by showing you this, Tillah, but it's important that you understand why I keep insisting that Olla'set join us inside the bubble. Reality is much more than our aggregator thinks it is.

So there is a higher dimension than ours?

I'm afraid so.

With superior beings in it, observing us?

Yes.

How can you be certain, Demonai?

How do you think I was able to remove this bubble from Olla'set's collection sac without his knowledge? How do you think I even knew I ought to? One of those beings noticed that

I was behaving differently from the two of you. It studied me and eventually found a way to make contact with me.

And became your sidekick?

Yes, but that's not what is important. Tillah, the threedees consider the tiny creature under the microscope to be nonsentient because its life is limited to a small number of activities carried out in specific and unvarying ways, and it never tries to be more or better than it already is. Tell Olla'set that his observable life fits that description as well, and unless he is willing to join me, to learn and grow and become receptive to ideas that contradict his own beliefs, his very existence—our very existence—might be in danger.

Chapter Seven

2019
June 15

Several times each year, the O'Tooles and the Stedmans came together for a large family meal. Birthdays and anniversaries tended to clump together, and it was simpler to arrange one event per month with multiple cakes than to try to celebrate each milestone individually. February, August, and October were birthday months. The wedding anniversaries—all seven of them—took place in June and were commemorated with a sit-down dinner in the spacious loft Ellie's parents rented in the Corktown neighbourhood of Toronto.

Patrick and Teri O'Toole were theatre folk, well known in the Canadian arts community, so everyone was aware going in that any family event they hosted would include some kind of performance. Dinner conversations were always laced with quotations from plays they'd produced, or acted in, or both. One year, they'd adopted a Medieval England theme, greeting their guests in costume, calling everyone "M'lord" or "M'lady", and setting out a royal feast with only knives for cutlery. Between dinner and dessert there had been games, including some mock jousting and a sword fight with props borrowed from a local playhouse.

Ellie knew why her parents worked so hard to be entertaining at these gatherings—it was because her grandfather was in the audience, and they were desperate to get a smile out of him. In June especially, he was a hard crowd to please. One of the anniversaries being celebrated should have been his own, and seeing all the other happy couples together had to be a painful reminder that Gramma Kate wasn't around to share the occasion with him.

That was why Ellie had decided to wait until tonight to ask him about Demonai. It probably wouldn't make him relax, but thinking about her situation might just distract him from his own. At least, she hoped so.

This particular Saturday dinner was shaping up to be rather sedate for an O'Toole affair. Pat and Teri had transformed the loft into a banquet hall, with a head table for the two oldest generations and numbered round tables for the younger family members. White linen tablecloths, artful floral centrepieces, and ornately lettered place cards completed the illusion. Looking around the room, Ellie saw her parents, aunts, and uncles wearing tuxedos and cocktail gowns, and couldn't help wondering whether she'd somehow missed a dress code notification. Then her grandfather stepped through the door, clad in his judicial garb, and she realized: there was going to be a show, and the whole head table was in on it.

When everyone had arrived and was seated, Pat and Teri stood up, waving to get their attention.

"Welcome, honoured guests," Pat announced, instantly quieting the room. "Taking a page from the Dickens novel, *A Christmas Carol*, we will be going on a journey through time this evening, remembering past celebrations, enjoying this present one, and… well, I don't want to spoil the ending for you."

Everyone laughed at that. It was no secret that Ellie's cousin Danny had found his soulmate. Evidently, they were planning a wedding, and this dinner would be doubling as an engagement party. No, she amended, not everyone was laughing. The man in judge's robes sitting at the midpoint of the head table may as well have been presiding at a murder trial.

Teri noticed as well, but continued the preamble, unfazed. "Just so you know, this fine repast is being catered by our friends Lou and Carla Verelli. They've opened a brand-new *trattoria* in the Annex, and they would be most appreciative if you could help them out by posting a review or two. Or seven. Or ten." More laughter. "After the appetizer, those of us in costume will be filling the time until the main course is served by reminiscing loudly and interminably about our respective wedding days. In anticipation of that, enjoy!"

As promised, the food was amazing. Freshly prepared antipasto was followed by small bowls of penne *aglio e olio*, not enough to be filling but more than sufficient to whet everyone's taste buds for the rest of the meal to come. Meanwhile, Ellie kept an eye on her grandfather. Wearing an expression that would have made a felon tremble in his shoes, 'Mack Truck' O'Toole appeared to be passing judgment on every dish put in front of him. All that was missing was the gavel strike to punctuate the proceedings.

When the storytelling began he settled back in his seat, remaining determinedly silent. Apparently, they could persuade him to dress up, but not to participate. By now, the rest of the clan had evidently accepted that as a fact and moved beyond it. They recalled with great relish and amusement all the embarrassing moments from their own past weddings and simply left him be. It made the contrast between them heart-wrenching. Gramma Kate had been dead for going on twelve years now, and he still wasn't ready to share any happy memories of her.

Ellie watched her grandfather's expression close down as he retreated further and further from the moment. Would he ever be ready? Or was this the way his life would end, with him slowly and quietly spiralling into depression? *No!* She gave herself a hard mental shake. They hadn't lost him, not yet. This was 'Mack Truck' O'Toole, the toughest jurist to sit on the bench since anyone could remember. For someone like him to simply fade away would be—well, it would be unnatural. And for his own family to stand back and let it happen would be a tragedy.

After the main course of veal piccata, Danny and Luke made their much-anticipated announcement. The corners of the judge's mouth tweaked upwards, just for a few seconds. Ellie felt a flutter of hope in her chest. Then the dark clouds moved back in.

She couldn't stand it anymore. She crossed to the head table, leaned toward him, and said in a lowered voice, "Grandfather, I've met someone who claims you know him. His name is Demonai. He told me to ask you about him."

Unexpectedly, the judge's face lost three shades of colour. "He's back?" he whispered hoarsely. "I guess the other shoe has finally dropped." A pause, then, "I was afraid something like this would happen. I just wish I knew—! Never mind. If he's around, wishes are dangerous." Locking eyes with her, he said soberly, "We need to talk in private. Don't speak to anyone else about this. Come back to the condo with me after dinner and I'll tell you everything I know about him. And you can tell me how that monster introduced himself to you."

Judge O'Toole lived alone in one of the older condominium buildings along the lakeshore. The living room windows were bay, providing a panoramic view of Toronto Harbour. It was especially impressive at night, when Harbourfront and the majestic purple dome of the Rogers Centre illuminated the sky and painted the shimmering water with bold, multi-coloured ribbons of reflected light.

Ellie was drawn to this psychedelic display the moment she and her grandfather walked through the door of the condo.

"You're old enough to drink," he said behind her as she stood admiring the nightscape. "Care for one?"

"No, thanks," she replied over her shoulder. "I'm still

stuffed from dinner. Probably shouldn't have had any dessert, but each cake was different and they all looked so good."

When she turned around, he was sitting in one of the big leather armchairs, holding a glass half-filled with amber liquid. A bottle and a second glass were sitting on the low table in front of him. "You might change your mind about the drink once you've heard my story. Why don't you begin by telling me yours?"

Obediently, Ellie lowered herself onto the adjacent loveseat and described the incident at the laundromat. Nothing she said seemed to surprise him. All it did was make him look older and more tired.

"So, you wished for a bit of fame, and he made you an object of ridicule. Or tried to," he summed up. "Good thing your detective friend has his head on straight."

A terrible suspicion taking root in her mind, Ellie asked softly, "What did Demonai do to you, Grandfather?"

His expression contorted in pain. When the words came out, they sounded as though they'd been torn from somewhere deep inside him. "He killed my Kate. And I was responsible."

"No! You would never have wished any harm on Gramma."

"Not out loud, no. But I thought about it, Ellie. We'd had a really loud argument, and I was angry, and I imagined your grandmother weeping at my funeral, and two days later she was dead. The doctors told me she'd had a massive stroke during the night. They assured me that nobody could have predicted it, but I knew better. It was his doing. His or Olla'set's. They're cut from the same cloth, those two. And for all we know, there are others like them out there."

"I don't understand. You were imagining your own death, not hers. How could that possibly—?"

"He's a trickster. I was thinking about us being permanently separated, and that's what he gave me. And there's no way to take it back or undo it."

Claire Amory's voice surfacing in Ellie's memory, she recited, "He grants your wish but not in the way that you expect."

O'Toole stared glumly into his glass. "I've had to be really careful since then. It's been a preview of hell. Have you any idea what it's like to go through life terrified of your own imagination? Constantly having to remind yourself that anything you picture in your mind might be taken as a wish and twisted to bring harm to someone else? Not even daring—" He sobbed in a breath, then finished in a torrent of words, "—daring to wish happiness for a person you love on the chance that it could mean lifelong misery for someone else?"

His eyes were shining. Tears sprang to Ellie's eyes as well, as the truth dawned on her.

"Have you spoken to anyone about your feelings?" she ventured.

He recomposed his features and replied, "I tried to. At the funeral, I asked Slattery whether he'd heard from Demonai or Olla'set since—since the last time. He said no. Reminded me that they'd both promised to leave us alone. Then he suggested that I get grief counselling."

"And did you?"

He gave a one-shoulder shrug. "I went once or twice. It didn't do much good. I decided I needed to talk to the other two who were there. Russell and Perrone. I finally tracked them down, on the east coast. They've got a family law practice in Sydney. Separately and together they told me Demonai and his kind were history and I should focus on the future. So that's what I've been doing," he concluded bitterly.

"Waiting for the other shoe to drop. And you never went back to the grief counsellor?"

"I didn't want her to begin having doubts about my sanity. That's what tends to happen when you talk about hearing voices and blaming invisible beings for the death of a loved one."

"Grandfather, I wish I'd known much sooner."

"Then *you* would have thought I was losing my mind. I was a Superior Court judge, and whether or not it was true, I couldn't let myself be perceived as being emotionally unstable. I couldn't even risk telling anyone in the family."

"Of course not. Not until they'd personally experienced this… whatever Demonai is," she supplied.

He jerked himself erect, nearly spilling his drink down his shirt front. "Ellie, I did not wish this on you! You have to believe me!"

"I do," she assured him, as a plan began taking shape in her mind. "But it must be a tremendous relief to finally be able to talk about it. To know that you're not alone. Grandfather, this club has a lot more members in it than you think."

He gave her a quizzical look.

"There's a book you should read," she told him. "Afterward, we'll talk."

Chapter Eight

2003
Still March 18

He was returning to the scene of the crime. The last place Hollinger wanted to be right now was back in Claire's little purple room, but he'd said it himself: they had to stay together and find a way out of their predicament, and that meant packing a suitcase and moving into Boehm's apartment for the duration.

Hollinger climbed the steps and walked through the front door of the weary little building in the Beaches that was Claire Amory's fixed address. He was having flashbacks to that morning, and praying that he could dash in and out without running into anyone Claire knew. Any little thing might give him away: a wrong tone of voice, an uncharacteristic gesture of hands or head, a sudden, inexplicable "forgetfulness" totally unlike the woman he appeared to be. A tide of anxiety was rising inside him, tightening everything on its way up. He paused to collect himself at the foot of the stairs, beside a door marked A-l.

All at once, the door was flung open by a dumpy little woman who obviously hadn't been expecting to find anyone standing in front of it. She shrieked and jumped back a step.

"Claire!" she scolded. "You just took ten years off my life!"

"Sorry about that," Hollinger muttered.

"Actually, I'm glad you're back," the woman continued chattily. "Let me walk you upstairs to your room. I'm afraid you're in for a shock."

"Oh?"

"A man broke in this morning. He left your place a real mess."

Hollinger struggled, barely managing to keep a straight face.

"I called the police, of course," she went on, "but by the time they got here he was gone."

Hollinger had Claire's key in his hand but the woman whipped out a pass key and fitted it into the lock before he could make a move. "I never saw him, but I'm sure I would recognize that voice if I ever heard it again."

"Well, uh, thank you for telling me," Hollinger stammered uneasily. But the landlady remained just inside the door, watching him, like a bellhop waiting for a tip.

"Aren't you going to check that nothing is missing?" she finally asked.

The room was exactly as he had left it that morning, but Hollinger went through the motions of searching, since that was clearly the only way to get rid of this prepossessing busybody. When he had turned the place upside-down—again—and could tell her convincingly that nothing had been stolen, the landlady nodded grimly and left.

Alone at last, he thought, pulling Claire's suitcase down from the overhead shelf in the closet. The list of necessities she'd given him was short: some changes of clothing, all her toiletries, and her laptop. She had begun writing a story earlier, and she intended to finish it.

Hollinger set about assembling the specified items, adding a few extras that he figured would come in handy later. Finally, following her written instructions, he put the laptop into its shoulder-strapped carrying case along with the charger and cables, a mouse, a thumb drive, some hand-written notes, and a half-empty package of brown manila envelopes.

As he was zipping all the pockets closed, an unexpected

knock at the door froze him in place. Then he remembered whose body he was wearing. This was Claire's apartment. No matter who was standing in the hallway, and no matter how like an ill-fitting disguise Claire's identity felt to him, as far as the rest of the world was concerned he was *expected* to be here.

Right.

Hollinger went to the door and opened it—to a tall, red-haired woman who flung herself through the doorway and immediately began pacing back and forth, moaning, "Oh, Claire! It's unbelievable!"

It certainly was. Hollinger was beginning to understand why Boehm thought he'd been dreaming earlier. Resisting the urge to slap himself awake, Hollinger dragged in a lungful of air and addressed the amazon who'd just invaded his space.

"Umm, are you okay?"

"No, I'm not okay!" she declared loudly, pausing to rivet her gaze onto his face. "I've been attacked, Claire. By a weirdo in a dirty lab coat, in the hallway right outside my door. He knew my name, and he knew where I lived. How creepy is that?"

As her hands flew skyward, her all-weather coat parted at the bottom, giving Hollinger a glimpse of a white uniform beneath it. In that moment, pieces fell into place in his mind.

So this was the formidable Sophie Hopper?

Clearly distraught, she'd resumed pacing.

Hollinger cleared his throat. "Have you involved the police?" he asked, already knowing the answer.

"Of course. I mean, I called them, and they came and took my statement. But they're not going to do anything to him."

"Because you already did?"

"They said that I'd committed assault and battery on *him*, but if he decided to press charges against me when he regained consciousness, I was free to counter-charge. What sort of nonsense is that?" she demanded, finally plopping herself down on the edge of the bed with a huff. "Claire, would it be okay if I stayed here tonight? I know there's not much room, but I could camp out on the floor. I just don't feel safe sleeping at home with that maniac on the loose, and if I stay at the hospital—" She noticed the suitcase standing beside the folding bridge table. "Are you going away somewhere?"

Hollinger's thoughts were picking up speed. "Actually, I am. I have this friend who's asked me to mind his apartment for a while. You know, you could move in here until he gets back. If you think you can stand the decor for that long."

Her face brightened at once. "Are you sure? I still have the spare key you gave me for emergencies, but I would never just—"

"Of course I'm sure," he replied. "I'll let Mrs. Scotti know on my way out. Do you have what you need for overnight?"

"I grabbed a few things from my locker before coming here. I'm fine. And you're one in a million. Thank you, Claire!" Sophie cried, leaping up and catching him in a powerful embrace.

Taken off-guard, Hollinger had to force himself not to panic. It was, after all, a gesture of affection. He just wasn't accustomed to being the smaller, weaker one in a situation like this. Did women ever get used to it? He hoped he wouldn't have to find out.

After several seconds, Sophie released him.

"Well," he said shakily, picking up the suitcase and heading for the door. "I'd better be off."

"Oh, and you'll still be attending the meeting tomorrow night, won't you?"

His brain stalled. Meeting? Claire hadn't mentioned any meeting. But they had to keep up the appearance of normalcy at all costs, so, "Oh—sure," he stammered. "The usual place?"

"Right. Only don't forget that we're starting fifteen minutes earlier than normal."

"One way or another, I'll be there," he assured her, mustering a smile as he backed through the doorway.

≈

Boehm had returned to the penthouse, with Hollinger's list to fulfill and a large chip on his shoulder. He already knew that Hollinger was richer than Boehm would ever be. Sending him back to that huge walk-in closet to fetch what Hollinger had decided his body ought to wear for the next few days just added insult to injury. It felt to Boehm as though his nose was being rubbed in how robbed of choices he was right now.

He'd rather been hoping to find Roxanne waiting for him, but the apartment was empty. Boehm's only consolation, therefore, was that the "wealth guru" was currently on an identical errand, with a very similar list, in a neighbourhood he wouldn't want to be caught dead in.

Schadenfreude was evidently the only option Boehm had left. He might as well take it.

After opening Hollinger's suitcase on the bed, he set about assembling the items on the list. Two crisp white shirts. *Check*. Two pairs of elegantly tailored virgin wool trousers, one navy blue, one grey. *Check*. Half a dozen each of briefs, undershirts, and pairs of black socks. *Check*. One navy blue blazer. *Check*. One silk Armani tie to match the blazer. *Check*. Two casual T-shirts, one crew neck, one turtle neck. *Check*. One pair of black dress shoes.

Boehm hesitated. Dress shoes? Why would he need those, except—?

The telephone in the bedroom was ringing.

Warily, he stepped out of the closet, halting at the foot of the bed. Three rings later, he was still staring at the cordless receiver in its cradle on the night stand and dithering over whether to pick up. Then the answering machine cut in: "Hello, this is James A. Hollinger. Please leave a message at the tone and I'll try to get back to you as soon as possible."

"Don't bother, you scumbag creep!"

Boehm froze. The voice was harsh, even abrasive, but it belonged unmistakably to Roxanne. "How dare you! How *dare* you get your secretary to cancel your credit cards right after sending me out to shop with them? You bastard! And I'd just found the perfect dress to wear as your date to that fancy cocktail party. The police told me I must have misunderstood your instructions. I suppose I should be grateful she didn't tell them I stole the damned things. So what happened, you son of a bitch? Did you have second thoughts about taking someone like me to such an important do? Couldn't find the balls to tell me that to my face? Just like you haven't got the balls to pick up the phone and talk to me right now? Well, Jimmy, we're through. You hear me? I never want to see you or hear from you again." *Click.*

Jarred into action, Boehm dived for the phone, but he was too late. All he heard was a dial tone. So that was what Hollinger meant when he said he'd taken care of her! Roxanne was right. He was a bastard and a coward, and he definitely owed her an apology. And an explanation. That much, at least, Boehm could give her.

There was a coded number that would reconnect him to her, if he could just remember what that was. Star something. Wait a minute—the display on the phone had a menu on it. No good, it was numbers only. Damn these rich people and their complicated toys!

Finally, frustrated beyond belief, Boehm hurled the offending receiver across the room. He watched it hit the wall and land in three pieces on the berber carpet. Then he turned and sank down onto the edge of the bed with a defeated moan. Poor Roxanne. And poor Garry Boehm. Hollinger had managed to screw them both over with a single phone call.

"Is there something you'd like to tell me, Claire?" Hollinger asked her.

On her way to Boehm's bedroom with her suitcase and laptop, she stopped and turned around. "Yes. I've ordered a pizza for dinner. It should be here any minute."

"Anything else?"

"I called the number Garry gave me and spoke to his boss. Told him that I'd fallen and had a concussion and couldn't come to pick my stuff up. He said there's no problem. They're going to courier it over later this week."

"Coward. Anything else?"

She gave him a blank look.

"Like, about a meeting you're supposed to attend tomorrow evening?" he prompted.

"Oh, shit!" she muttered. "I'd completely forgotten about that. But how did you—?"

"Sophie reminded me when she stopped by your place. I told her I would be there. So, what's this meeting all about?"

Claire's eyes widened. "Sophie came to see me? Why?"

Hollinger dropped onto Boehm's easy chair. "She was pretty upset. It seems she was attacked by a weirdo in a lab coat this morning—her words, not mine—and because he knows where she lives, she's decided not to risk sleeping at home as long as he's at large. Long story short, she'll be minding your apartment for the next few days. Mrs. Scotti is okay with that, by the way. Now, tell me about this meeting."

Claire dropped her things off in the bedroom, then returned to continue their conversation. "Okay. It's a regular monthly meeting of an organization I belong to, called Women for Professional Equality. We're mainly concerned with labour laws and pay scales, and getting women a fair deal in a variety of professional areas," she explained. "We monitor the workplace, compile data, lobby for changes, that sort of thing."

"I wouldn't mind sitting through a session about that," he remarked. "It would definitely be more interesting than most of the board meetings I've attended. Okay. And I promise I won't volunteer you for anything."

She lowered herself uncomfortably onto one of the sofa cushions. "You wouldn't just be sitting through it, James. I'm supposed to be making a presentation to the membership tomorrow evening."

A pause, then, "You mean, like a speech?"

"More like a report about remuneration in the magazine industry. I have all the stats on my computer, and a draft of the text that goes with them. I'll print everything out for you, and we can practise it together. You'll be fine."

"You're assuming that I've agreed to do this. Claire, I know nothing about the magazine industry," he protested. "What if someone raises a question about something that came up in a previous discussion, or something simple that you should be able to answer but I can't? After all, the whole point of continuing to meet our day-to-day obligations is to maintain the illusion of normalcy, not to embarrass one another or make one of us look stupid."

Her lips contracted into a hyphen. "So, you're refusing to keep the promise that you made to Sophie?" she said coolly.

"I'm trying to preserve your reputation," he countered. "If we can figure out how to reverse the switch in time for you to attend the meeting in your own body, that will be great. In the meanwhile, I think you should accept the possibility that you may have to call in sick at the last minute. Maybe from a concussion."

Claire's face clouded over, but before she could respond, there was a peremptory knock on the door. She got to her feet and went to open it, calling over her shoulder, "I hope you like Hawaiian."

But it wasn't the pizza delivery person.

"You bastard!" exclaimed Boehm as he barrelled over the threshold. For a moment, he stood there, glowering as though he wanted to hurl the suitcase clutched in his right hand directly at Hollinger's head. Finally, he let the bag drop with a *bang* in the middle of the room.

"Do you know what he did?" Boehm snapped. "He invited Roxanne to be his date to a high society cocktail party. While she was out shopping for a dress for this gala affair, he cancelled the credit cards she was using. That's his idea of tying up a loose end. You make me ashamed to be in your body, Hollinger," Boehm declared, firing each word like a missile.

Eyebrows elevated, Claire took in the sight of her own face going pale.

"You spoke to her?" said Hollinger.

"No, unfortunately. I didn't have the chance. She left an angry message on your answering machine. It practically peeled the paint off the wall. So I guess you were right about her earlier, *Jimmy*. She never wants to see you again."

Claire was struck by a sudden thought. "So, James has a social obligation coming up? One he'll need his body to attend, with a date?"

"He does. And when exactly is this cocktail party?" Boehm demanded.

Hollinger evidently knew when he was outgunned. "Thursday evening," he replied with a sigh.

"So, there's no conflict. Perfect!" said Claire. "It would appear that what we have here is a *quid pro quo*."

"Oh?" said Boehm.

"Yes," she replied. "James here was being a little difficult about my body attending an important meeting of an organization I belong to."

"Really!" Boehm's eyes widened, turning Hollinger's face into a portrait of shocked disbelief. He was clearly enjoying the moment.

"Yes. Here is what I propose. If my body is a no-show at that meeting tomorrow night, then his body bails on the cocktail party. Fair?"

Boehm nodded sagely. "Fair enough. But let's take it one step further. I think the mind that goes with the body ought to accompany it, to provide guidance in case something unexpected occurs."

"Like a question that I can't answer. You're saying Claire needs to come with me to the meeting, and I get to be your date at the cocktail party," Hollinger mused, visibly warming to both ideas. "That works for me."

Now it was Claire's turn to blanch. "No, wait. Sophie will be chairing the meeting. As soon as she sees me in this body, she'll—!"

"No, she won't, not if you're there as my guest," Hollinger assured her. "After all, I did her a huge favour this afternoon."

"Yes, you gave her a place to hide… from *me*, dammit!" she pointed out shrilly. "If I turn up there, she's bound to think I'm stalking her. She has a green belt in judo, James. Violence will ensue! Is that what you want?"

"No, but here's what I think," he replied. "If you turn up there showered and shaved and reasonably dressed, and if you keep your cool and behave with respect, she may just change her mind about you. Who knows? She may even start to like you."

Defeated by logic, Claire warned, "You'd bloody well better be right about this, James Hollinger."

"I am. Now, where's that pizza?"

Chapter Nine

There was a spring in Marty Breck's step as he crossed the threshold of Lazy Susan's Bistro that afternoon. Ellie O'Toole had called him the previous day to request that they meet for coffee. She'd been on his mind a lot this past week, and not just because she'd walked off with his copy of *Three Heads Are Better* the last time they'd gotten together.

True to her word, Claire Amory had passed his phone number to the other two changelings, one of whom, James A. Hollinger, had contacted him that morning. Hollinger was spending a long weekend in his chalet near Blue Mountain, an upscale resort community on the shore of Georgian Bay, and he had suggested that Breck and Ellie join him there for Sunday brunch. The more Marty turned the prospect over in his mind, the more it felt as though he would be asking her on a date. And the more he thought about *that*, the more he found himself looking forward to the experience.

He was a little taken aback, then, to discover that she was not alone at their table on the patio. The older gentleman sitting beside her had probably been quite handsome in his youth. Now, his full head of grey hair, his broad shoulders, and the stern expression etched into his features made him a rather intimidating figure. Juridical, actually. That was when Marty realized that he was in the presence of Ellie's grandfather, the legendary 'Mack Truck' O'Toole.

Slowing his approach, Breck noticed a plate of muffins sitting in the middle of the table. He threw her an inquiring glance.

Ellie finished her sip of hot chocolate and told him, "We got three different kinds—carrot, blueberry, and apple oatmeal. I figured you had to like at least one of them."

"Have a seat, young man," the judge ordered him. Automatically, Breck complied. "You must be the detective my granddaughter has been telling me about."

"Yes, Your Honour."

Eyebrows rose in approbation. "I'm retired, son. Mr. O'Toole will do."

"Yes, sir."

"Ellie loaned me your book. I hope you don't mind," said O'Toole.

"No, sir, not a bit. What did you think of it?" he ventured.

"It was entertaining enough. Fictionalized, of course."

"Actually, sir, the author assured us that it was a truthful rendering of the events, not fabricated at all," Breck corrected him.

"I see. And have you found corroboration for that statement, Detective?"

"Not yet, but I still have witnesses to interview. The millionaire playboy character is based on James A. Hollinger. He's invited us to visit him and discuss his own experience with Demonai."

"So, you have no qualms about conducting an unofficial investigation. That's good, because there's a case I would like you to look into for me," said the judge. "A suspicious death. Problem is, I'm the only one who believes there might have been foul play."

Ellie rolled her eyes. "Grandfather, please!"

This had to be a test. Breck narrowed his gaze. "A suspicious death?" he echoed. "I gather you have a suspect in mind, sir?"

"Yes. I believe Demonai murdered my wife nearly twelve

years ago."

"Grandfather, there's no way to—"

He shrugged off her protest. "How would you go about handling such a case, Detective Breck?"

Marty thought for a moment. "It's a cold case, so I'd go back to basics. I'd begin by finding out everything I could about the victim. Was an autopsy performed?"

"No. As I said, nobody considered it to be in any way suspicious. The doctors found evidence of a cerebral hemorrhage. She'd been having problems with high blood pressure for years, so they called it a stroke due to natural causes, and that was what went on the death certificate."

"But you're not convinced that was in fact what happened. Why?"

"If you're looking for grounds to exhume her body, I'm afraid you're out of luck," O'Toole said. "The best reason I could give you would only cast doubt on my mental state, discrediting my reliability as a source of information."

"What about her medical records?" Breck asked, thinking furiously. "Was she allergic to anything? Was she on medications that could have combined or conflicted to produce a brain bleed? Had she recently undergone any procedures? Anything like that?"

"You think Demonai could have interfered with her medical treatment?"

Breck pulled out his little pad and slid it across the table. "I think we need to consider all possible suspects, sir, and all possible scenarios. Please list as many names as you can recall of the people who came into contact with your wife during the forty-eight hours before her death. Whenever I have a moment, I'll check them out."

O'Toole locked eyes with him. "You plan to rule them out as suspects so you can focus on Demonai?"

"I plan to go wherever the evidence takes me, sir,' he replied evenly.

It wasn't the answer O'Toole was apparently hoping for,

but it ended the exchange and got him writing. Meanwhile, Ellie cast a grateful smile Marty's way.

Once the pad was back in Breck's possession, the judge challenged, "What about Demonai? What do you do when someone points you at a suspect, Detective?"

"I try to find out as much as I can about both individuals," he replied truthfully. "For example, what reason do you have to accuse him? Has he made threats? Has he attempted to harm you or your wife in the past? Or have you perhaps made threats against him?"

"He never spoke to me. Demonai was Richard Slattery's genie. Rick and I became best friends in high school. We were like brothers, did everything together, even chose the same law school. When we were both undergrads there, Demonai helped Rick to pull off a series of brilliant practical jokes. They made the newspapers. They even attracted paranormal researchers. Then, in our final year, Rick decided he had to get serious and focus on his studies, so he called a halt. He fired his genie. About thirty years later, Demonai was back, with reinforcements—Olla'set."

Breck and Ellie shared a look.

"Thirty years to us, much shorter to a genie," she said. Addressing O'Toole, she added, "Demonai told us that his kind could travel up and down the timeline at will, and that twenty minutes for us could be much longer for them. That was how he learned to communicate with us so fast. He did his practising in some other time period."

"Demonai once told Rick that he was everywhere, all the time," O'Toole confirmed. "Like some kind of trickster god."

"And Demonai never spoke to you?" said Breck.

"Never. Olla'set did."

"Then what makes you so certain that Demonai is the one who should be held accountable, Grandfather?" Ellie cut in.

The judge's expression hardened. "Because Demonai was always the trickster. Olla'set was just a bully."

Marty swallowed hard. He knew a thing or three about

bullies.

"And because Demonai was the one who granted wishes, unlike Olla'set, who made demands and delivered punishment if they weren't obeyed," O'Toole went on. "He never demanded anything from me, although he did punish me once for accusing him of being a fraud. To demonstrate his power, he transported me from Rick's place to my own, in a split-second. For a single heartbeat, my body felt both completely numb and on fire at the same time. Then I was standing in my front hallway, minus my overcoat, trying to explain to Kate how I'd gotten back inside without using the door."

"It sounds as though we ought to be interviewing Mr. Slattery about this Demonai," Breck remarked, fishing a business card out of his breast pocket and sliding it across the table. "Mr. O'Toole, can you ask him to get in touch with me to set up the meeting?"

"I can. Are you going to tell him why you're investigating?"

Her cheeks dimpling, Ellie reached into the tote bag beside her chair and hauled out Claire Amory's book. "Not until he's had a chance to read this, Grandfather," she assured him. "He's sure to believe us then."

~~~

James Hollinger's chalet had appeared in several magazine spreads, and with good reason. It was an architectural and decorating masterpiece, using only natural, sustainable materials. And from the moment Marty's car pulled up in the driveway, he knew he'd entered another world, one solidly based on wealth and privilege.

It was a world he'd had occasion to visit once or twice in his official capacity, but always with that familiar awareness of being the outsider, the one who would never fit in. *Unlike Ellie,* he thought with a sigh, wishing he'd never done that
~~~

background check on her. She'd grown up well-to-do, the daughter of famous parents. She'd gone to school with the children of other rich and famous people. For her, a sumptuous home like this inspired no more than a curious glance as she preceded him along a series of artfully placed flagstones to the chalet's double front door.

It opened as they approached, and a pleasant-faced, bald-headed man stepped outside to greet them. He was casually dressed, in jeans and a green camo T-shirt, and he waved to them with something red and white that he was holding in his left hand.

"Please, come in!" he urged them. "You're Detective Breck, I take it? And this must be Ellie. The gods are already smiling on this visit. I cooked the whole meal and didn't set off the smoke alarm once."

The red and white item, it turned out, was an oven mitt. "You do your own cooking?" Marty said wonderingly.

"Up here, yes," came the firm response. "When I'm around, it's a no-staff zone. The whole point of having this place is to enjoy some privacy, and that's hard to do if you're tripping over servants. And," he added, nudging a door open to show them the location of the powder room as they passed, "I felt that any conversation involving Demonai ought to be kept private."

Breck couldn't argue with that.

Hollinger led them into the kitchen, a showy arrangement of stainless steel appliances and butcher block countertops, with a large island that today was doubling as a dining table. It held three place settings—each marked by a square white plate on a woven bamboo placemat—and a matched set of lidded serving dishes.

"This looks lovely," Ellie commented.

"I hope you're okay with crepes," said Hollinger. "It's my go-to dish for company."

"Not a problem," Marty assured him.

Ellie chimed in, "It's one of my favourites."

Hollinger brought a stack of the thin pancakes out of the oven where they'd been staying warm, then uncovered all the bowls and said, "I like being informal. Choose your ingredients, stuff them into crepes, and dig in."

Everything smelled delicious. Ellie made herself a couple of cheese blintzes, topped with applesauce. Marty went for the ham and steamed asparagus, smothered in cheese sauce. Hollinger chose ham and asparagus as well, with sautéed mushrooms and onions on the side. Not a word was said about Claire's book or Demonai the whole time they were eating.

After the main course, they carried their coffee mugs into the great room. Floor-to-ceiling windows framed a gorgeous view—a sun-splashed wooded valley with grassy rolling hills beyond. Marty and Ellie sat side by side on the sofa, facing the windows. Hollinger took the armchair adjacent to them and handed out coasters. Then he put his mug down on the lampstand at his elbow and said, "You indicated on the phone that you wanted to know about my relationship with Demonai."

Marty leaned forward. "Yes. Did he ever speak to you?"

"Outside of the events Claire recorded in her book, you mean? No, not a peep. As far as I know, he never spoke directly to any of us while they were happening, and none of us was ever bothered by him afterward. But I have to tell you," he added, picking up his coffee and holding it in both hands, "I've never been completely convinced that Demonai was responsible. I knew that something supernatural was happening—that much was indisputable. And I also knew without any doubt that I had zero control over any of it. That was the hardest part for me, letting go and accepting whatever was fated to happen. Meanwhile, Claire was the one who started connecting dots, and who concluded that Demonai had to be the cause of our predicament. And, having no better theory to suggest, I went along with hers."

"And Demonai never actually made contact with any of

you?" Breck persisted. "Never spoke to you, or gave you a sign?"

Hollinger leaned in as well, his interest visibly piqued. "Never. Why do you keep asking that? Has he spoken to you?"

"Ms. Amory didn't tell you?"

"Tell me what?"

Breck and Ellie shared a question-and-answer look. Then she replied, "He spoke to both of us, just a few weeks ago. Demonai's the one who told Marty to read Claire's book."

For a moment, Hollinger was at a loss for words. Eyes wide and jaw sagging, he fell back against his chair. "You're saying he's real? He exists?" he finally managed to get out.

"Yes. And it appears that Ms. Amory was right," Marty added. "Demonai was most probably the one who caused your body switch."

"Son of a bitch!" Hollinger muttered, glaring into his coffee mug.

"Besides that, how much of her story was true?" Ellie wanted to know.

"All of it," he said. "But she didn't tell the whole story in her book. Other things happened as well, things that couldn't be revealed without making me—making all three of us look like mental cases. And now that I know who to blame—!" His knuckles were whitening around the handle of his mug.

"—you still can't talk about them," Breck pointed out, "except to others who have had some experience with Demonai and his kind. We can help you out with that."

"Wait—and his *kind*?" Hollinger repeated, his voice rising in disbelief.

"There's another one, named Olla'set," replied Breck.

"And they've messed with others besides the five of us?"

"Four more that we know about," said Ellie, "and we're willing to bet they're just the tip of the iceberg. Demonai's been around for a long time."

"I'm curious about something," Marty said. "When we

spoke with Claire, she told us that all three of you had been changed for the better by spending time in one another's bodies. Do you feel that way?"

A pause, then, "To be honest, I don't think I do. Changed? Yes, we were all changed by the experience. How could we not be? But… for the better?" He shook his head. "It's tough, you know—having an experience like that, knowing it actually happened, but that nobody's going to believe you if you say anything about it. That's mainly why we stayed in touch. Why *I* did, anyway. For therapy."

"Has it been working?" she asked softly.

A haunted look came into his eyes. "Hard to say. I've always been good at keeping up appearances, so no one's had any reason to take a close look behind the curtain. Fortunately, I was fifty when it happened, the right age for someone like me to be planning for early retirement, and I took it at the first opportunity. I sank a couple million into building this place, then purposely lowered my profile. Now I spend my days managing my portfolio, staying physically healthy, and making regular contributions to the Hospital for Sick Children and various other organizations."

"And fulfilling all the social obligations pertaining thereto?" she said, her lips curving in a knowing smile.

His expression and his voice both seemed to sag under an invisible weight. "Some of them. That can be therapeutic as well."

"What do you think?" Breck asked her later, as they were driving back down to the city.

"I think I'm beginning to understand why Demonai chose to contact us," Ellie replied. "Claire Amory appeared happy when we visited her, but so far she's the only one. What if the trickster god realizes he's made a mess of things and he needs our help to put things right?"

"That sounds unlikely to me. Considering what his kind is capable of, why should he need any help at all?" Marty countered. "I agree that he probably had a reason for picking us. But as you said, he's a trickster, so I'm betting it's a lot more devious than simply wanting to make amends for some of his earlier wish-granting. In any case, you've pretty much committed us to finding the rest of the iceberg. That's not going to be an easy task."

"*Au contraire, mon ami*," she told him archly. "We don't have to go looking for them. They're already online, posting and commenting on videos of inexplicable events. We need only set up a few social media accounts, drop some carefully worded remarks, and let them find us. How does 'Friends of Demonai' sound as a user name?"

He made a face. "'Victims of Demonai' would be more accurate."

"Hmm. You're right, but it would be off-putting. I guess I'll have to let the idea percolate a little longer."

"Not that I disapprove of your plan, but are you going to have the time to monitor these social media accounts and respond to posts?" he inquired.

"Actually, I've got all the time in the world," she told him, studiously inspecting the position of her seat belt. "My summer job has gone away."

After meeting Dr. Phinegal, Marty wasn't surprised. The scientist's abrasive personality had rubbed him the wrong way almost immediately. "How come?"

"Phinegal had told everyone, including you, that the black hooded rat had either escaped or been stolen during a break-in overnight. But the security cameras showed no one entering the lab between the time he'd left it and my arrival the following morning."

"I know. I saw that footage. When it was clearly a rat hunt and no longer a break-and-enter, we passed the case back to Campus Security."

"Well, Phinegal knew why the rat would never be found, but instead of letting the matter drop, he claimed to the research committee that I must have left the cage unlocked, carelessly allowing the rat to escape."

Breck made a sour face. "Nice. He threw you under the bus."

"He tried. Would have succeeded, too, if I hadn't gone all CSI on the place right after the explosion. He thought he'd burned all the baggies holding concrete evidence, but I'd kept a couple back, and I had date-stamped video of the rat in the cage at the time the incident occurred. So, I could prove what had actually happened, which meant I could also prove that he'd lied to the police. If I brought the matter before the allocation committee, they would have no choice but to declare the experiment either a fraud or a failure. Bottom line: no more funding, and he leaves the faculty in disgrace.

"When I pointed this out to him, he became quite willing to negotiate a compromise. He's going to 'find' the misplaced rat, clear me of any blame, and abort the experiment voluntarily, since it wasn't producing any documentable results anyway. Once he's done all that, I'll give him the last two baggies to destroy."

"And the video?"

"There's no point. I told him I'd already uploaded it to the cloud. You can't put smoke back into a bottle."

"And did you? Upload it, I mean."

She made no response, but he could tell that she was smiling.

Breck threw her an admiring glance. "Wow. Remind me never to get on your bad side."

Chapter Ten

2003
March 19

At seven-thirty, the taxicab arrived to carry Claire and Hollinger to the meeting of Women for Professional Equality. Boehm hardly noticed their departure. He was sunk in longing thoughts of Roxanne.

Why had Hollinger placed that phone call to credit card security? The man was worth millions. Would it have killed him to buy her a dress? She said she'd found the perfect one, too. He hoped it was red. Red would have made her look spectacular. And now he would never get to see her in it, because his date for tomorrow was going to be... James Hollinger, damn him!

At that moment, Boehm would have sold anything he had for the chance to spend the evening with Roxanne instead. She had been his first. That made her special. Every time her blond loveliness appeared in his mind's eye, he felt a yearning beyond words. *Roxanne.* Just saying her name to himself was enough to make him ache in tender parts of his anatomy.

It was a good thing Boehm was alone in the apartment right now, because he was feeling an irresistible urge to wring Hollinger's neck. He couldn't actually do it, of course. Hollinger was currently in Claire's body, and Boehm was in Hollinger's. So, in order to kill Hollinger, Boehm would have to strangle two people, including himself.

Things had become way too complicated.

Boehm's itchings were rapidly approaching critical mass. Finally, he snatched a copy of Velikovsky's *Worlds in Collision* from the bookshelf and stalked into the bedroom to sublimate himself in science.

≈

The pay rates for staff writers and editors in the burgeoning magazine industry were abysmally low. After going over the presentation with Claire several times that day, Hollinger was brimming with confidence. He had all the numbers at the tips of his fingers, including some that didn't appear on any of the display charts. He'd also worked up a level of indignation that he wouldn't have thought possible, considering how far removed his own field was from hers. She'd been right about everything, though. He was better than fine. He was going to knock this out of the park!

Then they arrived at the venue.

Women for Professional Equality met once a month in the basement of an old church. Hollinger had no idea which church it was. There was no exterior illumination, so he couldn't read the plaque or the sign in front of the building. Claire had even given their destination to the cab driver as an intersection. Now Hollinger stood shivering on the sidewalk, cursing the pantyhose and knee-length skirt that she'd insisted he wear for this occasion. They not only offered no resistance to the wind, he could swear they were actively collaborating with it.

As Claire paid their driver, Hollinger eyed the gloomy structure with growing trepidation. For something purporting to be a place of worship and sanctuary, this church bore a striking resemblance to a castle from an old Boris Karloff movie. If he and Claire were characters in a cult film, the audience would be shouting at them right now to get back in the car and escape while they still could. If he were alone, he thought grimly, cocktail party or no cocktail party, that was precisely what he would do.

"Come on," said Claire. "The side door is over here."

She was pointing at a shadow cast against the building by two trees. It resembled a skull with horns. Of course it did. Hollinger swallowed his heart and followed her.

The church basement was almost as cold as the wind outside. A strange contradiction, Hollinger thought, since the room they were in was a perfectly constructed brick oven. A little kindling in one corner and they could have had a nice toasty fire. He was tempted to make the suggestion, but had promised Claire he'd take things seriously tonight. So instead, he snugged his jacket more tightly around his shoulders and crossed his arms over his chest.

A row of mismatched wooden chairs lined the front of a makeshift dais, a naked wooden platform several inches off the floor at the end of the room farthest from the door. More chairs were strung across the room at irregular intervals. Beside him, Hollinger heard Claire's soft gasp of horror. There were only four women there, not the crowd she had been expecting to cover her entrance.

The four women turned together at the sound of footsteps. One of them was Sophie Hopper. Her eyes glinted dangerously as they rested on the face of the man who had accosted her the previous morning.

"Oh, shit! She recognizes me. You said she wouldn't," Claire hissed through gritted teeth.

"I said she might change her mind about you if you showed her a different side of yourself," he replied.

"Well, she's headed directly for us, so I'm thinking maybe my back would be the best side to show her right now."

Before she could turn, Hollinger hooked his arm through hers and hung on tightly. "You're my guest tonight, and you are not going to run away and leave me here," he told her, deliberately enunciating every syllable. "It would be rude."

"Then do something," she urged in an undertone, "because I think she's moving in for the kill."

"Calm. Down. I wish I'd brought a paper bag."

"To put over my head?"

"To stop you from hyperventilating," he scolded. As Sophie approached, Hollinger tightened his grip on Claire's arm and asked, "Where is everybody? You told me to be here early."

"Yes, because I wanted you to be on time. You're usually fifteen minutes late. And I see you've brought a guest."

"This is Doctor Boehm. I believe you two have met," said Hollinger, "although under less than perfect circumstances."

"That would be putting it mildly." Sophie licked her lips, bringing to Hollinger's mind the image of a cat sizing up a mouse. "He's a friend of yours, I presume? And he's a doctor?" she said coolly.

"I'm a scientist," Claire cut in, finally finding her voice. Hollinger repressed a sigh of relief and let go of her arm. "And I wanted to apologize for my behaviour yesterday. I'm not normally like that. I'd just had an unusual experience and… I wasn't myself."

"So you were upset, and you came looking for me? Not Claire, who was your friend?" Sophie challenged.

Hollinger could practically hear wheels turning as Claire mentally drafted a story.

At last she replied, "Claire wasn't home. I was worried. And she once told me that if anything happened to her, you were her emergency contact."

"Then you should have led with that when you came to my apartment," Sophie informed her crisply. "It would have saved everyone a lot of trouble." Turning to Hollinger, she added, "Claire, you'll be sitting on the dais. I'll show you where. Meanwhile, Dr. Boehm can take a chair in the back row."

Halfway to the front of the room, Sophie paused and turned reproachful eyes on Hollinger's borrowed face. "I thought we were friends, Claire."

"Listen, Garry's not a bad person. Things have just been a

little weird for him lately and—"

"I mean, why didn't you tell me you were dating someone?"

"What? Wait a second. We're not dating."

"Why not? Is he married?"

"No! Not that I know of, anyway. And why are you—?"

A speculative gleam had come into Sophie's eyes. Cocking her head, she threw an appraising glance toward the back of the room. "So he's available? That's good to know. How did you and Garry meet, Claire?"

With effort, Hollinger corralled some of the thoughts that were stampeding around in his head. "Uh, he had found something of mine, and I went to collect it from him."

"I suppose that's as good a way as any to reel someone in," the amazon mused aloud.

"You're not going to hit on him, are you?"

"Of course, I am. He's a handsome, sexy, available man. And where is it written that a woman can't make the first move?" She licked her lips suggestively, nearly sending Hollinger into spasms of anxiety.

"But—But from the way you were talking to him just now, I thought you hated him. Sophie," he said, wincing inwardly at the pleading note that had crept into his voice, "you beat him up yesterday!"

"So?" the amazon said with a shrug. "That was then. This is now. A girl can change her mind, you know. And now I'm thinking I'd like to get physical with him in a much more pleasant way."

Hollinger played his last card. "You don't even know whether he's into women."

"No, but you do, and if he were gay, you would have told me that right away. So, stop sounding like my puritanical maiden aunt, please. I have a meeting to chair."

Stammering an excuse, Hollinger raced back to Claire and pulled her to her feet. "You need to leave. Now. Go outside, call a cab. I'll stall her as long as I can."

"You'll—What are you talking about?" she demanded. "She doesn't still hate me, does she?"

"Oh, it's much worse than that. Now she wants to get you into bed."

To his horror, the same speculative gleam came into her eyes as he'd seen earlier in Sophie's. "That might be fun, actually. I mean, we're already best friends."

"Except she doesn't know that you're you. She thinks you're a man she recently met for the first time. And she's probably straight."

"So?"

"So this is wrong, on multiple levels."

Something made Hollinger glance down then at the front of her trousers, where a bulge now appeared that hadn't been there before. His first thought was that Boehm's body appeared to be impressively endowed. His second was that the windbreaker Claire had grabbed on her way out the door provided no concealment whatsoever.

Cursing inwardly, Hollinger dropped onto a chair, pulling her down beside him.

"I thought you wanted me to leave," she said.

"You can't walk out of here with an erection. Not as long as Sophie is watching. It will just whet her appetite for you. Wait for the meeting to start. When everyone's watching the dais, you can sneak out the door."

"What about you?"

"A deal is a deal. I'll give the presentation, just as we practised it. Then I'll remember another engagement, get out of here as quickly as possible, and meet you and Garry back at the apartment."

People were starting to arrive, not all of them female. It appeared that some of the attendees had brought boyfriends and husbands along. They didn't look as though they'd come willingly. In fact, most of them wore expressions that were downright belligerent. It was an ominous sign. There would evidently be no good news or friendly questions at this meeting.

The first three rows of chairs had already filled up, and Sophie was rushing around greeting new and returning members. She was distracted. Maybe now was the time to—

"My Lord, there he is!" came a strident voice from the other side of the room. "That's the pervert who attacked Sophie yesterday! He's stalking her!"

Instantly, all eyes turned and landed on Claire's startled face.

"If you stand up, you're a dead man," Hollinger told her through gritted teeth.

"And if I stay here, I'm not?" she muttered tautly.

"Mrs. Griesdorf, it's all right," Sophie called to her. "He's—"

"Get him!" snarled a male voice.

"No, wait!" yelled Sophie and Hollinger in unison. They were both too late.

People were rushing toward Claire from all directions, their shouts splitting the air like battle cries.

"Call the police!" Hollinger shrilled to no one in particular. Then he watched in dismay as Claire closed her eyes and rolled limply off her chair to the floor.

~~

Velikovsky's book couldn't quell Boehm's primal urgings, so he'd gone on to even dryer, more technical literature. It was no use—he simply couldn't get Roxanne out of his mind. His memories of her were too vivid. The way she smelled first thing in the morning, the warmth of her in bed… the waves of sensation she'd sent crashing from one end of his body to the other. Just thinking about that was enough to raise aftershocks in his nether parts.

Unfortunately, Roxanne was gone, shooed away by Hollinger as though she were a mere inconvenience in his rich and powerful life—and just thinking about *that* was raising emotions of a different sort.

Distractedly, he glanced at the clock on the end table in the living room. He was stranded here alone, in Hollinger's body, and Claire's meeting could take hours. What he really wanted to do right now was break something, as noisily and violently as possible. But what? His conscience rebelled at the thought of destroying someone else's property, and he couldn't afford to replace any of his own. Not to mention that Rosseau would have a field day—and most likely a payday—if he found out about it. So, Boehm was trapped. Twice.

Or maybe not. A new pub had opened just a couple of blocks away. The Crown and Ha'penny. He checked inside Hollinger's wallet. The millionaire had removed most of his cash to a safer place, but there were still a few twenties in there. Enough for a night out. Since Boehm wasn't able to ignore or smother his sorrows, perhaps he could drown them.

Ever practical, he scribbled a note and left it on the kitchen table before heading out the door.

The Ha'penny was not so much a pub as a bar tailored for a young, swinging clientele. Its interior was green and amber. The walls were lined with small booths, separated from one another by stained glass partitions, but inviting intrusion from the large open area in the centre of the room. The owner, Ewan O'Meara, presided over his establishment from behind the long stand-up bar. And O'Meara's partner, Gunther Stark, a former heavyweight wrestler who had competed under the nickname 'the Teutonic Menace', presided at the door.

Boehm walked in quietly, took a place at the bar, and ordered a double Scotch. Stark had ignored him, for he was well-dressed and obviously sober. But while the bartender was serving him, O'Meara did a double take and waved his partner over excitedly.

"Gunther, do you know who that is?" he hissed into

Stark's ear. "Second stool from the end—that's James Hollinger. Jeezus, he could buy and sell us ten times over. I wonder what he's doing all alone in this part of town."

"Maybe he's slumming," Stark replied.

O'Meara shook his head. "Nah. That's not his style. There's got to be a reason, though. Listen, if any of our female clients notice he's here, they'll be all over him in an instant. Better keep an eye out, Gunther—we may have to hide him in a back room."

Meanwhile, oblivious to the conversations going on all around him, Boehm concentrated on downing his drink. His experience with hard liquor was quite limited, for he'd spent his teen years and most of his twenties in single-minded pursuit of scientific knowledge. But now that Roxanne had shown him some of the delights he'd missed by narrowing his sights at such a tender age, why shouldn't he explore the others as well? He'd never in his life been drunk. It ought to be a real trip.

As the Scotch whisky burned a path down his throat, he thought he felt Roxanne's grip on his thoughts relax a little. Encouraged, Boehm ordered another drink, this time a screwdriver.

Hearing this, the bartender made eye contact with O'Meara, who immediately took over.

"But, sir," O'Meara said respectfully, "you just had some whisky. Drinking vodka right after Scotch, you'll be seeing double in no time."

"Perfect," Boehm declared. "That's just what I want."

"You want to get sloshed? If you don't mind my asking, sir, why?"

Fixing O'Meara with a stern eye, Boehm slammed his hand down on the bar and said, "Because I'm not myself today, and that's what I've decided to do. Now, are you going to give me that drink or do I have to go somewhere else for it?"

"One moment, sir," O'Meara replied, stepping to the end

of the bar where Stark had taken up his post. "Gunther, Mr. Hollinger has come in with the express purpose of tanking up," he said in an undertone. "Why don't you take him into the back room with a bottle of single malt and try to find out what's going on? I'm sure he'd appreciate the privacy, too."

"Sure thing," Stark said with a nod.

O'Meara fetched the bottle of Glenlivet out from beneath the bar and placed it in front of their distinguished patron. "Let me get this straight, sir," he said pleasantly. "You're not here to pick up a date or socialize? You're not interested in action—you only want to get drunk?"

"Right!"

"In that case, Mr. Stark here will show you to one of our private rooms, where you won't be disturbed."

Boehm made no protest as he was led away from the bar, for the jolt of whisky he'd already consumed was having its effect. Suffused with warmth, with his limbs seeming to float beside his body, he simply could not imagine anyone intending him harm.

Not even the burly, scar-faced man who had taken his arm in such businesslike fashion and was now escorting him down a back hallway and into a tiny, windowless room.

The room contained a round poker table and half a dozen chairs. Assisting Boehm into one of the chairs, Stark told him, "Mr. O'Meara believes that serious drinking ought to be done alone. But if you don't mind, I'll just sit with you for a while."

Boehm shrugged. "If you like, sure."

Producing a glass from the inside pocket of his jacket, Stark wiped it with a clean handkerchief and poured the customer a double shot of whisky. Wordlessly, he watched Boehm swallow it down, then refilled the glass.

"We're a little curious, Mr. Hollinger," he said. "What brings you to our neck of the woods this evening?"

"I'm chasing oblivion," Boehm said, stumbling only slightly over the last word. (Was he drunk yet? He wasn't sure. He would have to drink more and find out.)

"Come on!" Stark prodded him. "A guy like you trying to lose himself in alcohol? And in a public place?"

Boehm heaved a sorrowful sigh and drained his glass again. (The liquor wasn't burning his throat anymore. Was that good or bad?) "There has been a drastic change in my life," he explained.

The scar-faced man looked suddenly attentive. "Oh?"

"I don't have one anymore. No control. No power. No warning, no 'pologies. Just ZAP! I wake up one morning and everything's gone." (Why was his tongue growing larger? His name wasn't Pinocchio.)

"Wow, that's terrible," the scar-faced man said.

Boehm felt deeply moved by this show of sympathy. Tears welled in his eyes. "I couldn't even keep Roxanne," he moaned.

"Who's Roxanne?"

"A blonde… gorgeous… tiny, perfect face… and large, perfect—" He held his hands out in front of him as though comparing the weights of two melons. Gazing wistfully into his upturned palms, he continued, "He erased her, like some adding mistake. No heart, no feelings. Made a phone call. Now she's gone."

"Roxanne is your girlfriend?"

"Not anymore," Boehm said.

"I get the picture," Stark told him grimly. "But why aren't you in your fancy penthouse? There's plenty of security there, and privacy."

Boehm leaned forward and replied in a stage whisper, "I can't hide there. It's the first place they'd look."

Stark's eyes opened wide. "Any chance they might follow you here?" he asked tensely.

"Oh, for sure they will," Boehm replied, now thinking of the note he'd left for Hollinger and Claire back at the apartment. "They've never cared about my mind, you know," he added bitterly. "What I know, what I feel, means nothing to them. Cold-hearted bastards. They just want my body in the right place, is all."

"*Jee*-zus!" Stark murmured. "Can you describe any of them, Mr. Hollinger?"

"Uh, there's a man, tall, lotsa blondish hair," said Boehm, concentrating with difficulty on the images of the other two bodies. "And a woman, short, with dark hair... wearing a red top-thing... knitted, I think. Anyway, they're together."

"I'd better get you a pot of coffee," Stark declared, scooping up the bottle and the glass and rushing out of the room.

It was half past ten. Stark and O'Meara had been waiting tautly for almost two hours while Boehm snoozed on a cot in the back room.

"This is crazy," Stark whispered across the bar. "I think we should call the police."

"And tell them what?" O'Meara snapped. "That James Hollinger came into our establishment to hide from a couple of syndicate hit men, who we expect to see at the door at any minute? They'd never believe that. I hardly believe it myself, for crying out loud! Are you absolutely sure that was what he said?"

"Positive."

Swayed by the firmness of Stark's reply, O'Meara went on, "Well, maybe we've lucked out and he actually managed to shake them before he got here."

"I'm afraid not, Ewan," Stark murmured. "Look over there."

Hollinger and Claire had just entered the pub. They paused near the door to let their eyes adjust to the lighting, then surveyed the main room, straining to discern a familiar face or waving hand among the many patrons.

"I don't see him," Claire said, frowning. "Are you sure you

read that note right?"

"It was quite specific," Hollinger replied. "How's your head, by the way?"

She shot him a disgusted look. "Still throbbing. And thank you *so* much for letting me hit it on the floor. As if the old lady's purse hadn't already done enough damage."

He returned the look. "You can be angry at me later. Right now, let's just find our prodigal scientist and take him home."

"Are you folks looking for someone?"

This sudden baritone voice behind them made Claire start and whirl around. "Yes," she said, wincing as the headache flared briefly, "a friend who was supposed to meet us here."

"Maybe you've seen him," Hollinger broke in. "A tall fellow, distinguished-looking, dark eyes and hair, greying at the temples?"

Stark gave him a broad grin. "You've just described half the men in this place, honey, including the owner."

"Perhaps if we just walked around," Hollinger suggested.

"By all means," said Stark, waving them into the dance floor area. Then he rushed back to the bar. "It's them, all right," he told O'Meara grimly. "They fit his descriptions to a tee. They claim he was supposed to meet them here. *Now* will you call the police?"

But O'Meara stood his ground. "No. Let them look around the place. As long as we don't act suspicious they've got no reason to figure we might be hiding him. When they don't see him, they'll leave. After closing time, we'll put him in my car and take him back to my house. *Then* we'll call the police."

Stark acquiesced with a shrug.

Meanwhile, Hollinger and Claire saw no sign of Boehm anywhere in the bar.

"Now I'm worried," she said. "You don't suppose he got tipsy and went for a walk or something…?"

"It's possible."

"Then he could be anywhere right now. He could be passed out or worse, lying in some filthy gutter at this very minute," Claire went on with growing agitation.

"What do you suggest we do?" demanded Hollinger impatiently. "Call the police? They'd never believe the truth, even if we were foolish enough to tell them. God, if only he weren't wearing my body!"

Claire felt her jaw clench but decided to let the remark pass. "Let's go outside. Maybe we'll find him puking in an alley or something."

O'Meara had been watching them carefully from behind the bar. "Here they come," he whispered to Stark. "They're leaving, just like I told you they would."

"What if they want to look in the back rooms?"

"As long as we smile at them and act all innocent they've got no reason to look too closely," O'Meara assured him. 'In a couple of hours we'll be home free."

Boehm awakened with the Sahara Desert in his mouth, camel dung and all. So this was what it was like to be drunk? His eyesight was haunted by ghosts. They kept moving things, leaving a series of outlines behind. His skin felt somehow wrong, as though he'd mistakenly grabbed someone else's on his way out the door. His skull was on too tight. It made his brain ache. No, not his brain. Hollinger's brain. Good! Served the bastard right if it was hurting.

Shakily, Boehm pushed himself up off his cot. Oops! His stomach didn't like that. It was doing cartwheels and loop-de-loops. He needed to get home so he could throw up.

Belching mightily, Boehm made his wobbly way to the door. With great effort he managed to fumble it open. Then he lurched into the narrow hall and around the corner of the bar, just in time to spot Hollinger and Claire heading for the street. As he opened his mouth to call out their names, however, Boehm's mind went blank.

Damn!

Desperate to get their attention, he shouted raggedly, "Hey, you two! I'm here!"

They spun around. "Thank goodness!" Hollinger declared.

Then a heavily muscled body stepped in front of them, blocking their way. "The exit is behind you," said the bouncer in a quiet, menacing voice.

Hollinger and Claire exchanged troubled looks. "But that's our friend," Claire said with a nervous laugh. "The one we came here to meet."

"He's no friend of yours," the ex-wrestler growled.

Hollinger frowned. "That may be true, but it's certainly not your place to say so," he pointed out recklessly. "Now would you mind getting out of our way?"

Claire could see Boehm swaying unsteadily behind this human wall that barred their path. The scientist was in no shape to come to them. Obviously, she and Hollinger would have to find a way to get to him instead. Claire was also aware that numerous pairs of eyes were now turned in their direction, watching this scene unfold.

Giving the bouncer what she hoped would register as an affable smile, she said, "There's no need to make an unpleasant fuss. Perhaps if we bought a drink or two…?"

But as she reached into a pocket for Boehm's wallet, she heard the human wall bellow, "I'll save you, sir!"

Startled, she glanced up just in time to see Stark barrelling toward her.

Claire sidestepped the charge. She watched with fascination as her would-be attacker plowed instead into a mixed group who had been standing around a booth holding assorted drinks in their hands. In an instant, people and drinks were mashed together and tossed in an untidy heap inside the booth.

Amid a rising chorus of angry shouts, Claire nudged Hollinger and said, "Let's grab Garry and get out of here."

And, as all hell broke loose inside the Ha'penny and O'Meara rushed to call the police, Claire and Hollinger each took one of Boehm's arms and hustled him out the front door.

~~~

By 1:00 a.m., the disturbance at the bar had finally been quelled and the last of the police vehicles was pulling away from the curb. But none of the changelings noticed. They were sound asleep, two blocks away.

James, in Claire's body, lay swathed in blankets on the living room sofa. Boehm's body, it was decided, must occupy the bedroom, within arm's reach of the telephone in case it rang during the night. As long as Claire's mind was inside that body, she was determined not to share the bed. So, Boehm, in James Hollinger's body, curled up on the carpet behind the sofa, where he lost consciousness and began snoring blissfully almost immediately.
~~~

In the Fifth Dimension

*T*hey're entertaining, I'll give them that.

Engrossed in observing the progress of his experiment, Demonai did not notice the intrusion of Olla'set's pod inside the bubble until it nudged his membrane to initiate communication.

Welcome, Aggregator, and thank you for accepting my invitation to join me.

That was no invitation, Demonai—it was a threat, one that I won't soon forget if you can't show me compelling proof that these creatures are truly as you claim.

Actually, Aggregator, I meant it as a warning. What you just communicated to me, however—that was a threat.

Demonai, please, begged Tillah, arriving third and joining the meld. *It took considerable persuasion to get Olla'set here. One disrespectful spark from you could undo all my hard work.*

You're right. My apologies, Aggregator.

Tillah has informed me that you are considered a god by the threedees, that you protect some of them and grant their wishes.

Tillah communicates the truth.

Then your collection sac must be uncomfortably full of their tribute.

I don't understand, Aggregator.

You frighten them with your power over them and they bring you offerings of coherent matter. That is tribute, he explained patiently.

That isn't the way I've been doing it, Aggregator.

Then you've been doing it wrong. Let me show you.

Before Demonai could react, Olla'set plunged a secondary pod numerous times into the third and fourth dimensions.

There. Temples should already be erected, overflowing with tribute.

What did you do, Aggregator?

I announced myself to a threedee and commanded it to honour me with tribute or be disaggregated. Then I appeared to it many times more to convince it of my great power.

Which threedee? demanded Demonai and Tillah in unison.

You wish proof? Fine. It was that one. By my third visit it was telling others about me. Implant yourselves and witness the making of a god.

Chapter Eleven

"Thank you for agreeing to see me in your chambers on such short notice, Your Honour."

Superior Court judge Cormac 'Mack Truck' O'Toole glanced up from the stack of papers on his desk, then leaned back in his chair and regarded his visitor narrowly. Round face, almond-shaped eyes, nervous hands gripping a brown leather zipper case. And much too youthful in appearance to convince anyone at first glance that she could be a second-year law student. A high school sophomore, maybe, but even that was pushing it.

"Your petition intrigued me, Ms. Perrone," he informed her sternly. "Don't get me wrong. I've seen—and done—my share of law school prankery, and I can smell public mischief all over this. But I admire the boldness and ingenuity you and your accomplices have demonstrated, and I wanted to meet you so that I could tell you that to your face."

The young woman's expression became even more strained. "I'm afraid this isn't a joke, Your Honour."

"Oh, no?" He read from the first page of the document his secretary had handed him earlier that day. "It says here that you're asking for an injunction against 'Olla'set the Magnificent, Megapotentate of the Twelfth Spatial Dimension'."

"That's just what he calls himself. But he's real, Your Honour, and he poses a genuine threat, not only to my client, but to all of us."

He shot her an incredulous look. O'Toole had checked her out immediately after receiving her petition. Paulina Perrone might not look it, but she was the real deal—23 years old, with a bachelor's degree in history and a year of law school already under her belt. Nonetheless, it was astounding to think that this little thing with the voice of a child and no standing whatever with the Bar Association could actually have a client.

Stubbornly, she continued, "Olla'set claims to be a god. He says that my client, Joseph Nathan Russell, has been neglectful by not paying tribute to him for the past ten years and now owes him 1430 glasses of homogenized milk, or the equivalent value in calcium and silica, plus interest."

"And does he?"

"Your Honour?"

"Does your client owe someone 1430 glasses of milk?" O'Toole repeated patiently.

"No! This is extortion, plain and simple."

"Hmph." He resumed flipping through the document in his hands. It bore a clerk's date stamp and initial, meaning it had actually been filed. So the courthouse staff were in on this? Now he *knew* they were getting close to April Fool's Day.

As stated, the purpose of the injunction was twofold: first, to prohibit this self-proclaimed god from harassing Mr. Russell until all claims and charges pertaining to the twelfth spatial dimension had been settled in a terrestrial court; and second, to stop Olla'set from taking any action that might result in "the disaggregation of the entire third dimension".

That last was the part that had gotten Paulina Perrone through the door of his office today. How could he possibly pass up listening to a plea for help to save not the city, or the nation, or even the world, but the whole damned third dimension? What breathtaking, lunatic audacity!

Minute by minute, his conviction grew: there was no way a second-year law student could have cooked this up by herself. Richard Slattery, the current dean of the law school, had to be involved somehow. The practical jokes he and O'Toole had orchestrated together in their undergraduate years there had been the stuff of legends.

O'Toole put on his grimmest face and motioned her to sit down.

"Tell me, Ms. Perrone, how does the twelfth spatial dimension concern my court, exactly?"

She swallowed audibly. "If you'll grant us the injunction, Your Honour, we plan to file criminal charges."

"Against a god?"

"Yes, sir. Olla'set's persistent, ongoing harassment of my client caused him to have a serious automobile accident three weeks ago. He just got out of the hospital."

This stunt had Rick Slattery written all over it. It was good to know that nearly thirty years spent immersed in the minutiae of jurisprudence hadn't been able to erode all the brilliant mischief out of him. And it was time for something like this. Slattery had been too quiet, for far too long. Refilling his tank, probably.

"So, you'll be charging Olla'set with…?"

"Criminal harassment and assault causing grievous bodily harm."

"And I presume you'll be seeking damages amounting to 1430 glasses of milk, to cancel out this would-be god's claim?"

To his surprise, the young woman replied, "No. Mr. Russell isn't interested in collecting punitive damages, Your Honour. He just wants Olla'set to back off and leave him alone."

"And not destroy the universe," O'Toole added, no longer able to keep a scowl on his face. "This has been a pleasant diversion, Ms. Perrone, but I have to get back to my real job now. Be sure to give my regards to Dean Slattery," he added, holding the petition out to her across his desk.

She stiffened in her chair. To her credit, there was steel in her eyes, but he couldn't help noticing that her chin was wobbling. "Would you be taking this more seriously if a member of the bar had presented it to you, Your Honour?" she demanded.

"Absolutely," he assured her. The document dropped forcefully onto his desk, making a sound like a face being slapped. "Any experienced lawyer who came to me with a tale like this would have been cited for contempt and recommended for disciplinary action within the first two minutes."

"How can I convince you that this is no joke?"

"The usual way, young lady: with arguments and evidence. You do understand the definition of admissible evidence?"

At that, she got to her feet, snatched up the petition and squared her shoulders. "I'll be back, Your Honour, with evidence."

Sure, you will, on April Fool's Day, no doubt, he thought, smiling to himself as he watched her march resolutely out the door. As it closed behind her, he punched the intercom key on his desk phone. "Elizabeth," he told his secretary, "get me Dean Slattery at Upper Canada University, Faculty of Law."

Paulina Perrone's visit had triggered an avalanche of memories: the law librarian's Mini Cooper, resting upside-down in the branches of a century-old maple tree; the registrar, staring aghast at his office door, which had somehow shrunk overnight to a quarter of its normal height, forcing him to go through it on all fours; five law professors, dumbly gazing at the place in the faculty dining room where the kitchen and serving area had been seamlessly replaced by banks of junk food vending machines, also overnight. There had been at least a dozen other pranks, each more insanely brilliant than the last, and all targeting the residents of what Slattery liked to call 'the pompous plane of existence'.

Slattery and O'Toole would imagine the prank together,

discuss it, revel in the thought of it for an hour or two. Then, Slattery would somehow manage to execute it, by himself. Like a magician, he never divulged how he'd done it, not even to his faithful co-conspirator. Whenever O'Toole, dying of curiosity, pressed him for details, Slattery would tell him with a wink, "See, I have this genie trapped inside a bottle." Then they'd have a good laugh, followed by a beer or three at the student pub.

They'd had a lot of good laughs together, before they'd graduated and gone their separate ways. Had it really been twenty-seven years ago? That was far too long a time between laughs, especially now that O'Toole himself was apparently residing on "the pompous plane of existence".

In the law school refectory, Paulina Perrone heaved a discouraged sigh as she dropped her zipper case onto a chair and shrugged out of her brown corduroy jacket. The eating area was almost empty. There were only a handful of students scattered about, most of them hunched over weighty-looking tomes and sipping distractedly out of institutional white coffee mugs. One young man, a teaching assistant she recognized, had spread his *Globe and Mail* out over an entire table. He glanced up long enough to wave cheerily at her before plunging back into the business section.

Oh, to have nothing more to worry about right now than a term paper!

She'd walked all the way from O'Toole's office at the court house, trying to think of some relatively painless way to break the bad news to Joey. Unfortunately, no epiphany had struck her en route. All she'd accomplished was to be twenty minutes late for her meeting with her client.

He sat across the table from her now, looking like an Edvard Munch painting with curly blond hair. Hollow eyes, hollow cheeks—and a thigh-high plaster cast on his left leg, which he'd elevated and was resting on the third chair at the small round refectory table. Joey wasn't the only one looking terminally sleep-deprived; it was crunch time for the students at the university, caught between essay deadlines and the looming shadow of final exams. Joey Russell, however, was caught in a much more desperate place. If a light did appear at the end of his tunnel, it would probably turn out to be the train.

He waited patiently for Paulina to hang and straighten her jacket across the back of her chair, move the zipper case onto the table, and sit down. Then he ventured a question. It was *pro forma*—the expression on her face had already given him the answer.

"Any luck?"

She shook her head sadly. "It's same old, same old, kid. Nobody wants to take this seriously. They think I'm playing an early April Fool's joke. O'Toole even told me he thought it was a very good April Fool's joke, and he ought to know. Then he threw technicalities at me—said he wouldn't lift a finger unless I presented him with hard evidence. Has Olla'set bothered you yet today? Preferably in front of several reliable witnesses that I can depose?"

"No, sorry."

Nodding philosophically, she accepted the lukewarm coffee that he handed her. Served her right for being late, she thought. "Don't apologize. In my experience, a serious bully doesn't give up. He'll be back." *...probably with a posse,* she nearly added, but stopped herself just in time. "None of this makes any sense, Joey," she said instead. "I mean, you expect to meet up with his kind in the schoolyard, demanding your lunch money. But years later, inside the toilet tank in your bathroom? Or threatening you at night from inside your closet? And why on Earth would a god want you to hand over every glass of milk you drank after school from fifth grade through twelfth?"

"It wasn't his first choice of tribute."

"What?"

"The first thing he demanded from me was a kilo of diamonds. I was just ten years old at the time, and terrified. If he'd asked for my bike, I would have handed it over. But diamonds? I told him he was being ridiculous, and he left. A month later, he was back, saying that out of the goodness of his heart he would settle for my weight in gold. Again, there was no way. I suggested politely that he go bother someone else for tribute." He paused, looking thoughtful. "That was probably my first mistake—saying 'please'. Anyway, he kept coming back, each time demanding something different. It was as though he was working his way down a list. It took him years to get to calcium, at which point I said, 'You mean milk?'"

"Your second mistake," commented Paulina.

"Yeah. And my third was letting slip that milk was a food, and that all the milk I'd ever drunk was stored in my bones and teeth," he concluded miserably.

"Well, you certainly made it easy for him to terrorize you," she agreed. "But I wouldn't be so quick to beat myself up if I were you. O'Toole said that he could smell public mischief all over this. What if he's onto something?"

Joey's eyes widened, then narrowed. Leaning as far over the table as he could, he hissed vehemently, "It's not a joke, and I'm not crazy!"

"I know you're not," she assured him, "but—"

"There has to be someone who will help us," he went on raggedly. "My mom's been after me to see a psychiatrist. If I thought being in a mental hospital would keep Olla'set away from me, I'd commit myself in a minute. I'm just glad you were there that day, Pauly, when he threatened to turn me inside out."

Actually, it hadn't been the threat so much as the way Olla'set had levitated Joey and made the skin and muscle seem to disappear for a moment from his entire left side. All the bones had been fully exposed, and the morbid thought had occurred to her that anyone, including herself, could have touched them, wiggled them, even plucked them right out of his body. Just remembering that moment now was making her a little queasy.

"Yeah, it was lucky that I was there," she agreed uncertainly.

"So what's our next step?"

"Dean Slattery, I guess."

"Great! Another legendary prankster."

"Well, Joey," she told him, "I don't know what else to do. Maybe this *has* all been some elaborate practical joke, and someone like Dean Slattery can debunk it for us."

In the Fifth Dimension

I don't *understand, said Olla'set. It worked all the other times.*

So you did communicate with the threedees? Demonai said.

Not at first. Not by making sound waves. I just shook the ground or exploded a mountain, to see what the creatures would do. Later, I singled out individuals and made my demands to them from inside various objects. Their reaction was always the same: build a temple, fill it with tribute. That was my experiment, and I believed it had been successful.

Well, the threedees are driven to study and understand their reality, Aggregator. Before they knew what caused such things as floods and quakes, they were fearful. They imagined that these disasters must be the work of powerful beings who needed to be appeased. However, the threedees have learned a great deal since then about the nature of their world. The farther along the timeline they are, the harder they are to frighten, and the less submissively they respond to threats.

And if Olla'set had studied them instead of bullying them, Demonai mused, he would already know that.

The female speaks of 'debunking'. What does that mean?

It means she doesn't believe that you are real, and she hopes the other threedee can help her prove that what you've done is simply an act of mischief by a third threedee.

That's ridiculous! Of course, I'm real!

You persist in denying that they are intelligent. Now they plan to use reason and logic to disprove your very existence. That seems fair payback to me. Tillah, what do you think?

Wisely, Tillah ignored his question and instead posed one of her own. *Demonai, the 'legendary prankster' the female plans to consult—that wouldn't be…?*

It would. I am his sidekick. I expect he'll be contacting me very soon.

How would he do that? she wondered.

You'll see.

Chapter Twelve

It was one o'clock in the morning, and he was quite literally about to let the genie out of the lamp. Again.

Richard Slattery had no idea what nearly thirty years of solitary confinement might be like for a supernatural being like Demonai. He only knew how angry he himself would feel after just one day of it. According to legend, a genie had to obey whoever owned his receptacle, but legends had been known to be wrong. What if Demonai, once freed, turned his powers against his supposed master?

Slattery shuddered at the thought, but his resolve held firm. After the phone message from Mac and the story he'd heard a few hours ago from Paulina Perrone, he knew that it was a chance he would have to take.

Wearily, he sank onto the brown leather armchair behind the heavy oaken desk in his study. He let his gaze wander across the desktop, past the marble pen-holder, the embossed leather CD case, the half-empty whisky bottle, and the recently refilled shot glass. His attention finally came to rest on the smudged and tarnished object occupying the middle of an otherwise pristine emerald green desk blotter.

The first time he'd seen the lamp, at a flea market in Wasaga Beach, it had looked like something straight out of the Arabian Nights. Now, after all the years it had spent in a straw-filled wooden packing crate in his mother's—now his— attic, it reminded him more of an armour-plated gravy boat.

Slattery glanced sideways at the shot of whisky—his third in the past thirty minutes—and let his lips quirk into a faint, rueful smile. Liquid courage, O'Toole had once called it. Tonight, that was exactly what it was.

For he'd concealed the lamp not to keep it safe from the world, but to keep the world safe from it—or, to be more accurate, safe from the powers possessed by the being it contained. Demonai had made a car fly across a street and land upside-down in the topmost branches of a tree. He'd melted an entire wall of the registrar's office and reshaped it to Slattery's specifications. He could even get inside people's heads, read their thoughts, make them hallucinate according to a script.

Slattery wasn't sure exactly when it was that he'd realized he had a proverbial tiger by the tail. He only knew that he'd awakened one morning in a cold sweat, with the sound of Demonai's laughter ringing in his ears and shreds of a horrific nightmare sliding off the edges of his memory. From that moment on, the very thought of summoning the genie from the lamp had been enough to tie his stomach in knots; and the thought of someone else doing it had turned the knots into ice. Slattery had channelled Demonai's powers into harmless practical jokes. The lamp's next owner might have plans that weren't nearly as benign. So, wearing thick gardening gloves, he had carried the beautiful old antique up to the attic and disappeared it, for the good of all humankind.

And now it was out of its crate and sitting in the middle of his desk, waiting with a disconcerting air of expectancy for him to work up the nerve to pick it up and stroke its sides. If he was lucky, he wouldn't be destroyed by Demonai the moment the genie emerged. If he wasn't… well, that was what the third shot of whisky was for, to help Slattery get past thoughts like that and do what needed to be done.

Earlier, law student Paulina Perrone had come knocking on his door with a story about a friend of hers, one Joseph Nathan Russell, who had been living a nightmare for the past ten years with a genie of his own. This genie had a sadistic streak and no lamp to hold him captive. Why he had chosen this particular boy to terrorize, Slattery couldn't even begin to guess. But as he listened to Paulina describe Joseph Russell's situation, a single thought sank bulldog teeth into Slattery and refused to let go: *There are more of them out there!*

He had always assumed, perhaps naively, that there was only one genie in the world, and that he'd prevented Demonai from ever doing any harm by shutting him away in the lamp. Now, learning about a second, evil genie, Slattery was forced to rethink his earlier strategy. Clearly, he would have to release Demonai—sooner rather than later—and pray that all those years of confinement hadn't turned his good genie into another Olla'set.

Paulina had spoken about injunctions and countersuits. She was an excellent law student, at the top of her class, but she obviously had no idea what they were dealing with, and he couldn't tell her without revealing the existence of the lamp. In fact, he couldn't even let her know that he fully believed her story. Making vague promises to do whatever he could, Slattery had ushered a very discouraged-looking Paulina Perrone out of his home. Then he'd fetched the whisky bottle and shot glass out of his bottom right desk drawer.

All right. He'd wasted enough time.

In one smooth motion, Slattery scooped up and swallowed the third whisky. Then he slammed the empty glass down onto the desk and reached with both hands for the lamp.

No longer bright and gleaming, the metal surface felt rough, even a little sticky to the touch. Slattery was glad to be wearing a long-sleeved shirt as he cradled the lamp in the crook of his left arm and began gently stroking its exposed side with his right hand. Three times... four times... nothing.

He felt a sudden chill. What was he doing wrong? Did genies hibernate? Did they sicken and die of neglect? *Was* there still a genie inside this lamp? Because it would be just like Demonai to let Slattery believe for almost thirty years that he was imprisoned here when in fact he was—where? Where could Demonai be?

Muttering darkly under his breath, Slattery got to his feet, still cradling the lamp. A horrible possibility had just occurred to him: What if Demonai and Olla'set were the same being?

"Come on," Slattery growled, trying once more. He took the lamp in his right hand and rubbed its other side, as energetically as he could stomach, with his left. Three times… four times… still nothing.

Frustrated, Slattery let the lamp drop back onto the desktop and fished around with two fingers in his pants pocket for a tissue to wipe his hands. "Come on out, Demonai," he challenged the air in the room. "Please! You have to tell me what the hell is going on. Who is this Olla'set and where did he come from? Can you help us to deal with him? Demonai, I need you. Show yourself, please!"

What in the name of the Universe is happening to you, Demonai? demanded Olla'set.

Demonai felt the familiar, pleasant shudder begin to cascade through him and knew he would have to wait for it to subside before attempting to communicate. Then another shudder, deeper and stronger than the last, surged from one end of his essence to the other and back, igniting a storm of sparks in all three of the melded beings.

Tillah was alarmed. *Demonai, communicate with us! What is that?*

A secondary pod… Slattery is touching… aah. And the final ripple of sensation flattened and disappeared, somewhere in his midsection.

Disgusting! You don't actually let the threedees—let them

TOUCH—? Olla'set was too repulsed even to complete the thought. But Demonai couldn't help noticing that the aggregator had made no effort at any point to withdraw from the meld. Evidently, there had been some pleasure in the experience for him as well.

No, of course not! Demonai reassured them. *The pod is implanted in an object, and the threedee is touching the object. Well, he's rubbing it, actually. It's how I've taught him to contact me.*

Of course, commented Olla'set, *you would teach them that. Excuse me, Aggregator, but I need to answer this call.*

⸜⸝

At last, a familiar voice flowed out of the lamp:

Yo, Ricky! Long time, no nothin'. Whassup, bro?

Stunned, Slattery froze in place. These were hardly the wrathful outpourings of a powerful genie who had been kept cooped up, incommunicado, for twenty-eight years. He sifted his mind for something intelligent to say and came up completely empty.

The genie made a sound like a sigh.

Oh, right—you're a big shot now. Greetings, Dean Slattery. What can I do for you today?

Slattery could hardly believe this. It was as though no time had passed at all. Perhaps, from Demonai's perspective, none had. Maybe that was one of the perks of being a genie.

This had better not be a crank call, man.

Slattery hastened to reply and heard words tumble out of his mouth in no particular order: "N-no! It isn't, D. I just—I was sure you'd be—Because it's been, what? Twenty-five years? More? And you're not even a little upset that I—? What were you *doing* in there all that time?" he finally blurted out, feeling a heat in his cheeks that was only partly owing to the whisky.

In the lamp, you mean? Didn't I tell you? That's not the only place I hang out.

Slattery swallowed hard, willing the butterflies in his stomach to quit fluttering and settle down. "So, you… travel around?"

Not really. I'm just sort of everywhere all the time. But you were saying you have a problem?

"A young friend of mine is being harassed by a genie. At least, I think he's a genie—he seems to have the same powers as you do." Slattery drew a full breath and continued, crossing his fingers, "I was hoping that you could have a word with the other genie and… you know… make him stop."

All right, Rick, I'll help your friend. But I want to meet him. When Slattery hesitated, Demonai added, *The Russell boy already knows my kind exist, so you won't be revealing any secrets. And I want to hear his story for myself.*

"How—?" Slattery's throat slammed shut on the rest of the question. He started over, enunciating each word carefully: "How did you know his name?"

I told you, man. I'm everywhere, all the time.

"Demonai, what exactly are you? And what is Olla'set? Are you the same being?"

The genie chuckled, raising the hair at the back of Slattery's neck.

A lot has changed since the last time we spoke. You need to hop on the Internet, Richard.

"I'm serious, D."

So am I. Hop… on… the Internet. And set up a meeting for me with the boy. Ciao, bro.

Silence.

"Demonai?"

More silence. Intrigued now, Slattery booted up his laptop, opened his browser, and keyed in Demonai's name for a search. Moments later, he was staring incredulously at his computer screen.

"Son of a bitch," he murmured. "Worshipped as a deity…

special protector of prostitutes and concubines? Holy shit!"

$$\sim$$

Did that threedee just insult you, Demonai? Olla'set wanted to know. *Twice?*

If I say yes, does that convince you that he's intelligent?

It convinces me that he deserves to be disaggregated for showing disrespect to a higher-order being.

Demonai knew that before Olla'set would even entertain the notion of there being a higher dimension than his own, he first had to be convinced that the threedees were just as evolved and self-aware as himself. That wasn't going to be easy.

Demonai, Tillah broke in, *isn't there an experiment in progress that you want to show Olla'set?*

Ah, yes. He had almost forgotten about that. *I'm testing the ability of the threedees to find their way out of a predicament that seems to have no solution,* he explained, guiding the aggregator's pod to the melded essences of the three primary test subjects.

Olla'set wasn't as impressed as Demonai had hoped he would be.

Really! Asking three-dimensional life forms to think their way out of a fifth-dimensional trap is an exercise in futility, Demonai.

But if they were capable of imagination, Aggregator, shouldn't they be able to find a theoretical solution to their shared problem? Tillah pointed out.

Olla'set thought for a while before delivering his response: *Very well. If these creatures were actually to pass Demonai's test by theorizing, then I would be willing to give some consideration to the idea that they might possess an intelligence approaching our own.*

It wasn't much, but it was a beginning.

Chapter Thirteen

2003
March 20

Boehm was awakened by the sudden slam of the apartment's front door.

"Goddamned extortionist!" Hollinger fumed, flinging a morning newspaper down on the sofa. "Where's my other wallet? I need a hundred dollars."

Claire emerged from the kitchen, where she had been stirring oatmeal with a wooden spoon and monitoring the brewing of about a gallon of coffee. "You're kidding! A hundred bucks for a *Globe and Mail*?"

"No, a hundred bucks for Mr. Rosseau, the building superintendent. It seems he just happened to see us come in last night," Hollinger snapped. "He thinks it's deplorable that a man like James Hollinger would go out and get himself publicly wasted and have to be carried back here like a common drunk instead of being discreetly dropped off by a hired limousine. He also thinks it's newsworthy. But for an extra C-note, as he put it, he can be persuaded to keep his mouth shut."

As Hollinger extracted the bills from his second wallet, he quickly counted the remaining cash. "We've got almost seven hundred left. That ought to carry us for a while, unless our wandering friend here does something else that Rosseau can capitalize on." Still grumbling, he dropped the wallet on the end table in the living room and stalked out the door again.

As it crashed shut the second time, Boehm moaned and opened his bleary eyes on a world that looked better when he squinted, but felt better when he didn't.

"Good morning," Claire greeted him cheerfully. "How's your head?"

It was already aching. The sound of her voice just sharpened the pain. "It hurts," he replied in carefully modulated tones. "My tongue needs a shave. And my stomach is sending me poison pen letters. Am I dying?"

"No," she told him. "What you are is hung over."

"Hung over what?" he groaned.

She'd brought him a cup of something on a saucer. "A litre of black coffee and some rest and you'll be good as new," she promised, making an unholy din as she put the cup and saucer down on the end table.

He'd been sleeping on the floor. Claire took his arm and helped him to a seat on the sofa. Then she handed him the cup.

A second later the front door flew open again. "No, not that," said Hollinger. "Tomato juice is the best thing for a hangover."

Claire pressed the rim of the cup to Boehm's lips. "Black coffee is the traditional remedy," she observed tartly.

"Why not give him a hair of the dog then?" he retorted, slamming the door behind him and nearly sending the scientist into spasms.

Boehm's hands were trembling. "Please," he whispered plaintively, "could you make a little less noise?"

"No." Rising to Claire's full height of five-foot-three, Hollinger glared down at him. "After that escapade of yours last night, you deserve to suffer. Taking my body on an impromptu field trip to a neighbourhood pub, of all places! And getting sloppy drunk? What the hell were you thinking?"

"Don't mind him, Garry," said Claire. "James is just ticked off about the hundred dollars Rosseau siphoned out of his wallet this morning."

"You're saying I shouldn't be?" he challenged her.

"I'm saying that for you, it's always about the money," she retorted. "You never miss an opportunity to remind us about that. Meanwhile, Garry's the one who's hung over and I'm the one who keeps getting beaten up, but you're the one complaining the loudest. Are you really putting your pain on the same level as ours? Especially when you knew from the outset that staying here was likely to be an expensive exercise?"

"You said that paying him off was just business as usual for you," Boehm added, each word a struggle to get out. "You said it was just the beginning."

Hollinger let out an exasperated syllable. "Yes, but I was assuming that I'd be bribing him a little bit at a time, and that none of us would be doing anything stupid. At this rate, I'm going to run out of cash."

"Yeah, that can be a real problem when your credit cards aren't working," Boehm grumbled, pressing his hands to the sides of his head.

Hollinger watched him for a moment. "How about some of that coffee, Claire?"

"Get it yourself," she told him. "I only minister to the infirm and the dying, and you are neither."

Giving an impatient huff, Hollinger headed for the kitchen. "I'm curious, Garry," he called out a moment later. "Why did you go to that bar anyway?"

"Roxanne," Boehm muttered miserably.

Hollinger emerged from the kitchen then, stirring a cup of coffee with a clattering spoon that resounded in Boehm's head like Big Ben striking the hour. "Don't tell me you're still pining over her," he scoffed. "You have to remember whose body you're wearing, Garry. I'm a celebrity. People recognize my face. And you played right into Rosseau's hands, getting blasted like that last night!"

"It's not only about you, Hollinger," Boehm complained,

wincing at the loudness of his own voice. "Not that you'd care, of course, about Roxanne or me. It's Number One who counts, right? Well, one is a lonely number now. She's washed her hands of you. Of us."

Hollinger sank slowly onto the armchair. "Listen," he said wearily. "Maybe I'm jaded, but to me, Roxanne was just another attractive woman I could take places and show off and then make love to. We dated for fun and for mutual sexual satisfaction. End of story."

"Were you born a sexist pig, James, or did you have to work at it?" Claire interjected.

He batted her question away. Still addressing Boehm, he went on, "Obviously, in the several hours you spent with Roxanne, you established a different sort of rapport. I'm not knocking that. On the inside, you and I are two different people. But as long as you're occupying my body, friend, I'll thank you to keep your lovesickness entirely to yourself."

"Listen here, *Mister* Hollinger!" Boehm blustered. "You're worse than jaded. You're the most callous person I've ever met, and that's saying something. Before your despicable lifestyle was thrust upon me I'd never experienced—I never knew—" Something hot and rough was rising at the back of Boehm's throat. The effort of forcing words past it was making him perspire. "—how rotten a man could feel about wanting—"

Then he was done. His face the colour and texture of a giant pearl, the scientist leaped off the sofa and headed for the washroom, nearly tipping over his coffee cup as he brushed past it. Claire caught and righted it just in time to prevent a spill.

"It's a shame Roxanne feels that way," Hollinger murmured sadly. He heaved a heartfelt sigh. "We had a beautiful arrangement."

"Until you spoiled it. Right. So now what?" Claire wanted to know. "Are you going to go out and get smashed too?"

He physically shook off the moment. "Don't be

ridiculous," he snapped. "In our present situation we can't afford to indulge that kind of sentimentality. Garry's just going to have to realize that. So, Roxanne is history. Her choice."

He was contemptible. Disgusted beyond words, Claire leaned back in her seat. But Mrs. Griesdorf's purse had raised a sizable lump, and the spot was still tender. As it contacted the rear cushion of the sofa, Claire winced and clapped a hand to her head. "That old lady must have been carrying bricks in her purse," she moaned. "What happened after I passed out, anyway?"

"Just what I told you before. There were maybe two dozen men and women there, and they obviously had never seen a man faint, because the sight of you lying on the floor brought their little lynching party to an immediate halt. Sophie rushed over, of course, announcing her nursehood and talking about concussions. She checked your vital signs. She even produced a pocket flashlight from somewhere and made sure your pupils were equal and reactive."

"And?"

"They were. Then she offered to call an ambulance, and if you hadn't stirred and opened your eyes just then, I might have let her."

"You *might* have? Your concern for me is touching," she commented dryly, "but not especially credible, since you refused to escort me back here until after you'd made the presentation I prepared."

"Well, you kept telling me how important it was to you, and a deal is a deal," he said. "And after all the time we spent practising it—"

"You mean all the time you spent learning it," she corrected him.

"Okay, that too. The point is, I'd already decided I wasn't going to let anything stop me from holding up my side of the agreement."

"Even at the expense of Garry's health? James, you

seriously need to rethink your priorities," she declared.

Just then, two things happened. Boehm reappeared, still pale but looking a great deal more composed than he'd been when he left the room. And the telephone rang.

It was a land line receiver, plugged into a wall jack beside the door during the day and sitting on a small circular table. For several seconds they all stared dumbly while it rang twice… three times… Finally, Hollinger pointed out, "Claire, you've got the voice that belongs with the apartment. You'd better answer that."

"It could be someone at the research project," Boehm chimed in tautly. "They might be recalling me to work. Please!"

Acutely aware of the two pairs of eyes watching her, she picked up the receiver and said in her most formal voice, "Hello? Yes, this is Garry Boehm." When it dawned on her who was on the other end of the call, Claire nearly dropped the phone. Gasping her next breath, she pressed a silencing hand over the mouthpiece and hissed, "It's Sophie! How the hell did she get this number?"

"From the directory, I'd guess," said Hollinger. "Don't assume the worst. She's probably just checking to make sure you're all right. Talk to her," he urged.

Throwing him a dirty look, she uncovered the mouthpiece and said, "Sorry about that. I'm just a little busy right now, and—" Her eyebrows rose. "My wallet? What about my wallet? Found on the floor after the meeting?" she repeated for James and Garry's benefit. "Well, thank you for keeping it safe. I appreciate that."

She covered the mouthpiece again and asked Boehm conversationally, "Is there anything in your wallet that you're going to need right away? Because it's in Sophie's possession right now, and I suspect she's using it as bait to reel in your body and have her way with it."

At that, his eyes went wide as saucers. A second woman was after his body? "Damn! And I'm not even in it."

"I'll take that as a no." Claire unmuted the receiver and said, "Ms. Hopper, thank you for calling. I have company and can't come over there to pick it up right now, but… Oh, I think I can manage without it for a couple of days. Why don't you give me your phone number so I can call you when I'm available to meet? Uh-huh… uh-huh… got it. Terrific. We'll talk again soon. 'Bye." And with that, she hung up the receiver.

"You didn't write down her number," Boehm pointed out.

"We've been best friends for three years," Claire replied. "I know her number. I don't have to write it down."

"And if we get switched back into our own bodies tomorrow, and I want to collect my wallet…?" said Boehm.

"Then Claire will give you the number," Hollinger cut in. "For now, we don't need you getting any ideas about racing over there."

"Oh, shit!" muttered Claire, struck by a sudden thought. "He may not need to go there. There's no stopping Sophie once she sets her mind on something. And if she found Garry's number in the phone book, then she has his address as well. She could turn up here at any time."

"Giving Rosseau yet another reason to ding me for a bribe," said Hollinger sourly.

"Actually, I was about to say that she mustn't find me here alone," Claire informed him, "because I've decided that you were right earlier. It would be wrong for her and me to have sex while I'm in this body."

Claire was treated to the sight of her own face lighting up. "You decided that I'm right?" Hollinger echoed. "Quick, alert the media!"

"Don't let it go to your head, James. I still think you're a pig."

"I don't see what the fuss is all about," Boehm said. "I mean, what's this Sophie going to do? Kick down the door and carry you off like King Kong?"

Hollinger and Claire exchanged looks. Hollinger's

contained a question. Claire shook her head in response.

"Besides," Boehm continued, "we're all going to be here together for the duration, so why worry about it?"

Now Claire's features were contracting into a pained expression. "That's not entirely true," said Hollinger.

"Which part isn't?" Claire demanded. Then, all at once, she remembered: "The fancy cocktail party. It's this evening, isn't it?"

"Garry and I will be gone for just a couple of hours. You should be okay," Hollinger assured her.

That sounded like wishful thinking to her. However, James *had* been right twice now. Sophie had changed her mind about Boehm. And having sex under false pretenses *was* morally wrong. Maybe the pig was on a roll. "Okay, I'll give you the benefit of the doubt," she told him. "But bear in mind that two hours can be an awfully long time to wait."

"It will fly by," he assured her. "Trust me."

～

On arriving in the city, Claire had quickly realized how expensive food could be if she relied on others to prepare it for her. Consequently, she'd invested in some basic kitchen equipment and dusted off the cooking skills that she'd acquired in high school Family Studies classes. Three years later, using only a two-burner hot plate, a bar fridge, and a plug-in toaster oven, she had absolutely nailed breakfast, could throw together a tasty light lunch, and was the queen of one-pot dinners. She also knew that if James and Garry found out how good she was in the kitchen, meal preparation would become her full-time job.

So, she purposely burned the oatmeal two mornings in a row, motivating Boehm to take over for the rest of the day. That freed her up to work on her short story for Ralph Ignace.

Fortunately, her laptop had a full-sized keyboard. Even

then, it was a challenge at first, directing Boehm's large hands over the keys. However, within half an hour she was touch-typing with confidence as she put her initial attempt at lesbian porn through the second of three editing passes.

Ralph was going to love this story. It oozed sensuality. The prose was as purple as a fresh bruise. The sex scenes were explicit but tasteful. Best of all, it was completed by half past eleven, in plenty of time to be printed out on Garry's little inkjet, sealed in an envelope, and carried to the local post office for same-day mailing.

"Would you like me to drop that off for you after lunch?"

She swivelled her chair and saw Hollinger leaning against the door jamb.

"You're going out later, alone?" she asked. "After the hard time we gave Garry this morning?"

"He snuck off to a bar and got wasted. This is different. I need something to read besides back issues of *Canadian Geographic* and scientific journals, so I thought I'd find a drugstore and pick up some magazines. You're welcome to come with me if you'd like to take a walk."

Having just spent two solid hours sitting at the computer, she was sorely tempted to accept his offer. However, it would mean leaving Garry by himself again, and Claire wasn't sure that would be wise. So, after staring at the destination address on the manila envelope for several seconds, she said, "No, I think I'll stay here, thanks. But I appreciate your mailing this for me. I have no idea how much postage it needs, so it will have to be weighed."

"Not a problem. When I get back, I'll show you what I'm going to wear to the party tonight."

With that, he about-faced and returned to the living room. She said nothing, just stared speculatively for a moment at the place where he'd been standing. While unpacking the suitcase that Hollinger had brought back from her apartment on Tuesday, Claire had found her best dress and a pair of strappy high heels in among the underwear and toiletries. By then she'd already learned about the cocktail party, so she understood why he'd included them. And yet, just now he sounded as though he expected her to be surprised.

What are you up to, James Hollinger? she wondered.

Hollinger hadn't been completely honest with Claire about his destination that afternoon. A drugstore was just one place he intended to visit. As he read the street address on her envelope, he realized that he could hand-deliver this as well, without going too far out of his way. It made more sense to him to do that than to entrust the package to some postal clerk who would just drop it into a large bag and send it on an odyssey. Claire was no fool, after all. Given her choice between waiting days for her story to arrive via snail mail and having it safely in the publisher's hands within the hour, she was certain to pick the latter.

While walking to the Ha'penny the previous evening, Hollinger had noticed a pay phone standing across the street from the bar. Today, having transferred a couple hundred dollars from his second wallet to Claire's purse, he used that phone to summon a taxi.

Forty minutes later, it deposited him in front of a modern steel and glass office building on Eglinton Avenue. The ground floor was all storefronts. One of the windows bore a painting of a large pink kitten with bedroom eyes, striking a provocative pose. There was no company name spelled out around it. Then again, none was necessary. This had to be Pussyjoy Enterprises.

Then it hit him: Pussyjoy.

Damn!

Until that moment, Hollinger had had no idea what sort of publisher Claire was dealing with. Now that he knew, things were starting to fall into place. The taxi was waiting, its meter running. Meanwhile, he stood on the sidewalk, dithering. He was wearing Claire's body. Dicing with her reputation. If she didn't want to be seen entering a place like this, she probably wouldn't appreciate what he was contemplating doing. On the other hand, he was already here, envelope in hand. He might as well go inside.

Hollinger gave himself a hard mental shake. He was overthinking, making this much more difficult than it needed to be. Pussyjoy was evidently a business. That meant there would be a front desk, staffed by someone who could receive incoming parcels. Hollinger was simply delivering a piece of mail. He would slip in, drop it off, and be out again within seconds. No muss, no fuss, no questions.

Squaring his shoulders, he hauled open the front door and stepped into what should have been a reception area. Except it was a jungle. On each wall, a mural depicted several big cats staring hungrily at visitors from behind tall grass and trees. The sofa and chairs clustered together in one corner all wore zebra-striped upholstery. Beneath Hollinger's feet was a shaggy carpet the colour of grass. A glassed-in display of books and posters occupied another corner. An afterthought? No, he realized, it was a lure. This room had been set up to deliver a message to anyone who wandered into it: at Pussyjoy Enterprises, you were either predator or prey.

Before today, Hollinger would never have characterized himself as prey. However, the female body he was currently wearing possessed instincts over which he had no control. Adrenalin was already flowing—he could practically feel it racing along his limbs, making him restless and uneasy. If this was anything like what Claire had experienced at that meeting the other night, he decided, then he definitely owed her an apology.

"Ye-es?"

Absorbed in noticing the decor, Hollinger had forgotten to look for the receptionist. Now he pivoted to face the owner of that supercilious male voice. A tall, narrow-faced fellow with a smug grin, calculating eyes, and crimped dark hair, he had apparently been lurking behind his desk, watching how this visitor reacted to the environment. Classifying her as prey.

Hollinger frowned in recognition. He had dealt with this man's kind before, many years earlier. There had been a thin line between stripping and porn in those days, and the financial situation of exotic dancers had often been complicated, especially when greedy or abusive employers were involved. Sometimes, it had taken a personal visit from a confident, determined accountant to pry a correct T4 form from a strip club manager. Always, the manager was a man, wearing the same expression Hollinger now saw on this receptionist's face.

James needed to be that confident, determined accountant again. At the very least, he needed to try. So, pretending to himself that he was still in his own male body, he stepped closer and dropped the envelope onto the desk. "This is for Mr. Ignace. Please see that he gets it."

Just then, a door flew open, releasing into the reception area a man who resembled a large teddy bear. Ralph Ignace, Hollinger guessed. He'd seen too many of this type before as well.

"Nonsense, Claire!" Ignace declared, placing paw-like hands on Hollinger's narrow shoulders. "I hardly ever see you anymore. Come in for a cup of coffee and let's discuss your next assignment." His voice seemed to ooze out of some hot, wet place deep inside him. Hollinger had been propositioned in those same moist tones by the Harrington-Smythe sisters. It was a memory he wished would stay buried.

"No, sorry, I can't," Hollinger demurred, keeping his voice steady even as his skin crawled at the overly familiar touch. "There's a cab waiting for me outside. I need to go."

Ignace licked his lips. "If you hand-delivered this, you must really need the money. Stick around while I read it and I'll cut you a cheque to take with you."

"No, really. The meter's running and I have another couple of stops to make."

The teddy-bear face contracted with disappointment. "Well, I'm sure the quality of this piece will be just as good as your previous work. You really are an excellent writer. Claire. I can have the cheque ready by this evening."

"Sure, that would be great."

"Wonderful! Till tonight, then." That quicksand voice followed Hollinger out the door to the street.

Not until the cab was blocks away from the office building did Ignace's final words register in Hollinger's mind. Thoughts and stomach began churning in unison. Ignace was expecting to see Claire again that evening. What had Hollinger just agreed to? Had he promised to return later and pick up the cheque from the office? Or had he given Ignace permission to deliver it to Claire at home, on this worst of all possible nights?

Wait a minute—the return address on the envelope wasn't Boehm's. When Claire didn't show up at his office, Ignace would assume that she was still at her own place in the Beaches and go looking for her there. His knock at the door would be answered by Sophie, the green belt in judo who didn't like strange men making passes at her and let them know it in no uncertain terms.

Hollinger's lips curved slowly into a smile.

The teddy bear was going to be schooled tonight. Oh, to be a fly on the atrocious purple wall!

Chapter Fourteen

"James, is that you?"

He almost didn't answer Claire's question, for he'd just let himself into the locked apartment with Boehm's key, and not even Rosseau, the sleazebag super, had the gall to enter without knocking first. At least, Hollinger hoped not.

"Yes, it's me," he finally replied.

"You were gone for a while. I was beginning to worry," she said, emerging from the bedroom. "I meant to tell you to get a postal receipt, for tax purposes. Did you?"

"Oops, no, I didn't. Sorry! It wasn't much, though. A couple of first-class stamps," he lied, tightening his grip on the plastic bag from the drugstore.

Claire narrowed her gaze, then crossed the room to confront him. "For someone whose obsession is numbers after dollar signs, you're being very cavalier about this. What's up?"

"I told you. It was a trivial amount, and I decided to make it my treat. Would you like to see what I brought back?" He pulled four magazines out of the bag and dropped them side by side on the coffee table: *Globetrotter*, *Macleans*, *Cosmopolitan*, and *Logic Problems*. "There should be something for everyone there. Oh, and one more thing," he added, reaching to the bottom for the final item.

Claire gasped when she saw the signature silver-embossed

box. "You went to a jewellery store?"

"It's for tonight," he told her. "And it's rented, not purchased. I do this every year. After Roxanne shows me the dress she'll be wearing, I pick out a necklace and earrings to go with it."

A light went on behind Claire's eyes. "How many years have you been taking her to this cocktail party now?"

"About seven."

"In a row?"

He nodded.

"And you claim not to have a relationship with this woman?"

"I see her for two weeks once a year. Did, anyway," he added, "until now."

"For seven years in a row. I hate to break this to you, James, but that's the definition of a relationship."

Actually, he'd been doing Roxanne's taxes for a lot longer than that, but Hollinger chose not to correct Claire's statement. Instead, as he replaced the jeweller's box in the plastic bag, he said, "I'll model it for you later, when I'm getting ready to leave."

Claire had insisted he try on her party dress to make sure it still fit properly. Now, fingering the silk tulle of the full skirt as he inspected himself in the mirror, Hollinger made a face. "Was this your prom dress? Or maybe a bridesmaid's gown?"

Claire threw him a dagger-sharp look. "Neither. It was a going-away gift from my parents. They wanted me to look special at my very first book launch."

"Oh, it's special, all right," he muttered. "*Too* special."

"What the hell is that supposed to mean?" she demanded.

He paused, picking his words. "It means we'll be attracting lots of attention, when all we should be doing is making a *pro forma* appearance and then fading into the crowd." Hollinger glanced at the clock. "There's still time to shop."

"And do you still have a credit card that works? Because fancy cocktail dresses don't come cheap."

"Of course. I didn't cancel *all* my cards, just the ones that Roxanne—never mind. Boehm has the identity and I've got the body. We'll have to do this together."

"You're not shopping without me," she declared. "That's my body, not a dress-up doll for the two of you. Anything it ends up wearing should reflect my own tastes."

"Okay, then. Call a cab. We're going to Carewe's," he told her.

Carewe's, in Yorkville, was a transplant from Rodeo Drive in Beverly Hills. The simplicity of its exterior was deceptive. In the two modest display windows, three or four pantsuits had been tastefully arranged without the use of plaster mannequins. Only the absence of price tags suggested that they might be at all expensive.

The interior of the store, however, was an entirely different breed of retail environment, with carpeted risers, tiered platforms, gilded archways... more like a stage set for a musical number than an actual clothing business. Claire wasn't surprised to see it. She had been here several times before, usually with Sophie.

The first time, they had wandered in out of curiosity while window shopping. On subsequent visits, they had amused themselves by indulgently deploring the excesses of the very rich. After all, who but an inbred wastrel would spend over two hundred dollars on a plain white cotton blouse with a shawl collar and a Givenchy label at the back of the neck? When they'd tired of tut-tutting the exorbitant prices, she and Sophie would turn critical eyes to every other aspect of the boutique.

Now, as then, as far as Claire was concerned, Carewe's was found wanting in three essential areas. There were no straight paths to anywhere in the store, a minimal amount of merchandise was on display, and an elegantly attired saleswoman was staring at the three new arrivals in haughty disbelief. She looked ready to call the police to escort this riff-raff off the premises.

"I think she recognizes me," Claire murmured. "My body, anyway."

"Well," Hollinger murmured back, "we'll just have to redirect her attention, then." With a sudden sophomoric giggle, he grabbed Boehm's arm and wrapped himself around it.

Claire nearly swallowed her tongue. It was bad enough that she'd just heard her own voice utter a sound she'd never thought herself capable of making. Now she was having to watch her body rub itself suggestively against a male arm. If Hollinger's ploy didn't work, she was seriously considering outing herself then and there.

When the saleswoman finally noticed the famous Hollinger face, there was an almost audible *click* of recognition in her eyes. She strode across the store toward him, wearing a welcoming expression. An instant before she came within hearing range, Claire reminded Boehm in a hoarse whisper, "We're shopping for cocktail dresses."

"I know," he muttered irritably. "I'm not stupid."

The woman stopped at what seemed to Claire an excessive distance away. "Mr. Hollinger?" she said expectantly. "Did you have an appointment with us, sir?"

"Er… no, but this is kind of an emergency," Boehm replied. "I need to purchase a cocktail dress for my friend. For tonight."

Her gaze swept rapidly from the simpering female clamped to the Hollinger arm over to the tall, stern-faced man who appeared to be overseeing the proceedings. "Very good, sir." And to Claire's relief, the saleswoman subsided back into brisk officiousness. "You're in luck. A previous showing just ended and our mannequins are still here. Please follow me and I'll have several dresses modelled for you."

At the rear of the store was a small circular stage surrounded by dainty white wrought iron benches with pink silk cushions. Gesturing to her three clients to take seats, the woman disappeared behind a set of matching pink curtains. Scant minutes later, the fashion show began.

This was a side of Carewe's that the casual walk-in public never saw, and it explained everything: the sparse arrangement of lifeless garments on the counters out front, the half-hearted effort at retail sales, and the dismissive attitude of the staff. Claire fairly drooled as the models strolled past wearing wrapped satin, Georgette studded with cultured pearls, silk jersey that glowed richly under the fluorescent lights—the saleswoman referred to them offhandedly as "frocks," but Claire knew in her soul that not a single dress in the line could be bought for less than a thousand dollars.

After a dozen beautiful creations had been shown, the saleswoman asked, "Do any of these appeal to you, Mr. Hollinger?"

Claire had loved them all. She bit back a disappointed exclamation when James piped up, "Do you have something a little simpler? I'm looking for understated elegance."

Blinking with bewilderment, the woman turned to Boehm. "These are our most exclusive designer fashions, sir," she pointed out. "And you found none of them satisfactory?"

Once more, 'Hollinger' remained silent and it was the woman at his elbow who replied, "They're all very nice, but we want something a little less eye-catching."

The saleswoman nodded knowingly. "Of course, sir," she said, her voice tinged with disdain. Then she retreated behind the curtains once again.

Claire took advantage of her withdrawal to berate both men in whispers. "Are you crazy? They're gorgeous! And some of them did have understated elegance."

"You're missing the point," James told her quietly over his

shoulder. "Like I said back at the apartment, I can't show up wearing something that will attract attention, either positive or negative."

"But—!"

"That's enough, you two," Boehm muttered urgently.

All at once, Claire realized that the saleswoman was back, wearing a forbearing expression and flexing her fingers. She looked like a teacher waiting for an unruly class to notice her presence and come to order. "You'd better turn around, James," Claire whispered. "I think the fashion show is about to resume."

"We have three short gowns that might suit your needs," said the saleswoman, "from our lower-priced line. Suzanne?" she called.

The first model appeared in pale blue silk jersey with a handkerchief hem and a neckline that dipped almost to her waist. Wordlessly, James shook his head and the mannequin whirled and disappeared behind the curtain.

The second dress was salmon pink, with long sleeves slit from shoulder to wrist and teardrop-shaped openings in the sides of the bodice, exposing plenty of ribcage. Boehm leaned forward eagerly as the model approached his bench, but James muttered just loudly enough to be heard, "No way!" Then he added, as a reminder to Boehm, "It's the dress we're buying, not the girl inside it."

"Oh," said Boehm, his excitement rapidly fading.

Claire prayed that the last dress would be acceptable. It would be mortifying to have to request a showing of their third-best line and be informed frostily that Sears was having a sale that week.

The third model, named Starlight, came out in a white silk toga with a purple border. The dress was cinched tightly around the waist, falling in elegant pleats from the hips to just below the knees. It shimmered pristinely as she took long, feline steps toward them.

"That one!" exclaimed Hollinger and Boehm at the same

instant.

Starlight wheeled around, revealing nothing but purple lacing holding the bodice of the dress together at the back.

The two men exchanged a dismayed look. Then Hollinger said with a nervous little laugh, "I guess I'll be finding a warm wall and keeping my back to it."

As the saleswoman turned her attention to the model, Claire leaned over and prompted Boehm, "Now we need a matching wrap and shoes and a handbag."

But the saleswoman didn't give him a chance to speak. Addressing James, she asked briskly, "And what dress size do you usually take, dear?"

Here it comes, Claire thought dully. *He'll turn to me and ask what size he wears.*

He surprised her. With remarkable presence of mind, he smiled up at the woman and returned the question. "What size would *you* say I should try on?"

"How about an eight?" the saleswoman suggested.

"Okay," he replied, bouncing to his feet. "And I should probably have a wrap to go with that, and some shoes, and a bag." And, chatting animatedly, Hollinger and the saleswoman strolled behind the curtains, leaving Claire and Boehm sitting slack-jawed on their respective wrought iron benches.

"He's certainly getting into the spirit of things," Boehm remarked faintly.

Claire said nothing, but her head was full of doleful thoughts. Hollinger was having altogether too much fun inside her body. What if she never got it back again? If she was trapped in Boehm's body for the rest of her life, that would be a whole other closet to come out of.

⸺

Are you certain these threedees are even aware of the problem you have posed them, Demonai? They don't seem to be paying it much attention.

They have to work their way through other, smaller problems first, Aggregator. Be patient, please.

Don't even think about making contact with any of them, Olla'set warned. *I heard the hints you dropped to your sidekick earlier. 'I'm everywhere, all the time. Hop on the Internet.' If you violate the integrity of this experiment I'll disaggregate the bubble with you inside it. Is that understood?*

Understood, Aggregator.

Demonai was confident the experiment would succeed. Threedees were constantly learning. And he had already witnessed during his association with Richard Slattery what a talent they had for getting themselves in and out of trouble, without any assistance from a being such as himself. The three that he had melded were intelligent and would soon figure out who was responsible for the startling change in their lives, because that was how he had originally set things up.

Now he just had to keep Olla'set from realizing that the game was rigged in the threedees' favour.

Chapter Fifteen

Located on the Bridle Path, where homes worth millions of dollars hid from curious eyes behind artfully placed greenery, Hugh Rockaway's mansion was a showpiece. It flaunted itself. Rather than conforming to his neighbours' tastes and giving it a thousand-foot, tree-lined driveway, Rockaway had had his house constructed so close to the road that it was sometimes mistaken for a public building. But that was typical of the man. Half his acquaintances admired his panache, while the other half condemned him for being tacky and gauche.

Tacky or not, Hugh Rockaway was worth at least eighty million dollars, thanks to an enterprising spirit and James Hollinger's good advice. And he'd returned the favour many times over, with referrals and recommendations that had helped to build Hollinger's firm into a powerhouse.

Twice a year, June Rockaway showed off her home at an exclusive social gathering: in the spring, she threw a gala cocktail party for a hundred selected guests; and in the fall, she hosted a lavish costume ball. It was deemed a great honour to receive an invitation to one of these two annual affairs, and socially suicidal to decline or ignore it. And that was why, come hell or high water, James Hollinger plus date had to show up at the Rockaway mansion between six-thirty and eight o'clock that evening. They didn't have to make a splashy entrance or even a positive impression on the other guests. They just had to fit in, consuming their share of alcohol and hors d'oeuvres and conversing politely for some respectable length of time before eventually making their escape into the night.

As their taxicab pulled into the wide semicircular driveway that fronted Rockaway's stately grey brick home, Hollinger straightened his rented opal-and-diamond necklace, adjusted his stole, and prayed fervently that Claire wouldn't do anything rash while they were gone.

Boehm was preoccupied as well, but for a different reason. Hollinger had force-fed about fifty names and physical descriptions into the scientist's memory, and it was taking every bit of his concentration to keep them all straight. As his 'date' nervously tugged at the embroidered white wrap for the hundredth time, Boehm said irritably, "You look just fine. Relax!"

"I'm not worried about me," Hollinger exclaimed. "I'm worried about you. Can you remember all the information I gave you about the other guests?"

Boehm cast a beseeching glance skyward. "Probably not," he replied tightly, "but I think I've learned enough to get by."

Shifting uneasily in his seat, Hollinger swallowed a groan. Perhaps there was something worse than social suicide. Maybe he would have been better off forgetting about this evening after all.

A uniformed attendant opened the cab door for them. Boehm stood gazing up an Everest-like climb to the mansion's front door and felt his mouth go dry. What on Earth had he been thinking? It was one thing to pretend to be James Hollinger for a bunch of faceless strangers, but to do it at a cocktail party, among Hollinger's own friends and business associates? Nor was Boehm's confidence boosted by the peculiar effect surrounding the Rockaways' front door. Each time it was opened to admit guests, the light that spilled into the deepening night made it glow like the maw of a blast furnace.

"Come on, Garry, buck up," Hollinger whispered encouragingly as he took Boehm's arm and led him toward the hell's mouth at the top of the stairs. "We're in this together, you know."

Of course they were. The Dunberrys of the world, the dabblers, the sheep—those were the types who needed to flock together to do things. They "teamed up". They provided "collegial support". They were pathetic. A true scientist didn't need a cheering section or a chorus to be successful. Or a social calendar filled with gala events. Or—

He paused, recalling the time he'd spent with Roxanne. He might just make an exception for her. She'd taught him a lot about applied biophysics.

Strictly speaking, however, none of that was necessary to scientific discovery. Pure science happened in out-of-the-way corners, and a true scientist needed only to stay focused on those corners, carefully adjust the conditions, and wait. In science, as in any other field of endeavour, the most artful hunters worked alone.

Boehm hated to admit it, but he and Hollinger were alike in that respect, the one in pursuit of knowledge and the other in pursuit of profit. The difference, of course, was that people in power wanted people like Hollinger to be successful. Given a choice between funding a series of nuclear fusion experiments and underwriting a potentially lucrative trade deal, the bankers and government types almost always chose the latter.

Boehm cast a glance at the apparent young woman on his arm. How he envied James Hollinger at that moment, pantyhose, mascara and all!

All at once, they were inside the door and being announced by a young man in green livery: "Mr. James Hollinger and Miss Claire Smith."

Boehm started. "What? Why did you—?"

Hollinger seized the scientist's arm and pulled him into the huge salon, where tray-bearing servers navigated adroitly between clusters of guests, offering them flutes of champagne and finger-sized delicacies. Not until they were standing on one of Mrs. Rockaway's prized Persian rugs holding drinks and hors d'oeuvres in their hands did he whisper an explanation: "I don't want anyone taking a fancy to Claire and tracking her down the way Sophie did you. There are a thousand Smiths in the phone book but not too many Amorys."

Boehm nodded distractedly in response. There was no point in arguing when he needed to concentrate on remembering.

A glance around the room showed him many of the people James had described to him back at the apartment. Bits of that interminable discussion repeated on Boehm like raw onions as his eyes alighted first on the Drysdales, Howard and Marie. ("...majority owners of a large meat-packing operation... be sarcastic if you talk to them at all.. we don't get along.")

Then he noticed a woman who had to be Doris Plisker. ("...loaded with affectations... wants desperately to be 'with it' but won't relax and let her natural charm come out... she was a different girl when her husband was alive... maybe that's why she still gets invited to these dos.")

Moments later, a man crossed his field of vision who fit Hollinger's thumbnail portrait of Richard Slattery—angular and distracted-looking, with a shock of greying hair, and wire-rimmed glasses, and a wooden pipe hanging off his lip. ("...the ex-brother-in-law... an academic who couldn't cut it in the courtroom, but he's apparently a genius at getting things done, so they made him Dean of the Faculty of Law at Upper Canada University. Hugh says he gives the event 'gravitas', although why a purely social evening would need that kind of weight is beyond me.")

"Da-a-ahling!"

Startled, Boehm nearly dropped his samosa. A statuesque woman with carefully sculpted bleached-blond hair was swooping down on him, in a blue dress that even sported a wing effect, arms outstretched in obvious expectation of a big, insincere hug. He searched his memory frantically for a second. James had described this person to him. Now who the hell was she?

"That's your hostess, June Rockaway," Hollinger hissed beside him, and all at once everything came back. This was Hugh Rockaway's third wife, the one who was into charity work and who spent most of her vacations with her widowed sister on Majorca.

"Jimmy!" she reproached Boehm fondly. "Sally is going to be terribly disappointed that you've brought a date. She's been telling everyone how she intends to monopolize you this evening." Boehm must have looked distressed, for Hollinger patted him reassuringly on the arm as their hostess burst into delighted laughter. "Heavens, it's nothing to worry about," Mrs. Rockaway continued. "She knows she has to be in bed by ten-thirty. I imagine she'll find someone else to corner until then. But she does have an overpowering crush on you, Jimmy, so try not to brush her off entirely, all right? By the way, I see you still have the same excellent taste in young ladies. Ah, someone else has just arrived. Will you excuse me?"

As June Rockaway breezed off carolling another "Da-a-ahling", Boehm turned sheepishly to Hollinger. "Sally is the Rockaways' ten-year-old daughter," he said, having just that moment recalled the information.

Hollinger nodded. "Give her another ten years and the whole world will be eating out of her hand. She already has the makings of a natural beauty, and if she's inherited even half of her mother's personality, look out!"

"I quite agree," said a tall, distinguished-looking man suddenly standing at Boehm's elbow. He was wearing a charcoal grey and silver pinstriped suit, and his hair and moustache had to be prematurely grey, for his face was unlined and there was the twinkle of youth in his clear blue eyes. Boehm conducted a rapid mental scan of all the descriptions he'd memorized, but this fellow wasn't among them. Instantly, the scientist relaxed.

He was in the presence of a stranger. And if Hollinger had never met the man, then Boehm didn't have to follow a script.

Boehm extended his hand. "I don't think we've met, Mr…?"

"Oberer," the man replied. "Roger Oberer. I'm the newest member of the board of Remstock Financial Services."

Even though the name meant absolutely nothing to him, Boehm tried to look knowing. "Oh."

"I came over just now to get a rumour confirmed," Oberer continued.

"Oh?" said Boehm.

"The pundits on Bay Street are predicting that your company is about to close a merger that'll shake us all to the very roots. There's some speculation that you're even using your personal fortune to anchor it."

"Oh?" Boehm hadn't an inkling of what this chap was talking about. At his side, Hollinger grinned mischievously.

"Okay," Oberer said. "Since you obviously intend to keep this firmly under your hat until the *fait* is *accompli*…"

Finally, Hollinger spoke up. "Jimmy," he cooed, "you promised there would be no shop talk while we were on vacation. Can't you two discuss something else for a while and just enjoy the party?"

Boehm turned and smiled a question at Oberer.

After a moment's hesitation, the other man shrugged slightly and replied, "Sure, why not?"

In a general conversation that he could occasionally steer to the margins of popular science, it was soon obvious that Garrick Boehm was well able to hold his own. So well, in fact, that Hollinger began to feel restless. He decided to leave Boehm with Oberer and do some mingling.

The room they were in was immense, and while its

dimensions weren't exactly lost on him, it happened to be one of many such salons that James Hollinger had had occasion to visit. In the circles in which he customarily moved, marble floors and ornate ceilings were the rule rather than the exception. Hollinger had reached the point where he enjoyed spacious surroundings, elegant furniture, and original works of art without being particularly conscious of them. People, however, were another matter.

The way some might avidly devour books, James Hollinger was a voracious reader of people. He couldn't help noticing that there seemed to be an entire school of them, drifting through the salon and library and great room of the mansion as though swept by an invisible tide. And so he strolled around, smiling pleasantly, joining conversations when invited, giving his assumed name when asked, and watching and listening and making copious mental notes.

All at once, he found himself standing in front of a large, simply framed, pen-and-ink drawing representing a map of the city as it must have appeared around the turn of the twentieth century. It was a quaint reproduction, with important buildings actually drawn in miniature, rather than being depicted as shaded outlines, as later became the practice. Intrigued, he stepped up for a closer look.

City hall was physically at the centre of the town in those days. Distributed equidistantly around it were the university, the port and customs office, and the main post office. In fact, he mused, if lines were drawn joining those three locations they'd form a triangle, with the city hall somewhere in the middle.

Hollinger caught his breath with a shrill gasp. "Oh, my God! That's the answer!" Whirling excitedly, he looked for Boehm. The scientist hadn't budged from his conversation with Roger Oberer. Hollinger made his way purposefully across the room, moving as quickly as he could without attracting too much attention. Once at Boehm's side, however, he tugged urgently at his arm and blurted, "We have to leave."

"What?" Boehm said, startled. "But I was just—"

"It's an emergency," Hollinger insisted, his voice trembling with suppressed excitement. "I'm sorry to have to take him away like this, Mr. Oberer."

"I'm sorry too," said Oberer, perplexed. "What's the matter? Aren't you feeling well? I'm sure our hostess wouldn't object to your lying down in one of the bedrooms—"

"I appreciate your kind offer, but I—it isn't me. It's—it's a family thing," Hollinger stammered. Then, turning to Boehm, he added beseechingly, "Please, Jimmy, I really have to go home. Right now."

Boehm was nonplussed. James had drilled him so insistently on protocol—when to arrive, the earliest they could leave, how and to whom to say goodbye when they did leave, even how much they could eat. He'd put the scientist in terror of inadvertently committing a grievous social gaffe and possibly ruining Hollinger's career. And now here was Hollinger himself, tossing the entire litany out the window. However, since the urgency appeared to be genuine, there was nothing to do but follow James's lead.

"I guess I'd better take her home," he said reluctantly to Oberer. "Do you see Mrs. Rockaway? I'll have to make my apologies to her."

"Don't worry about it," Oberer assured him. "June and I are old friends. I'll explain that an emergency forced you to leave early. I'm sure she'll understand."

The butler was happy to call a taxicab for them. As soon as the vehicle was rolling down the street, Hollinger leaned forward and instructed the driver to stop at a gas station.

Struggling to fathom his companion's suddenly irrational behaviour, Boehm blurted resentfully, "A gas station? What for?"

The taxi driver was only slightly more polite. "I've already got a full tank, lady."

"It's not to gas up," Hollinger insisted. "We have to pick up a map of the city." Turning to Boehm, he lowered his voice and went on excitedly, "I know how we can locate the source of our problem. We triangulate ourselves. I can't believe I didn't think of it before."

Thoroughly perplexed, Boehm shook his head. "You're not making sense."

"Never mind. Once I've got the map I'll show you."

The apartment was dark and quiet. Shortly after the other two changelings had departed, Claire had turned out the lights in the kitchen and living room and had sequestered herself in the bedroom to await their return. For about an hour, she lounged on the bed, long legs outstretched, back propped up by pillows, and brain engrossed in solving a challenging-level logic problem. Then the beast in Boehm's belly growled, demanding its evening snack.

Padding barefoot in the dark, Claire went to the kitchen to find a piece of fruit. Or a bag of potato chips… a package of cookies… anything with calories in it. She'd eaten only a couple of hours earlier, and yet she was hungry again. Claire had often shaken her head at the sight of men consuming large amounts of food. Now she understood why they did it. The hyperactive male metabolism—they burned calories while sleeping, for heaven's sake!—had to be one of the great injustices of the universe.

Just as she was reaching for the light switch, there came a gentle tapping at the apartment door that froze her outstretched arm.

Instantly, her thoughts were racing. That was not Sophie—her knock would be much more aggressive. And Garry and James had keys to let themselves in. No one else was expected.

Leaving the light off, Claire made her way to the cutlery

drawer and eased it open. She hoped she wouldn't need one, but there were things here with which she could defend herself. Carefully, she felt around, her fingers finding forks, tongs, a meat thermometer…

She heard a scrabbling sound at the lock. Someone was breaking in.

Damn!

The doorknob was turning. Finally, her hand closed on the wooden handle of a steak knife. Clutching her weapon, Claire tiptoed back to the kitchen door. The light from the kitchen was strong enough to illuminate the living room as well. Perhaps that and the element of surprise would drive the intruder off.

With a gentle creak, the apartment door swung open and then closed again. The latch whispered shut. Her breath turning to dust in her throat, Claire reached for the light switch. *I'm a big, tall man,* she reminded herself sternly, *and that's what the burglar will see. A tall, angry man with a knife.*

Steeling herself, she flicked the kitchen light on.

Two people gasped simultaneously.

Caught like a fly in a bead of amber by the brightness pouring through the kitchen door was a short, potbellied man wearing jeans and a matching denim shirt. His greasy hair was slicked right back from his face. His eyes were wide and his jaw hung slack with fear and astonishment.

"Rosseau!" Claire exclaimed indignantly. "What the hell are you doing here?"

"I—well, I—I thought—"

"You thought the apartment was empty and decided to do a little snooping," Claire accused him, shifting her grip on the knife and deliberately bringing it into view. "Maybe lift a few souvenirs?"

"I'm the superintendent of the building," Rosseau squeaked. "It's part of my job to keep track of the tenants. And when only two of you go out and the place seems empty… for all anyone knows you might be murdered or something. Didja think about that?"

"I think your vigilance would be much more praiseworthy if you weren't being paid so damned much to look the other way," Claire rasped. "What you just did is called breaking and entering. The police frown on it and so do I. I'd advise you to think about *that*. Now get out of my apartment! And stay the hell out!"

Claire only had to advance a couple of steps with the knife in her hand to send Rosseau scurrying back the way he'd come, quaking in fear for his life. As the door slammed shut behind him, she let out a sigh of relief. And then she laughed.

Chapter Sixteen

Coffee at Lazy Susan's Bistro was becoming a regular Saturday afternoon date for Breck and Ellie. Her hot chocolate was topped by orange marshmallows today. Marty had stepped out of his comfort zone and ordered a cappuccino. And neither of them had heard from or spoken to Demonai since that day at the laundromat.

"I want to thank you for helping my grandfather," she said between sips. "Even if nothing comes from your investigation, just the fact that someone is taking him seriously has already made him feel better."

"That's good, because I've been going through Mrs. O'Toole's medical records and researching the drugs she was on."

"And?"

"Speaking circumstantially, I don't believe supernatural forces had anything to do with your grandmother's death."

"So that's it? He's been making himself miserable for twelve years for nothing?"

"I didn't say that."

"But—"

"Ellie, it's an ongoing investigation. Your grandmother's case was not handled to his satisfaction, denying him closure. So, I've promised him that I will get to the bottom of things, and that's what I'm doing, by considering all possibilities and following the evidence wherever it takes me."

"And where has it taken you so far, besides away from Demonai?"

"Until I can prove otherwise, I'm operating on the assumption that there may be some basis for his concern."

She halted with the mug halfway to her lips. "Meaning what?" she said. "You think someone may have murdered my grandmother?"

"Not murdered. Certainly not intentionally. But I've identified several points on the timeline where someone could have slipped up or made an error in judgment, ultimately resulting in her fatal stroke. For example: people bring their expired or leftover medication to the pharmacy all the time. Then they walk away, trusting that those pills or that cough syrup or whatever will never again see the light of day."

Ellie knew where this was going. "But some of it does?" she ventured.

"I'm not saying this actually happened," he warned her, "but what if there were a mix-up at the pharmacy? What if things were crazy busy one day and a new employee made a mistake? What if they misread a date, or they got confused and emptied a bottle of expired pills into the wrong container?"

"…from which my grandmother's final doses of blood pressure medication might have come?"

"Now, admittedly, it's an extremely remote possibility, but one that I've yet to rule out. Because this is an off-the-books investigation, I can't get a warrant to examine legal records. However, I can still move forward by asking carefully worded questions and making polite requests for cooperation. Dropping the judge's name has opened a lot of doors for me this week. I've also learned that your grandmother's last prescription was not filled at her regular pharmacy. That gives me another couple of people to interview."

"You're being very thorough."

"I have to be. Whatever I put before Judge O'Toole needs to be convincing enough to have stood up in his courtroom. Especially if my final conclusion is that the doctors were right and his instincts were wrong."

"Another remote possibility?"

"Growing less so the deeper I delve, I'm afraid."

"Well, I've got some happier news to report," Ellie told him. "Dean Slattery got in touch with my grandfather the other day. He's read Claire Amory's book, and he's ready to sit down and talk about it."

Marty frowned briefly. "I was sort of expecting him to call me directly, but… this works. When and where are we getting together?"

"Your next off-duty day, at three p.m., in the library of his home in Thornhill."

<center>~~~</center>

Tucked away in a cul-de-sac just north of Highway 7B and just west of Yonge Street, Richard Slattery's current residence, a grey brick-and-siding, ranch-style bungalow, was clean and well-tended. It was part of an older housing development, with a wrought iron gate at the foot of the paved driveway, mature trees in a spacious front yard, and hanging flower pots overflowing with pink and white blooms, located to either side of a double front door.

As he climbed broad concrete steps to the porch, Marty couldn't help recalling what Claire had said earlier about buying her dream home in Caverley Corners. Breck had a dream home too. Unfortunately, he lived and worked in the Greater Toronto Area, where even a small semi-detached house cost far more than he could afford. Maybe, if he won a quarter million dollars in the lottery, he'd be able to put a down payment on something. Until then, the dream home would have to remain just that, a dream.

The man who ushered Marty and Ellie inside had a full head of straight, white hair framing a sombre face. Everything about him was tidy and compact. Wire-rimmed glasses, a wooden pipe, and a cardigan sweater over an open-necked shirt completed the stereotypical image of a retired academic. This was Rick Slattery, reportedly a legendary practical joker in his youth but now a stalwart pillar of the legal community. Every word he spoke came out sounding as though he were addressing a lecture hall full of students.

Slattery led the way into a room lined with floor-to-ceiling wooden bookshelves and took his seat behind an impressive oaken desk. "So, you're Mac's granddaughter," he said, indicating with a gesture the two guest chairs where they were to sit. "And you must be the detective who's setting his mind at ease about the circumstances of Kate's death."

"Detective Martin Breck, sir, of the Toronto force," Marty responded, trying not to sound too official.

Leaning back in his chair, Slattery lit his pipe and puffed out a small cloud of smoke. "I've read Claire Amory's book, as Mac requested. He tells me she's claiming it's factual."

"She's not exactly claiming, Dean Slattery," Ellie corrected him, frowning. "As far as the reading public is concerned, it's a comic fantasy. But when we asked her point-blank whether the events in her story had actually occurred—"

"She said they had, and you took that as truth. Or perhaps 'mistook' is a better word."

"You know Demonai is real, sir. You even had a relationship with him," Breck pointed out. "What do you find so difficult to believe about Claire's account?"

"Demonai appeared to me as a ball of light and spoke to me from an antique lamp. According to Mac, that's how it went when Demonai contacted you as well. Not from a lamp, of course, but from a different type of metal container. Seeing and hearing him is how you and I know he exists. In this woman's book, there is no actual contact, only a lot of imagination and guesswork. Therefore, my theory of the case would be this: that the author was surfing online, discovered information about an idol that had been unearthed by an archaeological team, and used it as the basis for a fantastical narrative."

Marty and Ellie exchanged a look.

"Dean Slattery, the three main characters in the book are based on actual, living people. Detective Breck and I have interviewed two of them so far, and they both swear up and down that the events they experienced were real. In fact, one of these people is still dealing with post-traumatic stress as a result." She paused for a breath. "Would you be open to hearing some first person, eyewitness testimony regarding this matter? I can assure you that he's reliable."

Slattery narrowed his gaze. Before he could respond, however, Marty cut in, "Demonai's the one who told me to read this book, sir. Why would he do that if it wasn't a true account?"

"I don't know, Detective. You would have to ask Demonai that question, but personally, I would not advise it. Demonai and Olla'set have godlike powers. There's no other way to describe them. The less contact our kind have with theirs, the safer humanity will be."

"Forgive me, Dean Slattery, but I'm curious to know what brought you to that conclusion," Ellie asked.

"Nightmares, Ms. O'Toole." He shuddered visibly. "Demonai was my sidekick for three years—that was his word, not mine. We cast ourselves as underdogs and played practical jokes on the powerful elite who I believed were holding me back. Then I realized: Demonai was never an underdog. He just wanted someone to play with. That's all we are to them, you know—playthings." He made a face. "Living action figures. I had nightmares about him my entire final year of law school.

"Thirty years later, he was back, with Olla'set, and so

were the nightmares. For six months, I didn't sleep well. Then Mac approached me at Kate's funeral, asking about Demonai. More weeks of nightmares. And now you and this damned book. Demonai and Olla'set. Each time their names come up, it's as though evil spirits are being raised to haunt my dreams."

"Well, since the damage is already done, sir, we'd appreciate knowing anything you can tell us about Demonai and Olla'set," Breck told him. "For example, did you summon him? Or did he just appear when he chose to?"

Slattery paused, puffing thoughtfully on his pipe. "Years ago, he kept a presence of sorts inside the antique lamp that I'd found at a flea market. At least, that was what he led me to assume. He said I could summon him by stroking the outside of the lamp. I know, it's a cliché, but at the time it worked. He's not in there anymore, but I doubt whether it matters. He told me later on that he and Olla'set are everywhere, all the time, and I have to say, I'm inclined to believe it. I think if you went somewhere private in the vicinity of an enclosed metal container and called out his name, Demonai would answer… as long as he felt he could have some fun with you."

"Well, Demonai or not, whatever supernatural power switched those three minds into other bodies was certainly enjoying itself," Ellie remarked. "When you're having nightmares, do you ever—discreetly, of course—seek professional help?"

"No. It's a waste of money when you already know what's causing them and can't discuss the experience without appearing to have lost your marbles." A pause, then, "You mentioned that this other individual is suffering from PTSD? That's the reliable eyewitness testimony you want me to hear?"

Ellie smiled. "It is. We can put you in touch with him, if you're amenable."

Slattery nodded slowly. "All right." He reached into a desk

drawer and produced a card with nothing on it but an email address. "That's my private address. Use it to send me his. Maybe the two of us can set something up."

"So, how is your social media project coming along?" Breck asked once they were headed back down to the city. Rush hour was hectic going in any direction, it seemed, and at the same time maddeningly slow-moving.

Beside him in the front seat, Ellie pulled out her phone and accessed the Internet to show him. "I've set up three accounts, and am following about a dozen others. The main page has collected nearly two hundred likes so far. What do you think?" She turned the screen so he could see it.

He glanced over, then did a double take. "*Demonaimania?* I think you've got your work cut out for you, moderating a group with that name."

"Maybe, but I made sure to pin a warning at the top, and it seems to be working. There haven't been any serious problems so far," she assured him. "No weird religious stuff or political trolls, not since I bounced a few of them, anyway. There have been a number of posts from people claiming to be sex workers or concubines, asking when the first prayer meeting will be held. That's to be expected, I guess. And an archaeology post-grad student has weighed in with some interesting links to papers and such. I've been throwing a hook into the water every couple of days, mentioning strange recorded occurrences and speculating as to whether they might be the work of ancient gods."

"And you don't think that qualifies as 'weird religious stuff'?"

"Not when I add 'LOL' at the end. In any case, we have to be patient. Two pigeons and one rat can't be the only animals that blew up while Demonai was learning to talk to us. Sooner or later, someone will get in touch. And then there will be others, I'm certain of it. It's the way of the web."

"Uh-huh." He slid her a sidelong look. "You're having fun with this. Sort of like Demonai."

"Marty, if we can't laugh about what's been happening lately, we're going to cry," she told him. "Personally, I prefer to laugh."

Chapter Seventeen

Claire was still chuckling to herself twenty minutes after Rosseau's hasty departure. That was when Hollinger and Boehm stormed through the front door of the apartment.

"What are you two doing back so soon?" she exclaimed. "Not that I'm unhappy to see you, but I thought—"

"Never mind that," Hollinger snapped, clearing the coffee table with ruthless efficiency.

Claire raised an inquiring eyebrow at Boehm, who merely shrugged in reply. Meanwhile, Hollinger had dropped a folded road map on the table and now rushed off into the bedroom, imbued with grim purpose.

"James? What's going on?" Claire demanded.

All that came out of the bedroom was the sound of an apartment being ransacked, so she turned to the scientist and repeated her question in a more threatening tone of voice.

"He says he's going to triangulate us," Boehm replied. "That's all I know."

"Right. So how was the cocktail party?" Claire asked.

"I'm not sure. It was my first, so I have no real basis for comparison. To be honest, though, it felt more like a performance than a party. I followed a bunch of rules for nearly an hour. Then we left. How has your evening been so far?"

"Rather exciting, actually," Claire replied proudly. "I scared off a burglar."

"You *what*?" Boehm cried.

Something heavy crashed to the floor in the bedroom.

"Got it!" Hollinger proclaimed triumphantly in Claire's voice.

But Claire and Boehm were by now too involved in discussion to pay much attention to him.

"Did he get inside?" Boehm demanded. "What did he take?"

"He didn't take a thing. He wasn't more than a couple of feet past the door when I grabbed the steak knife and confronted him."

"You confronted him? Good Lord!" Pasty-faced, Boehm grasped the back of the sofa for support before asking tightly, "Was there a struggle?"

Hollinger burst from the bedroom into the middle of this dramatic tableau but ignored it, being too preoccupied with unfolding the map on the coffee table. Without a word, he began drawing bold lines with a ruler and the stub of a soft pencil.

"No, there wasn't a struggle," Claire explained patiently. "But I was sure glad to be wearing your body, I'll tell you."

"Well, *I'm* not glad you were!" Boehm snapped. "What if this burglar had been armed with a knife himself, or carrying a gun?"

"Then I wouldn't have shown myself. I'm not stupid, you know!" was Claire's irritated response. "But as soon as I saw that it was only Rosseau—"

Boehm was aghast. "Rosseau broke into the apartment? Rosseau, the superintendent? Oh, my God, what next?"

"He didn't come to steal your stuff or mine, I'm certain of it," Claire assured him. "I think he just wanted to lift something of James's that he could sell back to him at some outrageous price later on. Rosseau's a weasel, Garry. He goes in for extortion and blackmail because he hasn't got the stomach for grand larceny. Now, would you please calm down?" she pleaded. "You're making me nervous."

"Aha!" Hollinger crowed, startling them both. "What's on the southeast corner of Bloor and Parliament?"

"Hell, I don't know," Boehm replied.

Finally taking notice of what Hollinger was doing, Claire and Boehm stared over his shoulder at the map. "That area is coloured green," Boehm pointed out. "It has to be some kind of park."

"I think it's a playground," Claire chimed in. "What about it?"

Exhaling with satisfaction, Hollinger dropped the pencil stub beside the map and leaned back into the sofa. "Whatever switched us around the other night is located in that park."

Claire nearly choked swallowing a laugh. "James, as weird as our experience was, I doubt that it could have been perpetrated by a sandbox, a slide, and a set of swings."

"Maybe not," he returned, "but are you sure there's nothing buried underneath them?"

"Are you prepared to go there after dark with a shovel and dig up the ground to find out?" she demanded. "And explain yourself to the police when they catch you at it because someone called them to report suspicious activity? How did you figure this out, anyway?"

"I made our three apartments the vertices of a triangle and then joined them to—"

"Of course!" Boehm exclaimed, smacking a hand to his forehead. "Well, at least we know where you went wrong. I wasn't here when the change took place."

"That's right!" Claire said. "I woke up in a building situated... here." She picked up the pencil stub and marked the block with an X. Occupying her petite body, Hollinger was easily muscled out of the way as Boehm and Claire took over the map, redrawing the triangle and joining all three vertices to the mid-points of the opposite sides to discover its exact centre.

"There!" said Boehm with some satisfaction when they were done. Then he amended and repeated Hollinger's previous declaration: "Whatever switched us around is located at the southwest corner of Bloor Street and Avenue Road."

The changelings fell silent for a moment.

"Garry," Claire pointed out reluctantly. "That's the Royal Ontario Museum."

"The ROM?" he echoed.

"The same. And not the same," she told him. "It's undergoing a huge renovation right now. Part of it is being torn down. Some exhibits have been moved, and others have simply been packed up and put into storage. Searching for something in that chaos is going to be nearly impossible."

"Then we mustn't waste any time," he declared, his voice rising with excitement. "We'd better get over there right away."

"Relax, Garry," she said. "It's after hours. And anyway, I've got a better idea."

Hollinger had just had the same thought. "The Internet."

Working quickly, Claire brought her laptop into the living room and plugged it into the electrical outlet nearest the sofa. "Since we can't go to the ROM tonight anyway, why don't we see if there's any enlightenment to be found on their website? If nothing else, it'll kill some time."

A few minutes later, Claire had accessed a wireless network, and the computer screen was filled with choices.

"Good grief," murmured Boehm. "Egyptian Exhibit, Hall of Minerals, the Bat Cave… There's so much here. Where do we start?"

"We can probably eliminate the Bat Cave," said Hollinger. "Unless you think the culprit might be a Transylvanian count?"

"Not funny, James," Claire muttered. She slid the grabby hand across the screen and clicked on *What's New at the*

ROM. "Hold on, this looks promising: 'New Finds from Iberian Dig'." *Click.* She scanned the repainted screen. "Well, it's not really an exhibit, but some of the pieces are currently on display," she told them. "And there's detailed information posted about several artifacts in particular, which means they're unusual. We're in the neighbourhood anyway—want to have a look?"

Without waiting for an answer, she clicked on the first one, *Demonai.*

There were pages of text about the little statue. Claire scrolled through them slowly, so that the other two changelings could read over her shoulder.

"Prostitutes and concubines?" Hollinger remarked. "Well, this is interesting, but not especially useful. Let's move on.'

"I don't know about that," Boehm countered thoughtfully. "We're in genie-in-a-bottle territory here. According to this mythology, Demonai traded favours. You know, some ancient peoples believed that deities could be enslaved—trapped inside containers and forced to grant wishes."

Hollinger opened his mouth to utter a sarcastic reply, then thought better of it. Wasn't that exactly the way he'd been feeling lately—trapped and tapped?

"Hey, look at this," urged Claire, pointing at the colour plate of the statue on the screen. She clicked on a button beside the image and a mischievously grinning face appeared on the figure's head. "Maybe there really is a little god inside this thing."

"And maybe you're both letting your imaginations run away with you," Hollinger said disgustedly.

"Come on, James, loosen up," Claire told him. "There's nothing we can do about anything right now, so let's have a little fun."

"As the scientist in this triad, I'm beginning to formulate a theory," Boehm announced.

"Yeah? Based on what?" challenged Hollinger.

"Based on the fact that I distinctly remember making a

wish on the afternoon before the switch, and got exactly what I asked for. I'll bet that if you search your memories, you'll find that sometime that day, you made wishes too, and they've been granted. Maybe not in the way that you expected, but—"

"That's crap!" Hollinger declared. "I never made any wish."

"I did," said Claire wonderingly, "now that I think about it. Three days ago I was trying to force my way through a writer's block, and I realized that what I really needed was to step out of my daily routine and have an adventure. And if this isn't an adventure, I don't know what is. What was your wish, Garry?"

"I wished I could trade places with a rich and powerful man."

"Come on, James," Claire coaxed, becoming more and more excited. "You must have wished for something. Or thought about how great it would be to have something, or do something. Or even just wondered what it would be like?"

"Nope," said Hollinger firmly. "Not a damned thing."

Claire and Boehm exchanged a look. "Well, you've got something to wish for now," she told him, bouncing up onto her feet. "Keep this image of Demonai on the screen, Garry."

"What are you going to do?" he asked.

"Desperate times call for desperate measures. I'm going to find some candles and light them. Then we're going to have a little ceremony to butter up Demonai, before we ask him to put us back into our own bodies."

"You can't be serious!" Hollinger said.

"Hey, what would be the harm?" she demanded. "We're just hedging our bets. If Demonai is for real, then maybe he'll grant our wish. If he isn't, at least we can say we tried. It's not like we don't have the time. You have to learn to go with the flow, James. That's what people do who aren't in control of every situation. And in case you haven't noticed…?"

"All right," Hollinger conceded reluctantly. "I guess it makes about as much sense as anything else we've done the last few days."

In the Fifth Dimension

I had nothing to do with this, Demonai declared. *It was all their own idea.*

Really? What about that map on the wall at the gathering place, the one that gave them the information they needed to locate your likeness?

What about it, Aggregator? That map has been hanging there for a long span of time. It was a happy coincidence that the threedee noticed it and was able to make a connection between the drawing and his predicament. In fact, that's the way many problems get solved in the three-dimensional world.

And you can truthfully say that you did not cause the map to appear just at the moment when it would be needed?

I can, Aggregator.

But Olla'set was not convinced—his demeanour remained challenging.

Tillah reminded him, *The threedees are gathering trappings for a ritual, to ask Demonai to put them back the way they were. Doesn't that prove something, Aggregator?*

They haven't reached any conclusions, he pointed out. *They're guessing. And they're desperate enough to try anything, even a ritual that none of them actually believes in.*

But they can't perceive that their essences are melded, so guesses are all they can make, argued Demonai. *And if they guess correctly, I need to let them know. It's how these creatures learn, by trial and error.*

It's part of the experiment, Tillah chimed in. *You did state *that the integrity of the experiment had to be preserved, Aggregator. So far it is proceeding exactly as Demonai planned it.*

Olla'set's essence went still, but he did not withdraw from the meld. *So you are saying that the subjects of this experiment are expected to learn something from it as well? When did you decide to tack this on, Demonai?*

When you threatened to destroy the bubble, Aggregator. These beings may need some time to prove to you that they are, indeed, evolved. I didn't want the experiment to conclude before that happened.

An honest response. How refreshing. All right, then, I rescind my earlier decision. If these creatures cannot pass your test, I will not immediately disaggregate them. However, I will reclaim the bubble as my property and return it to my collection sac.

And if they are able to demonstrate the same thinking skills as ours, Aggregator?

In that unlikely event, you may decide what to do with the bubble.

What about the wishes? Tillah wanted to know. *The threedees are going to ask Demonai to put them back the way they were. And he does need to let them know they've guessed correctly about the source of their problem.*

You can give them one hint, Demonai, warned Olla'set. *After that they have to figure things out on their own.*

Chapter Eighteen

Across the street, two men sat in the dark in a late-model sedan, watching shadows flow and sway behind curtained windows on the third floor of Boehm's building.

"You're sure these are the guys that snatched the millionaire out of the Ha'penny?"

"Yep. Gunther followed them here from the bar. Then he called Augie for help. Then Augie had to go to work, so he asked me to take over." He rolled his car window down and pitched a cigarette butt out onto the street.

"Bruno! What did we talk about earlier?" scolded the driver.

"Sorry." Hurriedly, the other man got out of the car and retrieved the butt.

"Jeez! It's a filthy habit to start with, but if you're going to litter the streets—!"

"Y'know something, Dougie? Ever since you got that job with Waste Management, you haven't exactly been a barrel of laughs. I picked up the effin' butt. Now shut up about it, and keep your eyes on those windows."

"That's all your boss wants us to do? Sit in the car and watch the place?"

"And follow the millionaire around if he comes out, at least until Augie can piece together whatever the hell is going on. Gunther is Augie's favourite nephew, but he's taken some knocks to the head and isn't the most reliable source of information, if you catch my drift."

Dougie nodded knowingly. "So the millionaire may not be Hollinger after all?"

"Oh, he's Hollinger, all right. Augie's been surveilling him, says he never goes out alone, and he always ends up back here. Whoever the other man and woman are, they haven't hurt him yet, but they're keeping him on a short leash, and Augie wants to find out why."

"Maybe we oughta go in there and bust the poor guy out."

"Dougie, Dougie, Dougie," said Bruno in a sad, singsong voice. "We're not in that line of work anymore, remember? Bustin' in on people is against the law."

"But what if they kill him while we're sitting out here watching windows? What then?"

"They'd have to be dumb as bricks to do it here. Nah. If they decide to snuff him, first they'll take him to an industrial part of town. Then they'll make him walk, at least a mile, to somewhere really private. A greenbelt area, maybe, or an abandoned factory… like that. And we'll be right on their tail the whole time. Those were Augie's orders."

The driver sighed. It was going to be a long night.

<div align="center">~~~</div>

Boehm was having another of those dreams. The three of them were kneeling at the foot of a huge faceless statue as a ring of candles burned around them. Claire held her laptop aloft, a finger poised to hit the delete key. She prayed to Demonai in a strange tongue. Sang him songs. Made extravagant promises. Sudden fear struck deep into Boehm's heart. What were they doing here? Demonai had been trapped inside that statue for centuries. What terrible vengeance might he wreak once they had released him?

"Claire—no!"

All at once… he was one hand clapping… he was hot buttered popcorn… he was old tennis shoes… he was one second too late. The key had been pressed, the pin had been pulled, his fate had been sealed. On the statue's blank face, the features of Demonai slowly appeared. They puckered and twisted, as though he were struggling to speak. At last, the huge crystalline lips parted—and Demonai stuck his tongue out at them, and laughed.

The laughter took shape. It expanded in all directions. It attacked and swallowed Boehm, surrounding him like a huge soap bubble, turning and tumbling him and pushing Claire and James out of his dream altogether. And it grew, and stretched, and finally burst, with a short, shrill scream that sounded as though it was right beside his ear. Then it screamed again, and again, pushing even Boehm out of his dream and following him into wakefulness.

It took him a moment to identify the sound. It was the telephone. But what was it doing beside him on the floor? Hollinger's voice couldn't answer the phone, especially not at this hour of the—Wait a minute, he wasn't on the floor. He was in his bed, in the bedroom. Did that mean he was no longer—?

The phone rang again. To shut it up, Boehm reached over and fumbled the receiver out of its cradle. "Hello," he croaked.

"Garry, is that you?" sobbed a female voice.

"I think so," he said, shaking his head to clear it.

"You've got to help me, Garry! I think I've killed a man!"

"You're not sure?" Who *was* this woman?

"I'm afraid to roll him over to check his heartbeat," she whimpered.

"Mm—What about the pulse in his neck, the carotid artery?" One by one, Boehm's thoughts were sorting themselves out. He glanced at the clock. It was just past one a.m.

"I don't even want to touch him!"

"Well, what did you do to him?"

"I flipped him, the same way I did to you, remember? Only he's hit his head on something and hasn't moved in almost five minutes and I'm scared, Garry! Please, come over," she pleaded.

Same thing she'd done earlier? But not to him. To his body. To Claire, then. The memory of a days-old conversation clicked in. Of course! The woman on the phone had to be Claire's friend, Sophie Hopper.

So he was back in his own body, and its erstwhile attacker was asking him to help her dispose of someone else's. This couldn't really be happening. It was classic dream logic, and he was lucid. That meant he could make choices.

"Okay," he said in his best conspiratorial undertone. "Where are you?"

She gave him an address in the Beaches. He hung up and immediately dialed for a cab, his excitement growing. Garry Boehm was about to have an adventure, on his own and in his own body. He hoped he didn't wake up before it was over.

Boehm had had some experience with lucid dreaming. Just to make sure that he was in fact still asleep, he performed some tests while en route to Sophie's location. First, the time compression test, in which he willed events to skip ahead to his arrival at her door. Nothing happened—the taxi ride continued. *Hmm.* Next, the do-over test. He willed events to skip back to a previous moment so that he could make a different choice. Still nothing. Traffic was light at this hour on a weekday. The cab rolled smoothly along Queen Street, headed east.

Oka-ay.

Finally, and most conclusively, the reading test. The driver's credentials were displayed on the back of his seat. In a dream, everything came from the dreamer's own mind and memories. That meant the only clearly legible words would be information drawn from that source. Everything else would be either blurred or gobbledygook.

Boehm read the text on the driver's taxicab licence. The name was unfamiliar, the data was complete, and the printing was clear and sharp. He looked away, counted to ten, then read the document again. Everything made sense, and not so much as a letter of it had changed.

He wasn't dreaming. This was actually happening. All at once, the world sprang into painfully sharp focus as Boehm realized that he was back in his own body, for real...

...and riding in a cab, on his way to help someone dispose of a body.

Holy crap!

Gazing out the car window as the vehicle pulled up at the curb, Boehm thought about the scene that he might be walking into in Sophie's apartment and instructed the cabbie to wait.

"The meter will be running, sir," the other man informed him. "Company policy."

Fortunately, Boehm had reflexively picked up Hollinger's wallet on his way out the door. There had to be *some*thing in there that would pay the fare. "Not a problem," he replied.

There was a male body sprawled on the floor of apartment 2-B, but thankfully, it wasn't a corpse. Not yet, anyway. Through the half-open doorway, Boehm could see—and smell—Sophie's unwelcome visitor. The man reeked of Scotch and aftershave, and he was twitching his limbs and moving his head from side to side, like a giant tortoise struggling to right itself after being flipped onto its back.

Holding his breath, Boehm stepped inside and shut the door behind him. Instantly, his attention was captured by the tall, red-haired beauty who stood on the far side of the little purple room. She was wearing what he took at first to be an apple green bikini, and she was staring with eyes wide as traffic lights at something around the level of his knees. Fortunately, he thought to look down. The obscenely perfumed tortoise had managed to roll onto its belly and was now attempting without success to push itself off the floor.

"I've never killed anyone before," Sophie whispered tautly.

"You still haven't," Boehm assured her. "But if he's been unconscious… how are his vitals?"

"Everything normal."

Boehm glanced up and met her gaze, which had now abandoned all pretense of anxiety. "So you brought yourself to touch him after all?" he said, putting a smile in his voice.

An answering smile appeared on her face. "I'm a nurse. What can I tell you?"

"You can tell me what happened here tonight."

"I was sitting up in bed, reading, and suddenly there was this urgent knock at the door. Well, I wasn't about to open it at that hour to someone I wasn't expecting, so I called through it, 'Who's there?' He said, 'I've brought Claire's cheque but I need to hand it to her in person. Is she in there?' I could tell from his voice that he was drunk, and that made me doubly determined not to let him in. I told him she wasn't here and he should just slide the envelope under the door. Then he got cute with me."

"Cute? How?"

"He was coming on to me from out in the hall, asking personal questions, like whether I was straight, and what I was wearing, and he was doing it all at the top of his lungs. I'm sure half the building could hear him."

"Most likely he wanted to embarrass you into opening the door, just to get him to stop."

"As you can see, that's exactly what I did," she concluded, glaring down distastefully at the dazed intruder. "And now it's time for him to leave."

"Come on, fella," Boehm said, grunting with the effort of

hoisting him to his feet. To Sophie, he added, "Help me find his credit cards."

She threw him a look. "You want to roll him?"

Down the stairs, maybe. "No, I just want him to pay his own way home. I left a cab waiting downstairs. It can take him to the ER to be checked out. And speaking of cheques…" Boehm had found a business-sized envelope in one of the man's jacket pockets. The envelope was sealed and had Claire's name printed on it in block letters. Handing it to Sophie, he remarked, "It looks like he really was delivering one to her."

"We're treating him better than he deserves," Sophie declared, crossing her arms over her deliciously ripe bosom. "I hate to think what might have happened if Claire had been here alone."

Boehm wasn't sure how to reply to that. However, by then he'd located the other man's wallet. So, he focused his attention on half-dragging, half-carrying the unwelcome visitor down the stairs to the street.

The cabbie's eyes sprang wide when he saw them staggering across the pavement toward him.

"What happened to *him*?"

"He got drunk and took a tumble," Boehm replied. "Hit his head on something. Now he needs to be seen by a doctor. Here's a credit card to pay whatever's on the meter when you drop him off at the nearest Emergency Room."

The driver inspected the card. "Ralph Ignace," he read aloud. "That's you?"

"No, it's him. The rest of his identification is in his inside jacket pocket."

"And d'you want me to come back for you right afterward?"

"No," said Sophie's firm voice from behind Boehm's shoulder. "He'll phone for another ride when he needs it."

Boehm's heart leaped in his chest. "You heard the lady," he said.

However, as the cab pulled away, he turned and found her standing on the topmost outer step, her lips a disapproving hyphen, her arms looking as though it would take a crowbar to uncross them again. "We need to have a serious talk, Doctor Boehm," she said sternly. Then she disappeared through the front door, leaving him no other option but to follow her back upstairs.

"What do I have to do to get a rise out of you?"

Boehm halted just inside the door to Claire's apartment. "Excuse me?"

"No, I will not excuse you," Sophie declared. "I want an answer. Do you really not find me attractive?"

He was at a loss for words. Fortunately, the question appeared to be rhetorical.

"You know how good I am at defending myself," she went on, "so you must have realized from the get-go that I didn't actually need your help, that I was just taking advantage of the opportunity to get you over here. And who the hell wears stuff like this to bed if they intend to sleep alone?"

She spread her arms wide, giving him the full, panoramic view of a well-endowed female body clad in baby doll pyjamas. The top was tight enough to be revealing, a detail that instantly dried Boehm's mouth, putting words even further beyond his reach.

Seeing his discomfort, Sophie inhaled sharply. "Ohmigod, I never even thought—But Claire brought you to the meeting and when I saw your—I mean, I just assumed that it was because—Garry, I'm so sorry! I honestly believed you were straight."

"I am!" he blurted, in desperation spitting out the first words that made it past his throat.

"Really? In that case..." Sophie took an even more aggressive pose than the one she'd struck before. Hands on her hips, bosom thrust forward, chin jutting, she pulled herself up to her full height and drew a slow, deep, magnificent breath. Boehm's body responded automatically, with an equally slow and magnificent erection.

It did not go unnoticed.

Her eyes glittering lustfully, Sophie glided across the room toward him. "Has anyone ever told you what a gorgeous hunk of man you are, Garry Boehm?" she demanded.

Not lately. He swallowed hard. *Not ever, in fact.*

Was this really happening?

Before his brain could respond, she closed the distance between them in one sinuous movement and wrapped both her arms around his shoulders. Planting her mouth on his, she gave him a kiss that he could feel all the way to his ankles.

Sophie yanked the bedcovers down with businesslike efficiency.

"You're overdressed," she murmured into his ear.

He nodded, unable to stop himself from grinning like a fool as, together, they set about removing his clothes.

Thinking about it later, he realized that Roxanne hadn't really been his first. She'd just made love to Hollinger's body, with Boehm's mind along for the ride. This time, in his own body, he had lost his virginity for real.

To a redheaded warrior princess.

Oh, yeah, baby!

⁓

The sun would be coming up soon. If Boehm had thought he could return unnoticed to the apartment, he was mistaken. The living room light was on. It was visible from the street. The other two changelings would be waiting for him, and they probably wouldn't be happy. With luck, their annoyance would be tempered by relief at finally being back in their own bodies.

Or maybe not, he thought as he let himself in the door.

Every room in the apartment was lit up. When Boehm hesitated on the threshold, Hollinger's large hand grabbed a fistful of his shirt (and some of the chest hair beneath it), and yanked him inside, then shoved the door closed behind him.

"Ow! You're awake," Boehm observed brightly.

"Phone rings in the middle of the night, I wake up in James's body on the living room floor, and you go sneaking off somewhere and come crawling home at dawn with a peculiar air of contentment. And it surprises you that we're not both sound asleep?"

Boehm was confused. "Wait a minute. You're not Hollinger?"

"Nope," said Claire. She jerked a thumb in the direction of her own body. "And he's not Claire Amory. You and I were the only ones who switched places. And now you're the only one who's where they're supposed to be. Demonai must like you, Garry."

"So where were you all night?" demanded James.

After a moment's pause, Boehm replied, "I was with Sophie. She phoned here, all in a flap. Something about a strange man in her apartment. She was afraid she'd killed him."

"Two things are wrong with that story," Claire pointed out in a voice that could have cut glass. "First of all, Sophie would never let a stranger into her apartment in the middle of the night. She's too smart for that. And second, she's not in her apartment tonight, she's in mine. So, tell us the truth, Garry. Where were you?"

"He *is* telling the truth," Hollinger said wearily. "I'm the one who lied."

"What are you talking about?" she demanded.

"I didn't mail your story. I hand-delivered it to Ralph Ignace. He wanted to pay you for it as soon as possible, but I couldn't wait around, so… he must have brought the cheque to you personally yesterday evening."

"To me at my apartment," she echoed tightly. "In the middle of the night."

"Drunk as a skunk and smelling as though he'd bathed in aftershave," Boehm supplied. "So, it's probably safe to say his intentions were not honourable."

"And Sophie killed him?" Claire whispered, horrified.

"No, she just—thought she did. He was semi-conscious, and she was concerned. I sent him to the ER in a taxi."

"That still leaves a chunk of time unaccounted for, Garry," Hollinger reminded him. "If you didn't accompany Ignace to the hospital, where did you go?"

Boehm felt a sudden warmth suffuse his face. "I went back upstairs to... ah... check on Sophie. She was very upset, you know."

"Oh, I can imagine," Hollinger assured him, now wearing a knowing expression. "And when you left her, she was all right?"

Boehm grinned. "She was outstanding." *...and she's mine, you money-grubbing bastard,* he added mentally. *This one you don't get to take away from me.*

Chapter Nineteen

Augie had once more taken point, assigning his two associates to follow whomever their leader didn't. This morning, their subject was the sandy-haired man Gunther still maintained was an assassin working for an unnamed criminal organization.

"He doesn't look like a hit man to me," Dougie opined.

Bruno turned the key in the ignition, ready to tail the taxi that their target had just climbed into. "Really! And what does a hit man look like, exactly?" he demanded. After an entire night without sleep, his voice was a little gravelly.

"Stone cold killers have total control over themselves. This guy is walking around with a big goofy grin on his face, spreading love to the whole freakin' world. I think he's going on a date. From the way he's acting, I'm betting it's his first date ever."

"Maybe you're right," Bruno conceded. "Maybe Gunther got high and hallucinated the whole conspiracy thing. But even if it's a crock and a total waste of time, we take our orders from Augie, and we follow them. That's what he expects us to do. He's not paying us to think. If you're not okay with that—!"

"I'm fine with it." Dougie shrugged. "You know me, Bruno. Sometimes I just say stuff, but I don't mean anything by it."

"Well, do us both a favour and shut up, will ya?"

The taxi dropped their hit man off in front of a relatively new medium-rise building on Dundas Street.

"Pull over," Bruno said, unfastening his seat belt. "He's going inside. I'm going to follow him. You keep driving around the block meanwhile. When I know which apartment he's in, I'll come back out and we'll call Augie for further instructions."

Sophie was conducting a final inspection of her living room. The last couple of hours had been a whirlwind of preparation. The furniture had been dusted and the martinis had been mixed. She'd slipped into something alluring and made up her face. Now, crimson lips pursed, she imagined herself entering the apartment for the very first time. What would he see when he walked in?

Her eyes went first to the gold and white French provincial sofa, and the martini pitcher and glasses sitting an easy arm's reach away from it on the gleaming walnut coffee table. Good. She'd just polished that table to within an inch of its life, so it had *better* be shining.

The tasteful arrangement of artificial flowers on the end table was doing its job as well, covering up evidence of damage from a previous water spill. Sophie wanted everything to be as close to perfect as possible when Garry Boehm walked through her doorway.

They were meant for each other, she was certain of it. When she'd invited him over for cocktails and lunch, his unhesitating acceptance had set her pulse racing. The moment he was out the door, she had tossed her things into a bag and rushed back home to set the stage for the most important seduction of her life.

At last, the doorbell rang. She gave a final pat to her halo of flaming hair before hastening to answer the chime.

Boehm had actually been outside in the hallway for a

while, rehearsing suggestive greetings and trying out devil-may-care poses. He was being silly, he knew. By all accounts, Sophie Hopper was not the sort to fake an orgasm or pull her punches. If he had disappointed her with his lovemaking, she wouldn't have suggested a repeat performance.

That was what he was telling himself at the very moment that his elbow accidentally pressed her doorbell. He barely had time to put on a leer and lean against the jamb before she cracked the door open.

"Hi there, beautiful," he said, trying for smooth but foiled by eager.

Sophie ran one manicured hand suggestively over the edge of the door. "Hello, yourself, handsome. Why don't you come inside and get comfortable?" And she nudged the door fully open with one exquisitely rounded hip.

The sight and smell of her were intoxicating. This was no longer a dream for Boehm—it was a dream come true. A gorgeous woman in a sexy dress was inviting him into her apartment, and there was a smouldering expression in her eyes that left no doubt whatever about her intentions. Being considered a sex object was a new and very heady sensation for him. Boehm was determined to enjoy every second of it, for as long as it lasted.

"Care for a drink?" she offered, gesturing casually toward the martini pitcher on the coffee table.

Not trusting his voice, he just nodded.

Next thing he knew, they were sitting side by side on the sofa, sharing a conspiratorial smile.

"To us," she whispered, delicately touching the rim of her glass to his.

All at once... he was chocolate custard... he was a mosquito looking for a snack...

"No!"

"Garry, what's wrong?"

Tentatively, Boehm glanced around him. He was in the arms of a beautiful redheaded woman in a flimsy blue dress which had crept nearly thirty centimetres above her knees. She was lusting after his body almost as much as he lusted after hers. What could possibly be wrong?

"Uh, nothing," he reassured her. *Except Demonai might be having second thoughts about me.*

What was THAT?

Demonai had to wait for the crashing waves of sensation to subside before he could even attempt to answer Tillah's question. *The lamp—someone's rubbing it.*

It was probably Richard Slattery, summoning him to talk to the Russell boy. His timing stank.

Without warning, another huge breaker swept through Demonai, powerful enough to ignite sympathetic energy bursts in the threedees' essence meld. The pleasure was so intense that it devoured every other feeling, blocked all conscious thought. For a moment, Demonai himself ceased to be, as electrical spasms whirled from one end of him to the other. Then, at last, the storm of sensation weakened and died.

Demonai forced himself to manifest satisfaction.

That is truly disgusting, remarked Olla'set. And yet, his pod remained melded to those of Demonai and Tillah. *Can't you do something about it?*

You're only communicating that because you've never experienced such pure sensory stimulation, Demonai replied. *It's a shame. You've missed out on so much… pleasure.*

Is that what you choose to call it? Olla'set retorted. *Because it doesn't look to me as though you're enjoying yourself, Demonai. Quite the opposite, in fact.*

Olla'set is right, Tillah chimed in. *You look as though you're being tortured, Demonai. It's that lamp, isn't it? You need to pull your pod out of it immediately.*

I can't. Slattery needs to be able to contact me and this is the only way he knows.

Then you need to find out who is rubbing the lamp and tell them to stop, said Olla'set. *Do it right now or I'll do it for you.*

Chapter Twenty

There was only one threedee in the dean's study, and it wasn't Richard Slattery. It was a female, short and plump, with her dark hair knotted into a bun at the nape of her neck. She was wearing a blue dress and a white apron, and she had just set the lamp—his lamp—carefully on a piece of newspaper on Slattery's desk. Curious, Demonai watched her use a piece of cloth to scrape up a blob of something from the bottom of a wide-mouthed jar labelled Tarnish-Off. As she grasped the lamp firmly with one hand, Demonai felt a shiver race through him and decided to nip this one in the bud, so to speak.

Let go of me!

The maid screamed and yanked her hand away from the lamp. At the same time, the cloth she'd been holding took flight, landing blob-side down in the middle of Slattery's probably expensive carpet. For a moment she stood frozen in horror, her lips working soundlessly as she stared wide-eyed at the lamp. Then she began touching herself lightly and rapidly with the fingertips of her right hand, in a repeating pattern. Forehead, chest, left shoulder, right shoulder, forehead, chest, left shoulder, right shoulder.

This was interesting. Demonai wondered what else he could make her do.

Who said you could polish me? he demanded.

Slowly, her face crumpled, and she burst into tears and

raced for the door, shrieking and waving her arms. At the threshold, she ran right into Richard Slattery, who was coming the other way.

"Flora, what's wrong?" he demanded, bobbing and weaving around her, his arms outstretched at his sides.

Amused, Demonai watched them do their strange little dance in the doorway to the study. Twenty-eight years earlier, Slattery would have simply grabbed this hysterical female and immobilized her against his chest. Now, he had to worry about being brought up on charges if he so much as laid a finger on her. Life in the threedee world had become very complex indeed.

"*Signor* Slattery, the lamp! It is possessed! I clean. I try to polish. It *speak* to me! It is a devil lamp, *signor*, a devil lamp!" wailed the maid.

Abruptly, Slattery stopped moving. "You tried to polish that lamp?" he said, his expression morphing from concern to dread.

She nodded energetically.

"Demonai," he muttered.

"*Si, si!*" she shrilled. "A devil!"

"Flora, I'll take care of this. Why don't you go work upstairs for a while?"

Stealing frightened glances over her shoulder, she let him persuade her toward the stairs. When she was safely on her way to the second floor, Slattery strode into the study and closed the door behind him.

"Demonai, that wasn't very kind," he said sternly. He addressed his reproach to the lamp, which was, admittedly, a lot cleaner now than it had been a short while earlier. It lay on its side as though waiting to be gift-wrapped in the newspaper.

And it was the height of consideration, I suppose, to put the law librarian's car upside down in a tree?

Slattery breathed a sigh… of regret? Or was it nostalgia? "That was a long time ago, D."

Yeah, tempus fugit, I get that. Nonetheless, you shouldn't have left my lamp sitting around where someone might get the urge to polish it, Ricky. That wasn't very kind—or very smart, for that matter—unless you wanted me to scare the living daylights out of that woman...?

Slattery's spine snapped erect, completely belying the expression of resignation on his face. "You're right, Demonai. You're absolutely right. I'm sorry about the false alarm. I'll tuck the lamp away so this can't happen again."

Chapter Twenty-One

With a rash of burglaries and a home invasion with fatalities to investigate, Marty had had to bow out of two Saturday coffee meetings in a row. Today would be different, he decided. He would dip into his personal leave if necessary, but what he had to tell Ellie was too important. He would not disappoint her a third time.

The weather was overcast and drizzly, making the patio an impractical choice, so he looked for her indoors. There she was, sitting alone in a corner of the room. She had her elbows propped on the small round table and both her hands wrapped around a large mug, and she was wearing a contemplative expression on her face. Marty bought two muffins at the counter, one blueberry and one chocolate chip, and carried them over to her.

The sound of plate landing on tabletop snapped her back to the moment. She glanced up and observed with a faint smile, "Hello, stranger. I hear they've been keeping you busy."

"They have. Summer is the high season for criminal activity in this city. I've been earning my pay and then some."

"So, I'm guessing you haven't been able to make any progress with my grandfather's project...?"

"I'm afraid not. Even if it were an official investigation, it would still be a very cold case, and Forensics would be handling it, not me. What about you? Has anything interesting popped up on one of your social media accounts?"

"You might say so. Lots of posts about birds exploding, some with video. I've suggested that something similar might be going on with rats, but so far no one has crawled into a sewer to find out. And someone with the username Calamity Jane insists that about five years ago, three balls of light grabbed her cat by the head, peeled its body like a banana, exposing all its internal organs, then made it disappear. Two days later, she found its corpse, completely intact, in her hall closet."

Breck repressed a shudder, recalling the judge's description of being "magically" transported home. "That sounds like something Olla'set would do. I don't suppose there's any way for us to contact this Calamity Jane and set up an interview?"

"I've messaged her, expressing an interest in knowing more details, but so far she hasn't replied. Can't blame her, really. By the time I'd read her post, a couple of trolls had already latched onto it and brain-shamed her. I banned them immediately, but the damage may have been done. Anonymity is both the blessing and the curse of the Internet, Marty. Calamity Jane still has hers, and she may ghost me in order to keep it. In any case, the next move is up to her. We'll just have to wait and see what it is."

"Speaking of next moves, I've finally heard from the third member of Claire's group. The scientist. His name is Garrick Boehm, and he's willing to meet with us at his home in Richmond Hill, any day next week."

"Will you be able to make the time?" she asked.

"Oh, I'll make it," he assured her. "My partner is trying to figure out what I've been up to, so I've given her a copy of Claire's book to read. When she's finished, I'll introduce you to her. Then all three of us will pay Garrick Boehm a visit."

Ellie frowned. "And what if she decides that we're all just a bunch of crackpots, or worse—jokesters playing an elaborate prank?"

"That's when we take her to the laundromat, put a couple of dollars into the dryer, and introduce her to Demonai himself."

~~~

The Boehm residence in Richmond Hill was a two-storey link home on a quiet crescent, with white siding, dark green trim, and a roofed porch with a child's pink and yellow tricycle parked on it. There was also a hand-printed sign taped to the front door: COME AROUND BACK.

Apparently, the scientist had a young family.

The three visitors rounded the side of the building and let themselves through the gate, into a fenced yard equipped with a set of swings and an oversized inflatable wading pool. Ellie counted five youngsters jumping in and out of the water and running around on the lawn. Meanwhile, another pair crouched beside the pool, conducting naval manoeuvres with plastic toy boats. Not one of these children looked older than five or six.

"Welcome!" That cheerful voice drew their attention to the shaded patio abutting the rear of the building. A tall, lanky man wearing khaki shorts, an unbuttoned short-sleeved shirt, and a broad, friendly grin was in the process of unfolding himself from an orange and white chaise longue. "I wasn't sure when you'd be arriving, so the refreshments are still inside. If you'll just keep an eye on the kids for a minute, I'll go fetch them."

"Are all these little people yours?" Ellie wondered aloud.

Boehm laughed. "Only one—the girl in yellow. Melissa is four years old. Her two big brothers are away at camp until the end of the month. My wife got called into work at the last minute. And it's our turn to host the neighbourhood play date. Hence, the crowded yard."

"Considering what we need to discuss, perhaps it would
~~~

be best to reschedule," said Breck, frowning.

"No, it's all right." Boehm consulted his wristwatch. "Play dates at this age don't last very long. They've been here for a couple of hours already. I expect we'll be alone by the time the cookies are gone. There are folding chairs in the bin over there. Please help yourselves to a piece of shade. And excuse me for a minute."

With that, he disappeared inside the house.

"He doesn't *seem* like someone who's had a traumatic out-of-body experience," observed Breck's partner, Detective Rosie Maranis.

Ellie had liked this woman immediately. Dark of eye, hair, and complexion, Rosie had a ready smile that lit up her face, and she projected a warmth that immediately put others at ease. Not exactly what Ellie had expected to find in a seasoned police detective. But what had really sealed the deal was the other woman's open-mindedness when Marty and Ellie described their shared experience in the laundromat. Clearly, Detective Maranis trusted her partner. Also clearly, to Ellie's mind at least, Rosie completed their threesome, just as Claire had earlier predicted.

Boehm's timing proved to be bang on. In less than a minute, he was back outside with a metal tray carrying a pitcher of iced tea, a stack of nested plastic tumblers, and a plate of store-bought cookies. He put the tray on a small circular table, then dragged it to a spot that was within everyone's reach. No sooner had Boehm finished serving the drinks than the first neighbourhood mom arrived to claim two of the children in the yard. Before the cookie plate was empty, the final small guest had departed, and Melissa was curled up on her father's lap, sleepily rubbing her eyes.

"Nap time," Boehm said. "Water park always wears them out. I'll be back in a minute or two."

"This man is depressingly normal," Rosie declared once the back door had closed behind him. "Not a bit like the scientist character in the book."

"Claire did say that they'd all been changed by spending time in one another's shoes, so to speak," Marty reminded her. "If her account is accurate, his mind was moved to another man's body. Unlike the millionaire, who got to be a woman for nearly a week."

Rosie grinned. "Yeah, that would mess with his brain."

True to his word, Boehm reappeared, bringing with him the rest of the bag of cookies.

"So, you've all read the book," he said, refilling the plate on the tray and then settling back onto his chaise. "And I gather it raised questions in your minds. Ask them."

"All right," said Breck. "From your point of view, how factual is Claire's retelling of the story?"

"The parts that I'm involved in are completely accurate, with one exception. Just before I woke up in my own body again, I was having a nightmare about the idol Claire had found on the museum's website. She left that out of the narrative because it sounded too contrived, even for a fantasy, and even though it actually happened."

"Did it speak to you? The idol in your dream, I mean," Ellie said.

"No, not a word. It just had a good laugh at my expense. But Claire tells me Demonai has spoken to *you*, Ms. O'Toole. That's why I agreed to this meeting."

"Are you still working as a particle physicist?" Breck cut in.

"No. The nuclear fusion project went dark when the government pulled its funding. However, with Sophie's help, I reinvented myself. Got into education. Now I'm the Head of Science at a STEM school—that's a secondary school with a special focus on science, technology, engineering, and mathematics."

"And is it co-ed?" Ellie asked.

"Sophie wouldn't have let me take the job if it hadn't been," he replied earnestly.

"So you and Sophie are still a couple?"

"Married for going on fourteen years now," he confirmed.

"And are you happy?"

"Yes. Meeting Sophie turned my life around. I'd spent so many years chasing theoretical goals and thinking fifty years ahead that I was letting the here and now pass me by. She opened my eyes to the fact that I could shape the future by making a difference in the present. You might say she got me to slow down and smell the roses."

"Sophie did this? Not Demonai?"

"Oh, he helped, of course, by making it possible for us to meet. My wish was to get a taste of wealth and power—I never wanted to make it my steady diet—and Demonai tried to grant it. He would have succeeded, if Hollinger hadn't been so controlling. But he was, with the result that the time I spent in James's body did nothing to change my world view, or who I was as a person. Sophie did that. Sometimes I wonder how things would have turned out for James if he and Roxanne had been able to get back together. He's still alone, and as far as I can tell, he's not a happy man."

"We know," Breck responded. "We've spoken with him. Ever since the laundromat incident, Ellie and I have been on a self-imposed mission. We're trying to identify others whose lives have been touched in some way by Demonai and his kind and put those people in contact with one another."

Boehm had been lifting his iced tea to his mouth. He paused abruptly, creating a swell inside his tumbler. "His *kind*? There are more of them?"

"Yes," Ellie replied. "At least one more that we're sure about, named Olla'set. But there could be an entire race of beings living on a higher plane, if you like, observing us without our knowledge, travelling up and down the time line, manipulating events…"

"Toying with us," Boehm summed up flatly. He replaced his beverage on the table. "Like the ancient deities. If I remember correctly, in every pantheon there was a troublemaker with a special connection to humanity. Also a trickster. Sometimes they were one and the same." He raised a speculative eyebrow. "Demonai?"

"That's the hypothesis we're working with," Ellie told him.

"And you want to bring his human victims together. For what purpose?"

"Let me ask you this first," Breck interrupted. "Have you told Sophie the whole story of what happened? Does she know about Demonai?"

"Of course. We have no secrets from each other."

"And has Claire revealed to her partner, Sarah Jane, that *Three Heads Are Better* is really a memoir?" Breck persisted.

"I believe so."

"Well, of all the people we've interviewed so far, you two are the only ones besides Ellie and me who are happily getting on with your lives."

His face lighting up with dawning comprehension, Boehm completed the thought. "…because we've been able to talk to someone about our experience?"

"Exactly," Ellie declared. "Someone who won't roll their eyes and think we're delusional."

"It sounds to me as though you're starting a support group," Boehm observed.

"That's becoming the general idea," Breck said. "Are you interested?"

Boehm nodded thoughtfully. "I'll have to talk it over with Sophie. In the meanwhile, pencil me in."

～～

"So, what do you think?" Breck asked Rosie as he made the turn onto Bathurst Street southbound. Rush hour was in full swing, and traffic was slow-moving. Two cars ahead of them, someone without air conditioning had turned their sound system up full blast and was treating the whole street to a heavy metal concert. Breck wasn't a fan of hard rock. He closed his car windows.

"I think there's more to it than just knowing you're not alone," Rosie replied after a pause. "Don't get me wrong. Sharing the secret and being believed would have certainly played their part, but the man we met this afternoon also made a drastic career change fifteen years ago. Whatever his motivation might have been, whether it came from Demonai or from Sophie, he reinvented himself around a life goal that would give him personal as well as professional satisfaction."

"The same thing happened to Claire," Ellie piped up from the back seat of the car. "She said Demonai gave her the push that she needed in order to rethink her goals. Once she'd moved back to Caverley Corners, she found everything she now loves about her life."

"So, by putting them in someone else's body, Demonai helped them to see the world differently, and that change of perspective made it possible for Boehm and Claire to make choices that would lead them to happiness," Breck summed up. "But not Hollinger?"

"In the book, the millionaire is the one who resists change," Rosie recalled. "From what you've told me about Hollinger, I'd say the lesson was wasted on him. He picked up his old life where he'd left off, but simply fast-tracked his retirement plan. And now he's miserable."

"I wonder…" said Ellie.

"…whether it's too late for him?" Marty ventured.

"Something Dr. Boehm said, about Roxanne and Hollinger maybe getting back together. She could be his Sophie. We need to find her," Ellie decided.

In the front seat, Breck and Maranis traded knowing looks.

"Actually," said Rosie, "I've already begun working on that. As soon as I have a last-known address, I'll let you know."

Chapter Twenty-Two

It was an unprepossessing little diner, set back from the main street and about a fifteen-minute walk from Boehm's apartment. The menu was limited, as was the seating—ten on swivel stools at the snack bar and about as many again at the several tiny tables that stood against the outside wall. As she and Hollinger walked in, wearing each other's bodies, Claire felt as though she'd been transported back to Caverley Corners, to the restaurant her father often referred to with affection as "the local greasy spoon". Instantly, a feeling of comfort and belonging came over her.

She turned to Hollinger and said with a smile, "I've been here before. Not this place, but one just like it. When I was younger, my father used to treat the family to Sunday brunch at the Good Eats Café. The service was friendly, and the French fries were always cooked just right."

"Yeah, we had a Good Eats Café where I grew up too, only ours was called Ginny's Kitchen," Hollinger replied once they were seated. "Best goulash I've ever tasted. Nowhere else has even come close." A pause, then, "This was a good idea you had, Claire."

"Well, we're in a strange situation right now—"

"Ya think?"

"—and with Garry back in his body and getting on with his life, I figured a change of scenery was just what we needed."

"A change that we chose for ourselves for a change," Hollinger remarked.

Claire ordered the "three-alarm chili", with a diet ginger ale to drink, and Hollinger picked the tuna salad sandwich, with fries on the side and a cola. Then the solitary server got busy, spreading the washable plastic cloth and setting the table. They watched her bustle around, fetching and depositing their flatware, salt and pepper, and a metal dispenser crammed full of skimpy paper serviettes. When the food arrived, it smelled and tasted delicious, but not only because of the way it had been prepared.

"Mmm… this is Good Eats," said Claire with a grin.

"Straight from Ginny's Kitchen," Hollinger confirmed, popping a fry into his mouth.

For a while, they ate in silence. Then, suddenly aware of her own eyes gazing intently into her face, Claire felt a flush of heat that owed nothing to her spicy lunch. She swallowed her mouthful of chili, then put down her spoon. "What?" she asked.

"Why do you think you and Garry changed bodies and I didn't?" he asked quietly. "And please don't tell me it was because Demonai liked you better than he did me."

"All right, then, I won't," she replied, and resumed eating her chili.

A few minutes later, he dropped a half-eaten fry back onto his plate and hissed across the table, "You must have some idea as to why it would have happened that way."

She took a sip of ginger ale to clear her mouth. "I have a theory, but you may not want to hear it."

"Try me," he grated.

"All right. You were the only one of us who denied making a wish the day the big change happened, remember? So, last night, when we asked Demonai to consider our wishes granted and put us back—"

"Claire, we were looking at an image on a computer screen. If Demonai even exists, and that's a very big 'if', I doubt whether he has an online presence."

She let out an exasperated syllable. "Have you ever, in your entire life, taken anything on faith, James? Just taken someone's word for something, or decided to believe in something, even though you knew it could never be proven?"

"Like religion, you mean? You don't seriously think that Demonai is a god, do you?"

"I don't know. Maybe he is, and maybe he isn't. Here is what I know from the museum's website: during the Iron Age, a being going by the name Demonai took prostitutes and concubines under his protection, and because he was able to do wondrous, terrifying things on their behalf, they worshipped him as a god. A trickster god, so maybe it was all a trick. Maybe he was a master of illusion. Or maybe he owned some extremely advanced technology for the times. Maybe, if you were transported a couple of thousand years into the past with a first aid kit, a taser, and a backpack full of batteries for it, *you* would be considered a god too."

"This is not the Iron Age, Claire."

"Quite true. However, a few days ago something wondrous and terrifying and *real* happened to the three of us, something none of us can explain. Whether or not it was accomplished using a technology beyond our comprehension, praying to Demonai had a positive effect on our situation. We may never be able to prove he exists, but I'm willing to take a leap of faith and believe that some higher power heard us and responded."

"To Garry. Not to us. What's your theory about *that*?" Hollinger grumped.

She thought for a few moments. "Garry's original wish was to change places with a very rich and powerful man. Other than the obvious reason, do you happen to know why?"

"He told me it was because he'd been thrown out of a job when the government funding was cut for a research project he was working on. He was feeling poor and powerless, and

I guess he thought having lots of money would make him feel better."

"But it didn't."

"Nope. And it didn't help when he discovered there was a downside to being James A. Hollinger. It really pissed him off."

"James, don't take this the wrong way, but I got the impression that the only thing he didn't like about being in your body was the fact that you insisted on micromanaging it."

"No, I didn't."

"Yes, you did. You couldn't do anything about the fact that he had your physical body—which you repeatedly reminded him was only on loan—but you made damn sure he couldn't access your fortune, and that kept him from exercising your power. It's no wonder he resented you, James. You prevented him from getting his wish."

As realization broke over Hollinger, Claire was treated to the sight of her own body sagging backward like a deflating blow-up doll. "You're right. I did. So now that you're the one occupying my body…"

"…am I going to get on your case about your hiding your extra cash and credit cards? No. I never wished for money or power, James. I wished for an adventure, and that's exactly what I got. And what about you? Are you still going to deny that you made a wish that day?"

"I guess there's no point anymore. I wanted to turn back the clock. I wished that I were back in my twenties."

"So Demonai put you into a more youthful body—mine."

"If he exists—and I am not yet ready to concede that he does—Demonai didn't just put me into a more youthful body. He put me into a female body. I don't call that granting a wish, Claire. I call that playing a dirty trick."

"Well, according to the write-up on the website, that's par for the course for a trickster god like Demonai."

"Oh, please!"

Claire gasped as a thought occurred to her. "Wait a minute, James. That could be it. I wished for an adventure I could write up for the glossy magazines, like winning the lottery or visiting the penguins in Antarctica. Instead, I've got a story that nobody in their right mind would believe. You wished for youth and got a gender change along with it. Garry wished for wealth and power but in your body he wasn't able to use any of it. I think we've all three of us been pranked by the trickster god."

Claire leaned forward and would have said more, but, all at once… they were ham and eggs… they were a cerebral haemorrhage… they were a bad case of acne…

Demonai! Again?

I can't help it. Anytime a threedee touches or moves the lamp I get a surge of energy. It will subside.

Meanwhile, it's raising sympathetic sparks in the threedees' meld and destabilizing it. Olla'set could decide that the experiment is being compromised.

Be patient, Tillah. Don't let him withdraw his pod from the bubble. The experiment is succeeding on more than one level, and I don't want our aggregator to miss any of it.

When the strange sensation had passed, Claire opened her eyes. She was holding a half-eaten tuna sandwich in one hand and a paper serviette in the other, and across the tiny table from her sat a tall man with thinning dark hair and a stunned look on his face.

"Oh. My. God!" she declared after a moment's silence. "We must have got it right!"

"Or maybe the effect of whatever was used on us has simply worn off," he muttered.

"You're still not willing to believe, are you? Everything has to have a logical explanation, a perceptible chain of cause and effect that you can follow back to a point of origin. Where's the wonder in a world like that?"

"I don't need wonder, Claire. I need order."

"And control," she added quietly.

"Yes, to ensure that there is order. That's the way my world has always been—rational and material."

"Until recent events threw everything out of whack."

Hollinger said nothing, just lowered his gaze to the plate in front of her and stared at the French fries as though mentally commanding them to fall into formation.

"Well, whether Demonai exists or not, let's drink a toast to being back in our own bodies," Claire said. She reached across the table for her ginger ale and passed him his cola.

Just as they touched the rims of their glasses lightly together…

…they were peaches and cream… they were Mutt and Jeff… they were measles…

Muttering imprecations under her breath, Claire stabbed her spoon into her bowl of chili as Hollinger leaned back in his chair with a sigh.

"Maybe there's more to this riddle than just figuring out whodunit," said Claire.

"What more could there be? Howdunit? Good luck with that."

She pursed and unpursed her lips. "Maybe whydunit. After all, there are more than two million people in this city, all making random wishes every day. So why us? What made our wishes so special that Demonai decided to grant them in a way that linked up our lives?"

Hollinger chuckled to himself, prompting Claire to ask, "What?"

"Demonai, if he exists, is supposedly the patron deity of prostitutes and concubines, right?"

"Ye-es."

"I started up my business doing tax returns for half the strippers in this city, and many of them weren't taking off their clothes because they had a passion for the stage. You're a good writer, Claire, but you're forced to pay your bills by writing and editing porn. Selling out your ideals by selling yourself is the definition of prostitution."

"And what about Garry?" she challenged.

He reflected for a moment. "I dealt with prostitutes in the past. You're prostituting your talent in the present. Garry was doing some noble and high-minded work until the rug got pulled out from under him. Maybe there's prostitution in his future. Maybe, in order to keep a roof over his head, he'll be forced to trade his dreams and ambitions for the security of a steady income."

"It's not a simple either-or proposition, James," she protested. "Artists have always had patrons."

"And scientists? And financial analysts? We have dreams too, you know."

Claire wadded up her serviette and slam-dunked it into her now-empty bowl. "Are you seriously putting yourself on the same level as Garry and me? I'm sorry, James, but it just doesn't wash. You're a successful financier, a celebrity in fact. Oh, you may have struggled at first, but I can't even imagine you being forced to demean yourself just to pay the rent and keep food on the table."

He stiffened in his chair. "I guess that depends on your definition of demeaning yourself. Some of the things I had to do to get my business off the ground would have—Never mind. Tell me more about your wish."

"I wished for an adventure because I've been living hand to mouth for the last three and a half years," she told him. "I figured if I wrote a first-person article about something unique and exciting, the piece would sell for sure to a major publication, and—Don't look at me like that, James. Toronto is an expensive place to live."

"So, when you asked for an adventure you were actually

wishing for money."

"Ultimately, yes. And the freedom it would give me to write what I wanted to instead of what I had to. We both know that Garry was wishing for power. And you were wishing for...?"

"Love," he replied uncomfortably after a pause. "I wanted to find someone who would be attracted to me, not just my money."

"You're joking," she blurted out. "You had Roxanne. And you threw her away."

"I had Roxanne once a year, for a couple of weeks, while I did her taxes. It was all she wanted from me, so I didn't press the matter."

"Oh, really?" Claire cocked her head, raised an eyebrow and said, "It was all she wanted? Are you quite sure about that?"

"Yes. She was always going on about her 'third career', as the wife of a wealthy man. She's had two husbands already, and is currently shopping for lucky Number Three. If she had ever shown any interest in me outside of income tax season, I would have known it. But she never did."

"Perhaps she was waiting for you to show an interest in *her*."

"It doesn't matter anymore. Roxanne and I met years ago, when I was still living 'hand to mouth', as you put it. We've had a longstanding business relationship, with side benefits. Unfortunately, I was forced to sever it. End of story."

"Not quite. It's sounding to me as though you had a concubine, Mr. Hollinger. Demonai is the special protector of concubines, so I think we need to consider the possibility that he may have been listening to four wishes that day, not just three."

The heart-shaped face went pale.

"Let's run this one up the flagpole. You see, I wished for money and an adventure because I didn't have any of either one. And Garry wished for money and power for the same reason. But you may have had what you wanted right under your nose—you just didn't realize it. In any case, you're the roadblock here, James. Garry's part in this is done, but my adventure can't end until Demonai is able to put us *both* back into our own bodies."

〰

…he was a bat in a belfry… he was a banana cream pie…

He was quivering like a plucked string.

Sophie's dress was bunched around her waist. Her nipples were hard little buttons beneath the fabric of her bodice. Boehm should have felt warm. Instead, he was breaking out in a cold sweat.

"Garry, what's the matter?"

"I think I need to go to the ROM."

"The museum? Now? Why?" she asked, frowning with concern.

"To pray…"

〰

All right, conceded Olla'set, reluctantly rejoining the meld. *So they're intelligent and they share information. And guesses.*

Demonai was too busy to reply. The ferocious current of sensation had begun coursing through him again. Every part of him was sparking. What in the name of the Universe was happening to that lamp?

Demonai, they're doing it! said Tillah. *They're thinking their way through their situation, just as you predicted they would. Demonai, are you all right?*

Chapter Twenty-Three

"Hello, Mac."

O'Toole had been expecting this call. It was the next logical step in the elaborate April Fool's joke that Paulina Perrone had set in motion in his office four days earlier. Slattery hadn't lost his dramatic touch—his voice on the phone sounded taut and a little ragged, as though he were being harassed night and day by Olla'set the Magnificent.

"Rick," he acknowledged. "How have you been?"

"I've been better, my friend. I'm actually calling to invite you to a small gathering at my home this evening at eight o'clock. Just five or six… people."

The hesitation caught O'Toole's attention.

"Oh? What's the occasion?"

"There's someone I'm ready for you to meet. Remember all those practical jokes we pulled off when we were at law school?"

"You mean those jokes *you* pulled off, without telling me how you did it."

"I had help, Mac."

"That much I was able to guess."

"I know it's short notice, but he'll be here tonight. Can you make it?" There was an unspoken 'please' at the end of that question that intrigued O'Toole while at the same time putting him on his guard.

"This is interesting timing, Rick. Should I wear armour?"

"Mac, trust me, this is not an April Fool's joke. I wish it were, but—" A pause, then, "You'll understand when you get here. If you're coming, that is."

O'Toole debated with himself for a moment, but curiosity won out. "Okay, I'll be there," he said, certain that if this did turn out to be a joke, at least it would be a damned ingenious one.

≈

O'Toole surrendered his topcoat to the manservant who had opened the door to admit him to the Slattery family mansion, and was shown with great deference into the drawing room. He'd often been a guest here while he and Rick were schoolmates. The old-money elegance evident in the quality and style of the decor had greatly impressed him those thirty years ago. Now Rick lived here alone, attended by a butler, a cook and a handful of maids, and Mac didn't know whether to feel sad or relieved that nothing about the house seemed to have changed.

Rick got to his feet and walked over to shake O'Toole's hand. "Thank you for coming, Your Honour."

The use of his title cued Mac to look for others in the room, and he soon found them, sitting goggle-eyed in two of the brown leather loungers arranged around the fieldstone fireplace. As he'd expected, this meeting was part of the joke.

Paulina Perrone leaped to her feet as though propelled by a spring the instant their eyes met. The young man made a *pro forma* effort—the cast on his leg made the gesture of respect impossible. O'Toole sorted through his repertoire of expressions and finally settled on his pronouncement-of-sentence face as he acknowledged each of them in turn. "Ms. Perrone… and this must be Mr. Russell."

"It's an honour to meet you, sir," said the plaintiff as

Paulina sank back onto her seat.

"Dean Slattery," said O'Toole, remaining in character as he returned his attention to the chief perpetrator of the prank. "When do I get to meet the genie?"

Rick's shoulders sagged. "Please make yourself comfortable, Judge O'Toole. I have a story to tell you, one you'll find very difficult to believe."

Chapter Twenty-Four

2019
July 30

Post retirement, James Hollinger had liquidated most of his real estate holdings, including the condo tower where his penthouse had been located. Once the chalet in Blue Mountain had been built, it became his primary residence. Meanwhile, he'd downsized to a smaller condominium near the lakeshore. Watching the boats come and go in Toronto Harbour had proven to be a soothing pastime.

Today, he was expecting a guest. It was a blind date, of sorts. They hadn't exchanged names, only communicated via email, enough back-and-forths to confirm for each of them that they had something life-altering in common, as well as a shared willingness to talk about it.

Hollinger gave his living room a quick visual inspection. He had received the call from the concierge. The visitor was on his way up. Coffee was ready. So was something stronger, if they should require it.

At last, there was a knock at the door. Dragging in a steadying breath, he went to open it. As he did, two pairs of eyes widened in mutual recognition.

"Richard Slattery? *You're* 'amicuscuriae'?" Hollinger exclaimed.

"And you're 'poundofflesh'," Slattery replied. "Small world, isn't it? Are you going to invite me inside? Or would you rather do this out in the hall?"

Hollinger snapped out of his daze and stepped aside to let the other man pass. "Of course! Yes! Please, come in!"

"By the way, you're living two floors below another of Demonai's victims. He's an old friend of mine, since high school. At some point, if you're agreeable to it, we can ask him to join us. After all, according to Ms. Amory's book, three heads are better."

Hollinger led the way to a cluster of easy chairs surrounding a large circular coffee table. "Let's see how things go between the two of us first. Quite frankly, you were the last person I expected to see standing there."

"Fair enough." Slattery eased himself onto one of the chairs and accepted the mug of coffee Hollinger had poured for him. "I had no idea you were one of his victims too. It's funny, isn't it, how easy it is to fool the world into thinking everything is business as usual. Sometimes, I can almost fool myself as well. Then the nightmares start up."

"You have flashbacks?" Hollinger took the adjacent seat but remained leaning forward. "Me too. When did Demonai make first contact with you?"

"In 1967. I was in my first year of law school. That wasn't where I wanted to be. However, I was the only male child and there was a family tradition to uphold. I didn't have the talent or the self-confidence to defy my father and choose my own path, so I'd taken the one of least resistance, the one he'd already picked for me. It was a difficult time. I was struggling just to keep my head above water. Then I heard this voice coming from an old lamp I'd bought to send to my mother for her birthday. Life was never the same again after that. What about you?"

Hollinger swallowed his mouthful of coffee and replied, "About sixteen years ago, I went to sleep in my own body and woke up in someone else's. A woman's. No warnings, no explanations, no contact at all. Just *boom!* and suddenly the world was a totally different place, and instead of being a predator, I was prey."

"Interesting that you would use those terms, James. May I call you James?"

"Sure."

"And you can call me Richard. So, are you saying you were a predator before this overnight transformation?"

Hollinger thought for a moment. "Financially and professionally, I guess I was. I had to be, to survive in that business environment. And I was famous, which tended to attract a lot of female attention. But those women weren't prey," he hastened to clarify. "We used each other. They used me to make them feel important, and I used them to make myself feel…"

"Feel what?"

He smiled ruefully. "Feel good about myself. As long as we're being brutally honest, Richard, and it's just between the two of us, when this body switch happened, I was at the top of my field and the top of my game, with nowhere to go but down. Always appearing in public with a different beautiful woman on my arm took my mind off that depressing fact. Keeping up appearances was becoming tiresome, though, and there were other things I wanted to do. I was making preparations for early retirement. Then the trickster god, or whatever the hell he is, came along and knocked me sideways, out of the game entirely."

"That must have angered you," Slattery observed.

"It did. But the most frustrating part for me was that as long as I was in Claire's body, I had no control, over anything. And every time Claire pointed that out and told me to give up and just go with the flow, I got angrier. Or maybe I was just scared that I might never get my own body back. The thought of losing it all and having to start over again, as a woman in today's messed-up world…!"

Hollinger had to put his mug down. His hand was shaking.

"Are you sleeping well?" Slattery asked.

"Not for years. I can't seem to relax. The longest I've slept at a stretch was three hours. I don't have nightmares, but I keep waking up, convinced I'm not alone in the room. Then it takes me an hour to drop off again. I've tried everything—warm milk, meditation, massages, even sleeping pills—nothing works. And my blood pressure is higher now that I'm retired than it was when I was working eighty hour weeks on Bay Street."

"I can relate to that," Slattery said. "My nightmares are about control as well, specifically about not having any over the genie in the lamp. I started having them in my fourth year of law school, when I realized what Demonai really was, and just how godlike his powers were. And yet, for those three years, we were co-conspirators. We played practical jokes together. He called himself my sidekick. Until I went to sleep one night, dreamed about Demonai causing the end of the world, and woke up in abject terror of him. Truthfully, I'm still terrified of him. And of Olla'set, and of the possibility that there might be others of his kind out there, any one of them with the power to wipe us all out of existence on a whim."

Hollinger shuddered. "How do you deal with the fear?"

"Day by day, by filling my mind with other, more immediate preoccupations. I give guest lectures at the law school. And I've been researching historical case law, thinking I might write a book or two. I keep telling myself that if I'm not actively remembering Demonai, maybe he'll forget about me as well. And when all else fails, I medicate myself out of the well stocked bar in my home office."

Wordlessly, Hollinger went to a wall cabinet and fetched a bottle and two glasses. "How do you like your whisky?"

Slattery gave him a sleep-deprived grin. "I thought you'd never ask."

〰

"You're absolutely sure that this is her?" Ellie said in a hushed voice.

It seemed appropriate to whisper here. There was a heaviness to this place, a cathedral-like solemnity that slowed movement and quietened thought. It was mid-morning. The sky was overcast, threatening rain, and they were the only two living souls in sight.

"Not absolutely," Rosie replied. "Without a DNA match, nothing is a hundred percent certain. But the dates fit, and her background comes closest to what we know about Hollinger's girlfriend." She pulled out her little pad and began rhyming off data. "She stripped at the Fun 'n' Feathers Club for fifteen years, then bought out the owner when he retired. Turned it into a profitable, quasi-respectable establishment. Then she did the same thing for two more burlesque houses. She was never rich-rich, but she lived comfortably. She was worth a couple million dollars when the cancer took her. Left no heirs. Everything went to charity."

For the space of two long breaths, the women stood staring at the information engraved on the headstone:

ROXANNE
FORSYTHE
born December 4, 1947
died June 30, 2003

"Do you think he knows?" Ellie wondered. "Do you think he tried to contact her once he was back in his own body?"

"Don't ask me," said Rosie. "I have no idea. But if he did, it was probably too late."

And that would explain a lot, Ellie realized. Shaking off the thought, she turned to the other woman and declared, "I have a sudden craving for some hot chocolate."

"Me too," Rosie replied firmly. "With whipped cream. A lot of it."

There was a Timmy's around the corner from the cemetery. When they were sitting at one of the small tables, sipping from paper cups, Rosie said, "There was a reason I didn't ask Marty to join us today."

"Oh?"

The other woman paused, just long enough for a cold knot to form in Ellie's stomach. Was this going to be bad news? Was he in trouble?

Finally, Rosie continued, "Detective Breck and I only recently became partners. I'd been on extended health leave and my previous partner was promoted to admin during my absence."

"What was the reason for the extended leave? If you don't mind my asking, that is."

"It was a car accident. I was in pursuit, with lights and siren blaring. Got T-boned at an intersection by a distracted driver. We both ended up in the hospital. Fortunately, I was off duty at the time and therefore alone in the car. The passenger side was crushed. Anyone sitting beside me would have died on the scene."

"That's terrible! But—wait—you were off duty and yet in pursuit? Of what?"

"Good question. I received a head injury in the crash and lost an hour of my life. The doctors called it 'transient global amnesia'. Basically, it meant I had no memory of the pursuit or what had caused it. Dispatch had a record of my call requesting backup, but it consisted mainly of, 'Ohmigod I don't believe this!' and a series of location updates. Not very helpful."

"Shouldn't Marty know all this already? It would have been officially reported, right?" Ellie pointed out.

"That's correct." She leaned in and lowered her voice, prompting Ellie to lean in as well. "But what I haven't told anyone else is that my memory has been returning. It began as flashes, the fog clearing for a few seconds at a time. Enough pieces have fallen into place that I now know what I was following that night. It was the same thing you and Marty saw in the dryer at the laundromat—a glowing yellow sphere. It hovered over the hood of my car for a moment, then it lit off. When I didn't go after it right away, it came back, hovered for another few seconds, then zipped away again."

Ellie's eyes widened. "Dogs do that when they want you to chase them."

"Finally I did. I thought at first it might have been a drone, but drone control is line of sight, and this thing was whipping around corners and leading me down alleys and side streets, always at windshield height. It was Demonai, wasn't it? Playing with me."

"It sounds like it. And you've said nothing about this to your superiors?"

"No. My doctor told me that in some cases the memories never fully return, so I've decided to be one of those cases. Flashes only, none of them adding up to anything that makes sense. If what I saw were to be revealed, I'd be declared psychologically unfit for duty. So, I'm relying on your discretion, Ellie."

"Of course. But why confide only in me? Why not Marty too, since he's your partner?"

"Because he's obligated to report me, and you're not, and police work is all I've ever wanted to do with my life."

"Well, your secret is safe with me." Ellie touched the rim of her cup to the one Rosie was holding. "Welcome to the club."

The world was becoming a very strange place. According to the posts and links on *Demonaimania*'s news feed, a total of thirty-seven pigeons had exploded in the past few weeks alone, in cities as far away as Moscow and Johannesburg. Calamity Jane's inside-out cat had been the first of nine pets to mysteriously disappear and then turn up dead, without a mark on them. Somewhere in California, a pack of dogs had been captured on video, first playing with and then fleeing from five balls of yellow light. There were no reports of rats blowing up, but that didn't mean anything. Ellie was certain there must be whole sections of sewer pipe painted with rodent blood.

Words like "plague" and "apocalypse" had begun popping up on social media, especially among the evangelicals. There had been a rash of sharing by followers of the *Demonaimania* page online. Many of the shared posts were trending.

And Calamity Jane had finally responded to Ellie's message. She was ready to meet, but not at either of their homes. Ellie had replied, *I'll be doing laundry Wed @ 7 p.m., Cornerstone Plaza.* Then she'd texted Marty, asking him to be there as well.

Anonymity was the blessing and the curse of the Internet. Calamity Jane could be anyone, and anyone could walk into the laundromat, claiming to be Calamity Jane. Ellie knew she was taking a huge risk, having this meeting on her home turf. However, it was also where Demonai had appeared to her, making it his turf too. He would most likely be monitoring whatever happened there.

She was a smart enough gambler to hedge her bets. Demonai was a trickster. If Calamity Jane turned out to be a knife-wielding psychopath, Ellie wanted both a god *and* an armed police detective on the premises.

Chapter Twenty-Five

2003
March 21

"Augie says that Hollinger and the brunette left together right after our guy did. Augie followed them, first to a jewellery store, and then to a diner, where he says they're having lunch together right now."

"So Gunther was wrong?"

"Not necessarily. Augie says this meal isn't looking like a pleasant social occasion for either of them. So, he wants us to bring the redhead's partner to him so he can get a few questions answered. And you know what that means."

Dougie grinned. "Now we can bust in on them."

<div align="center">~~~</div>

"Darling," Sophie said, "what's the matter? Your hands are shaking."

Boehm gazed up at her unclad loveliness and breathed a helpless sigh. "It's all your fault," he murmured, pulling her down on top of him again just as…

…he was a rotten tomato… he was a charcoal briquette…

…he was getting tired of the whole damned thing.

All at once there came a vigorous pounding at Sophie's apartment door.

"Open up!" commanded a deep voice from the hallway. "Don't make us break the door down."

"What the…?" she muttered darkly. "Garry, I'm sorry about this." Sophie covered herself with a blue dressing gown (which only half-heartedly masked her curves) and went into the living room.

Boehm raised himself lazily on his elbows, enjoying her exit.

Sophie made sure the security chain was fastened. Then she cracked open her apartment door and saw two burly men in business suits standing out in the hall.

"Are you Sophie Hooper?" one of them demanded.

"That's Hopper," she corrected him frostily. "And just who the hell are you?"

"We represent someone who needs to have a word with your friend," the other man said.

"I've got lots of friends," she replied. "You'll have to be more specific."

"Don't try snowing us, Miss Hooper. We know he's here, and we know what he's been up to," snapped the first man.

"Really! How psychic of you! No one comes in here without a badge and a warrant. Leave now or I call the police," she told them, putting a sharp edge on each word.

As she moved to shut the door, both men threw themselves against it, ripping the chain from the wall and bursting into the apartment.

"Ee-*yah*!"

The first man went flying through the air and slid into a heap behind the magazine rack.

"Ee-*yah*!"

His partner's body described an arc in the air and made a perfect landing on Sophie's French provincial sofa. There was a sharp *crack* as he touched down.

Overhearing all this mayhem, Boehm realized: Sophie was in full warrior princess mode. Best to stay out of her way. He lay back down, every muscle taut, and waited until a stillness had fallen in the other room. Then he swung his legs out of bed, pulled on his briefs and trousers, and opened the door.

As he walked into the living room, barefoot and bare-chested, Sophie whirled on him. "Garry, I know you're in some kind of trouble, and I'm on your side, but I can't help you if you won't talk to me. You were expecting these two to come after you, weren't you? That's why you were so distracted this morning."

Running a hand through his hair, Boehm looked at each intruder's face in turn. Then he shook his head. "Sophie, I swear to you, I don't know either of these men. I can't even imagine who might have sent them. Maybe we should call the police."

She wasn't keen on that idea, he could tell. Boehm watched a series of expressions parade across her face. Finally, she said, "The last time something like th's happened, I was the one who nearly got arrested. Let's just tie them up for now. When they come to, we'll question them. If they tell us who they're working for, we'll find that person and pound whoever it is into the dirt. *Then* we'll call the police. If I'm going to be charged, we may as well make it count for something."

〰

The chili had given Hollinger's body heartburn to go with the stress headache it had developed from switching back and forth across the table at the diner. Claire and Hollinger had traded bodies twice more after that, once while the bill was being paid and again in the taxi while returning to the apartment. By the time they walked through the door, wearing their own bodies, he was carrying on nonstop about his head and his stomach. Anyone hearing him would have thought that he was dying.

Claire was not impressed.

"Quit moaning," she scolded him. "And stop popping the pain pills. You've already got heartburn. Too many of those will give you an ulcer, and since we don't know for sure whose body will be whose when Demonai finishes with us—"

"Okay, fine!" he snapped, tossing her the bottle. "Maybe this little god of yours will reach the end of his attention span and decide to torture someone else before the dose I just took wears off." With that, Hollinger dropped onto Boehm's easy chair.

"Or maybe we can figure out what he wants from us and give it to him before he switches us again," she pointed out sharply. "Come on, James, think! At the diner, you finally admitted that you'd wished for something."

"For love," he supplied, wearing an uncomfortable expression. "Which you told me had been in my life all along. You were wrong about that. Greed and lust had been in my life. All anyone saw about me was the wealth, and the power that wealth could command."

"Why?"

"Why what?"

"Why couldn't anyone see the man behind the wealth?"

He paused. "I guess it was because I never showed them. I couldn't afford to."

"Why not?"

He closed his eyes and raised a hand to massage his forehead. "I was fighting to succeed in a cutthroat industry, surrounded by rivals who would have jumped on any perceived weakness and turned it to their own advantage. I couldn't risk giving them that opportunity."

"And yet, you took Roxanne to that fancy cocktail party… how many years in a row?"

"That was different. She was my 'plus one', nothing more."

He was infuriating.

"Why is it so hard for you to admit that you and Roxanne have feelings for each other?" she demanded.

"Do we have to go into this?"

"Do you want to end up in your own body?"

"I told you, she's been married twice. She enjoys appearing with me at a high society event, but she's been looking for love somewhere else."

"And not finding it, evidently, since those marriages didn't last. She was one of your earliest clients, right?"

He nodded wordlessly.

Claire pressed her point. "She could have moved her business to another firm at any time, but she didn't. She stuck with you. Spent two weeks a year at your penthouse. Even while she was married?"

He nodded again.

"Then I revise my earlier judgment. She's not your concubine, James. You're hers."

"What?!"

"And you've been denying the existence of your patron deity. No wonder Demonai is pissed at you."

Hollinger bounced to his feet. "That trickster is *not* my patron deity," he informed her. "And you're out of your mind if you think I'm going to—"

"So you do believe he's real?" Claire interrupted, her cheeks dimpling.

He let out an exasperated syllable. "The jury is still out on that," he told her. "But even if you're right about Roxanne and me, you heard Garry earlier. She never wants to see me or hear from me again."

"Men!" Claire said, purposely making it sound like a curse. "She doesn't want to see you again until she's forgiven you. That's what we women do, James. We vent and then we forgive. Humanity would have died out centuries ago if we didn't. Come on, now—are you going to let one angry voice message stand between you and what could be the love of your life?"

Hollinger sat back down. "You're determined to turn your adventure into a romance novel, aren't you?"

"Sure, why not? There's certainly plenty of material, what with Garry and Sophie, and you and Roxanne. It could be a duology."

All at once… they were overripe bananas… they were lightning and thunder…

Not again!

…they were wet socks…

"What the hell do you want?" Hollinger shouted at the ceiling as his body looked on wearily from the easy chair.

"Clearly, more than we've already given him," Claire said.

"All right, enough about me. Let's talk about you now," said Hollinger, remaining on his feet. "How good a writer are you, really? I mean, just because Ralph Ignace likes your style—"

"He's not the only one. You should read some of my fan mail rejection letters," she told him.

"Then why are you writing and editing porn?"

"Because I like to eat. Ralph pays me when no one else will—which happens depressingly often—and Toronto is an expensive place to live."

"So you've said. And that raises the question: Why are you here? Writing is a portable profession. You could have stayed back in…?"

"Caverley Corners. Population 4700. A main street six blocks long. Lots of rolling hills and farmers' fields everywhere else. And five doughnut shops, all doing a brisk business, thank you very much," she added.

"Were you happy there?"

"Most of the time. When I wasn't restless and wondering what life outside the small town bubble was like."

"And now that you know?" he prompted. When she didn't reply, he added, "Where would you really like to live, Claire? …because I've got a theory."

"Oh?"

"I think Toronto is the reason you're blocked. This place is a big pressure cooker. Stay here long enough and you'll fall apart."

The more she considered his words, the clearer it became

to her that he was right. Some people just weren't suited to big city life, and Claire was evidently one of them. She was what she was, a small town girl still struggling to fit in here after three and a half years. As she was psyching herself up to tell him so…

…they were corned beef and cabbage… they were dandelion seeds on the wind…

Demonai had had a plan, he was sure he had, but the crashing waves of sensation had so disturbed his essence that he was hard pressed to remember a single detail of it.

Olla'set, we have to do something. This is killing him.

Demonai brought this upon himself, Tillah. I warned him not to become so involved with the five-dimensional universe, but he ignored me.

It's the lamp. Demonai, withdraw from the lamp!

But he did not respond, and the others were afraid to touch him.

We must communicate with the threedees and get them to stop rubbing the lamp, Tillah decided. *Aggregator, you've communicated with them before. I haven't yet learned how. Please, do this now! We are only three. If Demonai dies, one third of our kind will cease to exist. Is that really what you want?*

Chapter Twenty-Six

"Give it up, Dean Slattery," said O'Toole wearily. "There is no genie inside the lamp."

"He was there two days ago," Slattery insisted. "He told me he's everywhere, all the time, and I don't understand why he isn't responding now, since he was the one who wanted to have this meeting."

"Maybe he didn't like being jostled around in the trunk of your car," O'Toole suggested.

Then a booming voice erupted from the fireplace:

PUT... DOWN... THE LAMP!

Slattery nearly jumped out of his skin. As he hastened to follow the command, he noticed that two of his guests had instantly blanched. One of them, Joseph Russell, was hyperventilating and looked about to faint.

"That's Olla'set!" hissed Paulina Perrone, casting anxious glances around the room, several of them at the young man resting his leg cast on Slattery's ottoman.

Meanwhile, O'Toole was leaning farther back in his chair, his arms crossed, his expression skeptical.

Slattery cleared his throat and asked, in the courtroom voice he'd often practised when he was younger, "Where is Demonai?"

Demonai won't be answering your calls anymore. In fact, he won't be speaking to you at all.

Involuntarily, Slattery shivered. "Is he dead?"

Of course not! Olla'set replied. *He has merely withdrawn from this place.*

Questions were crowding Slattery's mind, but before he could pick one and ask it, Paulina jumped to her feet, her fists clenched at her sides. "Olla'set!" she cried in the direction of the fireplace. "I represent Joseph Russell, the human you've been tormenting for the last ten years. Before you leave, we need to talk."

Then talk.

"You nearly killed this boy with your bullying and your threats. We want you to forget about your so-called tribute and leave him alone from now on. In fact, we want you to leave us *all* alone." And she closed her eyes, as though expecting to be struck down at any second.

Interesting, said Olla'set after a pause, and Slattery could swear he heard a smile in the genie's voice. *I was about to say something very similar to you. Demonai is right—your kind don't frighten easily anymore. Very well, then. Joseph Russell, I absolve you of any obligation to provide tribute and promise never to communicate with you or these others again. I promise also that Demonai will never contact the four of you again, under pain of punishment from me.*

Uttering an impatient syllable, O'Toole went over to the fireplace. He shot a look at Slattery before bending to inspect the hearth and the flue.

"What are you looking for, Mac?"

"The microphone. Honestly, Rick, I'm a little disappointed. This prank is nowhere near the high standard of mischief that I was expecting from you."

You think you can debunk me? demanded the voice from the fireplace.

"I think there's nothing *to* debunk. A child could have come up with this. In fact, I suspect a child did," O'Toole declared.

Olla'set chuckled, sending icy tingles across the back of Slattery's shoulders. Then five glowing white orbs appeared in the room. Hovering at chest height, they formed a ring around O'Toole, who stood frozen, his eyes wide with belated comprehension.

"Please, Olla'set, don't hurt him!" Slattery cried.

I won't harm him, Rick, the voice promised. *I'll just give him a lift home.*

As the orbs moved in, there was a bright flash of light. A second later, three people sat in Dean Slattery's study, staring in shock into one another's faces. It was a full minute before any of them dared to speak.

"What just happened here?" Paulina asked, her voice barely a whisper. "Is he gone?"

"They both are," said Slattery, finally understanding how Mac must have felt years earlier when Rick had told him there would be no more practical joking. Mac had talked about the end of an era. Feeling a strange emptiness inside, Slattery suspected they'd just experienced another one.

"I believe you've won your first case, Ms. Perrone," he told her, "although I wouldn't try putting it on my résumé if I were you. Now that I know for sure that it's vacant, I can finally polish and display that antique lamp. As for Judge O'Toole…"

Right on cue, the telephone rang in the vestibule and was answered by the butler. A moment later, he stepped into the drawing room and said, quite calmly, "That was Mr. O'Toole, sir. He told me to convey a message. He says congratulations, and he is sorry he ever doubted you. Also, he requests that you bring his topcoat to your office tomorrow morning so that he can pick it up."

Chapter Twenty-Seven

"**D**o you think she'll show up?" Marty asked, pointing to the clock on the wall. It was nearly 8:00 p.m. Rhoda was in her cubicle beside the door, placidly folding and stacking a quantity of freshly laundered towels with a hotel logo embroidered on them. Ellie was switching her second load over from the washer to the dryer. The three of them were the only living souls in the place.

Ellie closed the dryer door and slipped her pay card in and out of the slot. "I don't know. Calamity Jane never responded to my personal message."

A bell chimed.

"That's mine," said Marty. He dropped the gossip magazine he'd been reading onto a chair and went to get a metal cart. While loading it up with wet clothes, he remarked, "You know, we can only stretch this out for so long. If no one else arrives by the time we've finished folding, I'm calling it a night."

At 7:57 p.m., a woman walked into the laundromat with a basket of clothing wedged against her hip and an anxious expression on her face. Rhoda stopped what she was doing long enough to ask her, "Have you got a pay card?"

"N—no, I don't," came the reply.

"I'll help her, Rhoda," Ellie offered, adding with a beckoning wave, "The dispensers are at the back. This way."

Once they were out of the manager's hearing, she asked in a lowered voice, "Are you by any chance Jane?"

The other woman darted nervous glances around the room and tightened her grip on the laundry basket. "Calamity Jane," she stammered. "I'm accident prone, so when my husband set up the account, that was the user name he chose."

"Your husband set up the account?" Ellie repeated, her skin prickling a warning.

"He had to, because I'm too—"

Jane choked on the next words, but Ellie could guess what they were. Checking surreptitiously for bruises, she saw none. That didn't mean anything. Abuse didn't have to be physical to leave a scar.

Jane made a visible effort to relax. Wearing a smile that was just a little too bright, she asked, "Are you 'ratgoboom'?"

Ellie traded significant looks with Breck before replying, "Yes, and I'd like to know more about what happened to your cat."

The sound of the door slamming drew all eyes to the front of the laundromat.

"Hey, watch it!" Rhoda protested.

"Shut up, bitch!" said the large man who had just barged in. Rhoda's jaw clenched. She picked up her phone. Meanwhile, the man's glowering gaze scanned the room. "Who's the nutbar who's been filling my wife's head full of even more shit than was already there?" he growled.

Standing beside Ellie, Jane went utterly still. She looked like a frightened deer, ready to bolt or just collapse. "I'm sorry," she whispered tearfully. "He insisted on driving me here. He never said he was going to—"

Marty stepped forward, thrusting his badge ahead of him like a shield. "You need to calm down, sir," he said firmly. "And watch your language, please. There are ladies present."

"I'm calling the police!" Rhoda shrilled from her cubicle.

"They're already on the scene," Ellie called back to her.

The man turned on Jane with an expression that made her tremble. "Come on, bitch, we're leaving."

"At least let her do the laundry first," Ellie piped up, matching his stare with a defiant one of her own, "since that's why she's here." *Demonai, you'd better be watching this,* she added mentally.

"And let her talk to you?" he sneered. "Not gonna happen! She's mine and I'm taking her home. Move it!" he added, addressing Jane once more.

At that moment, a light went on inside one of the dryers. Ellie caught it at the corner of her eye. Marty had noticed it too. He put himself in the man's way and said quietly, "I don't think so."

"Oh, yeah? Who's gonna stop me? You?"

All at once, five glowing spheres popped into existence, forming a circle around him.

"No, but I believe *they* are," Marty replied.

The man flailed his arms, trying to shoo the lights away. "What kind of bullshit is this?" he spat.

Jane gasped at the sight of them. "It's them, Jerry! I told you they were real. They're what peeled my cat!"

"*You* killed that cat, you crazy-eyed bitch! You gave it the wrong food or something and then made up a story to cover your ass."

"Look around you, Jerry," said Breck, as the spheres closed in. "This is no story. This is really happening. So you'd better watch your language, or Demonai may decide to peel you too."

Practically foaming at the mouth now, Jerry snapped, "Demonai doesn't exist. This whole thing is a con game, and I don't care if you're a cop, you motherfuckin' bastard, I'm gonna—"

DEMONAI EXISTS! thundered a voice from the dryer. Instantly, the scene in the laundromat became a tableau. *And so do I. I am Tillah. The female you call 'bitch' is no longer yours to abuse. She is now under my protection, and anyone who attempts to harm her will be answering to me.*

"This is a fucking trick!" Jerry declared, an instant before the spheres all converged on him at once. In a blinding flash, the man and the orbs were gone.

"I *told* him to mind his language," Marty commented mildly. "Some people just never listen."

"Where'd he go?" yelped Rhoda, her face a portrait of dismay.

"Home, probably," Ellie replied. That was where Olla'set had taken her grandfather, at least. "Or maybe Tillah left him outside in his car. I'm sure he's not dead. Well, pretty sure, anyway. Right, Tillah?"

As if in answer to the question, the light inside the dryer went out.

Meanwhile, Jane had fallen to her knees, shaking her head and murmuring incredulously, "It was real. I didn't imagine it like he said I did. I didn't fake it. It really happened." She turned awe-filled eyes to the row of dryers at the back of the laundromat. "Demonai is real. Tillah is real. And they live… here."

Marty observed her for a few seconds, then leaned toward Ellie and asked, "So, what do you think?"

"I think the cat got peeled because Demonai or someone like him was figuring out how to move living creatures through time. I think Jane is going to be doing her laundry here on a regular basis from now on. And I think that after my next post on the *Demonaimania* page, this place is going to see a lot more walk-in business throughout the week. But first and foremost, I think we all need to finish doing our laundry so that we can get home at a reasonable hour. Jane may need a ride."

"Not a problem. I'll be her police escort."

Rhoda was excitedly brandishing a cell phone. "The owner wants to know what the hell just happened. I was on the line with him when I threatened to call the cops and he overheard me. *Now* what am I supposed to tell him?"

Marty grinned. "Tell him that everything is okay, and that cleanliness really is next to godliness."

"Oooh, that's bad," Ellie groaned.

"Sorry, I couldn't resist."

How was that, Demonai? Tillah's essence was glittering with pleasure. As he had already discovered, the rotating drum of a dryer provided a much gentler version of the sensations he'd experienced with the lamp.

Not bad for a beginner. You imitated my vibrations almost perfectly. However, now that you have decided to watch over endangered threedee females—

And their offspring.

And their offspring, he acknowledged, *you will have to improve your communication skills. That will mean spending a great deal more time in compacted form, inside this five-dimensional bubble. How do you feel about that?*

She paused to consider. *I think I would like to wait before answering, until Olla'set has made his decision regarding the disposition of these creatures.*

He'd been afraid of that.

The following evening, Marty and Rosie paid a visit to Judge O'Toole at his home.

"Are you here to give me an update on the case I asked you to investigate?" he asked, once introductions had been made and they were all seated in the living room.

"Actually, sir, we're here to present you with our final report," Marty told him.

"I'm only interested in knowing one thing, Detective Breck. Did he do it?"

Marty pressed his lips together and threw Rosie a look. She reached inside her jacket and produced a business-sized envelope, which she then handed to O'Toole.

"What's this?" he demanded, scowling.

"It's a sworn statement from one of your late wife's doctors," Rosie replied. "You should read it, sir."

Grumbling under his breath, O'Toole tore open the envelope and unfolded the sheet of paper it contained. After perusing its contents for a moment, he glanced up at her, puzzlement in his eyes.

"Dr. Kevin Joyce? I don't recognize this name," he said.

Marty leaned forward and explained, "That's because Mrs. O'Toole didn't want you to know that she was seeing him. It was that final prescription for blood pressure meds that led us to him. Her regular doctor had written it, but she filled it on the first floor of the medical building where Joyce's office was located."

"Once the diagnosis had been confirmed, she stopped going to him, but not before making him promise never to tell you about her condition," Rosie added.

"A brain aneurysm," O'Toole murmured brokenly. "But why would she keep that to herself? Why carry that burden alone?"

"Dr. Joyce asked her the same question," said Marty. "When we interviewed him, he told us her answer. It was inoperable, and her symptoms were mild. She not only wanted to enjoy whatever time she had left, she wanted you to enjoy it with her. If you'd known about the ticking time bomb in her head, you would have stressed and worried constantly, and that would have made both of you miserable. In a way, this was her final gift to you, sir—three happy years before her fatal stroke."

"She should have told me. I would have been prepared for what happened. This way—!" Tears were welling in the judge's eyes. "And Demonai had nothing to do with it," he added in a monotone voice.

"Not a thing," Rosie confirmed.

"So I've been living like this for twelve years, for nothing. Thinking that it was my wish that had—! *Damn* that Demonai! Letting me go on suffering like that… He should have told me!"

The two detectives exchanged helpless glances.

"Forgive me, sir," Marty ventured, "but didn't you say that Demonai had promised never to contact you again?"

"I did," O'Toole admitted. "But Demonai never actually made that promise. Olla'set was the one who spoke to us that evening, and Olla'set promised to punish Demonai if he ever bothered the four of us again."

Since the judge was now visibly calmer, Breck continued, "You know, time works differently for them than it does for us. A short time for us can be a long time for them and vice versa. Maybe Demonai did find a way to tell you, through Ellie. But he couldn't possibly understand how the time delay would feel to one of our kind. I don't think any of them do, to be honest. One of the drawbacks of being extradimensional, I guess."

O'Toole got to his feet, tears now flowing freely down his cheeks.

It was their cue to leave.

"Are you going to be all right, sir?" Rosie asked.

"Yes. Thank you, Detectives. I appreciate your hard work. And I think, for the first time in twelve years, that I am finally going to be all right."

In the elevator, Rosie turned to Marty and said, "What you told him back there…?"

"I have no idea where that came from."

"Well, it was perfect. The next best thing to an apology from Demonai himself."

Demonai, who had been prevented by Olla'set from ever bothering O'Toole again, even if it was to set things right and say he was sorry. Marty had been wondering what his own part was supposed to be in the unfolding of this O'Toole family drama. Perhaps he'd just now played it, acting as Demonai's proxy. And if so, he could finally—

"Listen, I'm probably overstepping my bounds by saying this, but based on what I've learned from Claire's book, I would be remiss if I didn't point something out," Rosie continued in a rush. "I've seen how you are around Ellie, and how she is around you. If you have feelings for that girl and are waiting for just the right moment to tell her…? There is no right moment, Marty. There's just now. Don't wait, or you could end up like Hollinger, full of regret because you didn't speak up sooner."

He gave her a curious look.

"We found Roxanne. Ellie and I paid her a visit. She's buried in Mount Pleasant Cemetery. When the events in the book took place, she was dying. Hollinger couldn't have known it, but that fancy cocktail party was the last one she would ever have the chance to attend. And when he cancelled his credit cards while she was shopping, it was too hard a blow to forgive.

"The point is, we always assume there's more time, but we don't actually know how much we've got, or how much others have. So, if you want her to know how you feel, don't waste precious time. Talk to her." Rosie shifted her stance uncomfortably. "You can be pissed at me if you like for saying that, but I just had to get it out."

"Wow. You don't mince words, do you?"

"Not anymore, I don't."

In the Fifth Dimension

All right, Demonai, said Olla'set. *I have observed enough. Your experiment is over. Dissolve the remaining melds and let these creatures get on with their lives.*

Are you convinced of their intellectual equality with us, Aggregator?

No.

But you communicated with them yourself, protested Demonai. *You have observed that they are self-aware, that they can reason and form theories, that they experience emotions and can both plan for the future and remember the past. They learn and evolve. They question and explore. How can you say that they are not intelligent?*

While it's true that they do display most of the characteristics of higher intelligence, I'm afraid the most defining one is missing: the ability to create life in lower dimensions.

How is a three-dimensional creature supposed to create life in only one or two dimensions? wondered Tillah.

Exactly. And that is why the Universe only bestows this gift on the highest order of beings. There is no life in one or two dimensions. Therefore these threedees, while near-perfect counterfeits, cannot actually be considered our equals in mental ability.

I disagree, Aggregator, declared Demonai. *They are as highly-evolved as we are, and I can prove it.*

Chapter Twenty-Eight

. . . he was rice pudding with raisins…

Boehm felt the moment pass and resumed breathing. He was still in his own body, thank goodness!

Sophie and the two men tied up with clothes line in her living room were all staring at him curiously.

"Are you quite done now?" Sophie wanted to know.

"Hey, cut the man some slack," scolded the one on the floor. "He isn't well."

"Shut up, Dougie," growled the other man from his seat on the broken sofa.

"Dougie?" Sophie echoed. "Cute name. Now, if you've finished sniping at each other, perhaps you'd be good enough to tell me why you're here."

The man on the floor had struggled to a sitting position. "We were ordered to bust in here."

"Dougie—!" warned his partner. Sophie turned and scowled darkly at him.

"Our boss just wanted us to follow him and make sure nobody got killed."

Now she did a double take. "Killed?" she echoed.

The thug on the sofa cursed loudly and began thrashing around in his bonds. "Dougie, if you don't shut up right now—!"

"You've been following me? For how long?" Boehm

demanded.

"Since right after you and your partner kidnapped the millionaire out of the Ha'penny."

"The Ha'penny? This is about the Ha'penny?" Boehm said, his voice rising in pitch as everything suddenly became clear.

However, Sophie remained mystified. "Garry, what the hell is he talking about?"

"A huge misunderstanding. It's easy enough to straighten out. We just need to get the other two over here. If you'll excuse me, I have to make a phone call."

<center>~~~</center>

"What do you think?" Claire wondered. "Was that it?"

Hollinger looked himself up and down in the mirror. "Well, we're back in our own bodies, and that's a good thing."

The telephone shrilled, startling them.

"Oh, Lord," groaned Claire. "And Garry's not here to answer it—"

Hollinger crossed the room in two strides and snatched up the receiver. "Hello?" he barked. As Claire watched tensely, he listened for a couple of moments, then said, "We're on our way."

"On our way where?" she demanded.

"That was Garry. He wants us to join him and Sophie at her apartment. Apparently, there are two men over there who need to be straightened out about what happened at the Ha'penny."

"James, I'm not sure myself what happened at the Ha'penny."

"So? You're a writer. Make up a story. We can figure out the details during the taxi ride."

An hour later, they were knocking on Sophie's door.

The first thing Claire saw when they were welcomed inside was two rather large men with their wrists and ankles bound, sitting side by side on a broken sofa and glaring at each other.

"Sophie, what—?!"

"Please, Claire, don't ask. Just listen," Sophie begged her. "These men are under the impression that you and Garry are kidnappers. They're claiming that you snatched some millionaire out of a bar—"

"Yeah, that would be me," Hollinger interrupted.

Sophie stared him up and down. "You're the millionaire?"

"I wish!" he said, laughing. "But I look just like him. I'm his double. I'm the one he sends out the front door to keep the paparazzi busy while he sneaks out the back. I'm George, by the way. George Hastings."

Hollinger had missed his calling, Claire mused. With that acting talent, he belonged on a sound stage.

He offered Sophie a hand for shaking, and after a moment's hesitation, she took it.

"Wait a second," said one of the thugs on the sofa. "So that was you getting blasted at the bar the other night, not James Hollinger?"

Claire nearly rolled her eyes. Not exactly a quick study, that one.

"You didn't think it was strange that Hollinger was there all by himself?" Hollinger returned.

"Well, yeah, but… we heard from the manager that you were going on about your girlfriend getting erased, and someone wanting your body to be found in the right place. Our boss figured you must have gone there to hide out. From them." His hands being unavailable, he pointed with his chin in the direction of Boehm and Claire.

"No, that's all wrong," Hollinger told him. "These are my friends. I was in a bad way, and they were meeting me to try to cheer me up. Admittedly, I wasn't expressing myself very well that night. I'd had a drink or two before I got to the bar, and it kind of messed with my brain."

"So who's the bunch you were complaining about, the

ones who took everything away from you and didn't care about you as a person?" the second thug put in.

Hollinger shot a sharp glance at Boehm before replying, "Hollinger's lawyers. I'm an actor, on a retainer to impersonate Hollinger whenever he needs me, and there's a clause in my contract that forbids me to make any public appearances as myself."

The thugs exchanged a look. "That makes sense," said the first one.

"Maybe, but it means I don't have a life. My girlfriend left me because I could never take her out anywhere. And when I was offered a movie role in Asia, the damned lawyers invoked the contract and forced me to turn it down. That's why I was at the bar, feeling sorry for myself and drinking until my friends could join me."

"So this was all a misunderstanding," the second thug said.

"I'm afraid so," Hollinger replied with a disarming shrug. "I'm sorry that you've gone to so much trouble, but as you can see, no one's been kidnapped."

"…that we know about," said the first thug, wearing a scowl that made him resemble a bulldog. "If you're the double, where's the real Hollinger? 'Cause we happen to know that he's not at the penthouse right now."

Hollinger's face acquired a strange expression. Clapping a hand to his stomach, he said, "I need to use the washroom.'

Wordlessly, Sophie pointed the way.

As soon as he'd closed the door behind him, he was surrounded by five glowing spheres.

〜〜〜

O'Meara nearly dropped the glass he was holding when he saw Hollinger walk into the Ha'penny. "Gunther!" he whispered urgently. "Look! He got away from them."

"He doesn't look so good, Ewan. I'd better call my uncle

again."

Meanwhile, Hollinger had set his sights on the nearest bar stool. With luck, he would reach it without throwing up. He had no idea how he'd arrived on the street outside the pub, but the fact that he *was* here had given him an idea.

Mustering a weak smile, he nodded at the man behind the bar. "I'd like to speak with the manager, please."

"That's me, Mr. Hollinger. It's good to see you again."

"This is actually my first visit. But I understand you've met George Hastings, the man I hired to impersonate me occasionally and whom I intend to fire for getting sloppy drunk in your establishment Wednesday evening."

O'Meara looked puzzled. "That wasn't you that came in the other night?"

"No, it was my disgruntled employee, drinking and bitching about how cruel the world has been to him." Hit by a wave of nausea, Hollinger gripped the edge of the bar with both hands to avoid falling off his perch. When he could once more trust his voice, he added, "I understand he set off a brawl as well. Embarrassing."

"Yes, it was. If you don't mind my saying so, Mr. Hollinger, you look like you oughta be in bed."

"As a matter of fact, that's where I've been for the past several days. Then I heard about what happened here and decided I had to come and tell you… I take full responsibility for what happened to your bar. I want you to send me a bill for whatever it costs you to… put things back the way they were. And you can add a few thousand as compensation for the business you lost as a result. Fair enough?"

O'Meara was grinning from ear to ear. "Thanks, Mr. Hollinger. That's very generous of you."

"Do you want me to call you a cab, sir?" Gunther asked.

Hollinger thought furiously. Whatever had brought him here was no doubt more than capable of returning him to Sophie's apartment, unseen. But would it do that? If Claire was right and Demonai was orchestrating everything, and if

Demonai was a trickster, as she claimed… Too many ifs. They were overheating Hollinger's brain.

He swallowed hard as another wave of nausea rippled through him. "No, thanks, I've got a ride already waiting." Mentally crossing his fingers, he slid off the bar stool and made his unsteady way back onto the street.

As he walked away from the bar, the sick feeling gradually subsided. Hollinger made a couple of quick right turns, then paused to get his bearings in the entrance to an alley. Now what? He could take a cab back to Sophie's building, but by the time he arrived there, someone was bound to have discovered that he was missing. And in any case, he couldn't simply walk in through the front door. Maybe it would be best all around if he—

In mid-thought, he blinked… and found himself lying on a hard floor, staring up at the underside of something round and shiny. A toilet bowl.

There was a pounding noise. It went through his skull like a spike. "Hey, Ja—George! Are you okay in there?" It was Boehm's voice.

"Yeah, I just—I think I passed out," Hollinger replied, pulling himself to his feet and untwisting the lock.

The door swung inward.

"Man, you look terrible," Boehm remarked. He took Hollinger by the arm and helped him to a seat in the living room.

The thugs had been untied. One of them was talking on a cell phone. He spun and gave Hollinger an appraising stare. "Yeah, this George guy is looking under the weather too," he said into his phone. "Probably caught the bug from his boss. Sorry—his ex-boss."

"I've been fired?" Hollinger said, feeling genuine misery. "Perfect."

The thug concluded his call, then announced, "Okay, folks, you're all off the hook. The real Hollinger just left the Ha'penny, and nobody can be in two places at the same time. And Augie says that since the rich guy is picking up the tab for repairs to the bar, you should ask him to pay for a replacement sofa as well."

"Thanks, I'll do that," Sophie said, opening the apartment door and standing beside it with her head tilted toward the hallway.

Her body language sent a message that Bruno and Dougie received loud and clear.

Once they were gone, she closed the door with exaggerated care. Then she turned to face the group and demanded tightly, "Was he right? Are you infectious, Mr. Hastings?"

Hollinger buried his face in his hands. Oh, what a tangled web this was becoming!

"He had extra-spicy chili for lunch," Claire piped up. "It's probably just indigestion. But I think I'd better get him home."

"Good idea," said Boehm. "Take him to his own place. I can bring his things by later on today."

They were talking about him in the third person, as if he weren't even there. Damn! He was back in his own body and *still* had no control over it!

Hollinger forced himself to stand up straight. He recomposed his features and informed them in as firm a voice as he could muster, "I appreciate your concern, but you needn't bother. I'm perfectly capable of seeing myself home, thanks."

Claire gave him a narrow look. "At least let me walk you to the elevator," she said.

"We just want you to arrive safely, George," Boehm added. "You're not yourself right now."

Hollinger levelled a dark look at the scientist's face. "On the contrary. I'm more myself now than I've been for the past several days." Sparing a glance at Sophie's sagging sofa, he added, "Ms. Hopper, when you've replaced that, send Hollinger the bill."

"And he'll pay it?" she said, both eyebrows raised in

disbelief.

"He's worth millions, and he'll want all this to go away, so, yeah, he'll pay it," he assured her on his way out the door.

"Sophie, I'm sorry. He's not usually that rude," said Claire, preparing to follow him. "He's just having a really rough day. He'll be in a better mood once he's had a chance to rest in his own bed."

"No, I won't," he grumbled once they were out in the hall and walking.

"Yes, you will."

"No."

"Yes!"

He smacked his palm against the elevator call button, then wheeled to face her. "This is more than indigestion, Claire."

"You think I don't know that?" she scolded him quietly. "There's only one way you could have travelled to the Ha'penny and back in less than a minute: Demonai must have moved you around. Just from looking at you, I can imagine how terrifying that must have been. But it's over now."

"Is it really? What guarantee do we have that this force or entity won't decide to play with us again? How are we supposed to live our lives with *that* hanging over us?"

"It's been hanging over us since the day we were born," she told him. "We're just aware of it now, and we have to find a way to get past it if we're going to move forward."

"Get past it?" he echoed leadenly. "And how do you suggest we do that?"

The elevator door slid aside. She followed him into the car. As he pressed the button for the ground floor, she replied, "We each have to find our own way, James. I'm moving back to Caverley Corners. I realized that you were right about me. I'm not cut out to live in a big city. And after the turmoil of the last few days, I've decided that I deserve to be happy. Garry has found Sophie. She's already making him happy.

And you—"

"Are you really putting your pain on the same level as mine?" he demanded, parroting her earlier challenge back to her in a steely voice.

Her chin came up as she visibly chose her words. Finally, she said, "You deserve to be happy too. Listen, our three lives are joined in a way we can't fully explain and no one else can possibly understand. So, I want you to promise me something."

"What?" he growled as the door slid open again and they stepped out, into the lobby of the apartment building.

"No matter what else happens from now on, no matter how our paths may diverge, we have to stay in touch with one another. I'm going to phone you and Garry once a week, just to make sure you're all right. Garry's going to phone you too. And if you're not all right, if you need to talk about something, then I want you to phone one of us. Or email us. Promise you won't make me come into the city to check up on you in person, James Hollinger. Because I will. I'll crash right into one of your board meetings to find you, if necessary. That's how much this connection we have means to me. And it's my promise to you."

Her eyes were shining. "And one more thing. You know deep down that Roxanne is the key to your happiness. Promise me that you'll at least try to talk to her. Say it!"

Grudgingly, he repeated, "I'll try."

Any control he'd thought he had over his life had been an illusion. He realized that now. Hollinger stared into the face of this woman who had literally walked in his shoes, who was young enough to be his daughter but was much stronger and wiser right now than he might ever be again. The moment felt incomplete, but he was at a loss for what more could be said.

At last, he murmured, "Goodbye, Claire." Then he turned and walked out onto the street.

In the Fifth Dimension

*S*o *they are capable of deception,* said Olla'set. *Other life forms on this world practise it as well, and without any assistance from you, I might add.*

I realize that, Aggregator. I had a much different proof in mind.

Demonai selected his spot and implanted a sense pod. Tillah and Olla'set did the same.

What is this place, Demonai? Olla'set demanded.

Threedees come here to amuse themselves, Aggregator.

Then where are they? All I see are transportation devices, lined up in rows.

Demonai, observe! said Tillah, sparking with excitement. *On that two-dimensional surface. Aren't those...?*

...two-dimensional creatures that the threedees have made, he confirmed. *Threedees come together in their transportation devices so they can take pleasure in observing the activities of their creations. There are other gathering places as well, inside shelters, where threedees without transportation devices can go.*

Doesn't this prove Demonai's theory, Aggregator? Aggregator?

Very interesting, remarked Olla'set. *These twodees appear to be indestructible. After disaggregation they are able to reaggregate themselves and continue their activity. And some of them are very strangely made.*

Have you seen enough, Aggregator?

Not yet, Tillah. Be patient. I wish to observe Wile E. Coyote and Roadrunner some more.

Eventually, Olla'set declared, *These twodees are definitely not intelligent. They keep performing the same activities over and over, without deviation.*

Much as we did, before this five-dimensional bubble was placed in our way, Tillah remarked.

Demonai noted the nuance in her communication and was pleased.

And the threedees, Aggregator? Demonai wanted to know. *Are you finally convinced?*

As reluctant as I am to relinquish an object that has afforded me so much pleasure, I am forced to agree with you, Demonai. I'm not sure why the Universe chose them to receive such a gift, but I cannot deny the evidence. The threedees are fully intelligent. The bubble is yours to dispose of.

Mine to study, Aggregator. Yours and Tillah's to share and enjoy with me. After all, we're gods now. We can't just abandon the beings under our protection.

We can only be gods if we are worshipped, Olla'set pointed out. *I see little evidence of that in the so-called modern threedee world. And who exactly are we supposed to be protecting?*

Patience, Aggregator. Like all self-actuated beings, the threedees have choices. And so do we. We can protect whatever and whomever we want. And they will worship us in their own ways as well.

Chapter Twenty-Nine

"Calamity Jane has been busy since Wednesday," Ellie remarked as Marty set his coffee down and took the seat across from her at their table on the patio of Lazy Susan's Bistro. When they no longer had to text each other to confirm the date and time of their meetings there, it would officially qualify as their haunt.

"So has the laundromat, I would imagine," he said. "Especially if any of the dryers are lighting up. What about Jerry?"

"Jane messaged me that she found him in the closet when she got home. Not dead, thank goodness! He was curled up in the fetal position and whimpering. And his underwear was a mess. My guess is that it took Tillah longer to find his house than it took Olla'set to find my grandfather's, and whatever was in the in-between frightened Jerry out of his mind. He's never going to bully anyone again. Of course, he may never work again either. That's a different problem. But at least Jane is out from under his thumb and getting the support she needs to live her own life."

"And is she posting all over social media about her encounter with a real live god?"

Ellie swallowed her mouthful of hot chocolate. "Oh, yes! Proselytizing with great enthusiasm. The trolls are having a field day with this. I've managed to keep our accounts free of them so far. And the *Demonaimania* group membership is growing, not by the leaps and bounds I'd hoped for, but still steadily."

"So, you were right—we are just the tip of the iceberg?"

She responded with a shrug. "Time will tell, I guess. Meanwhile, classes resume in a month, and that's going to cut into my availability to moderate our various pages. I'm thinking I'll need an assistant. Maybe I'll find one this Wednesday."

"What's happening on Wednesday?"

Her cheeks dimpled. "In response to the many online requests I've received, we're having our first prayer meeting at the laundromat. I've already cleared it with the building's owner. No alcohol allowed, but there will be fruit juice and cookies. And each attendee has been instructed to bring at least one unique piece of clothing, to be washed and dried as part of the ceremony. No underwear, unless it's really distinctive. People need to be able to reclaim their own items once the dryer cycle is over."

Marty chuckled.

"What?" she asked.

"I'm just wondering who's going to write the book about this."

"I'm sure someone will. Meanwhile, every shared encounter is being recorded on the wiki."

He frowned. Al Gerber was worse than a troll. He was Marty's personal nemesis. And if he ever found out—! "Including what happened to us?" Breck said warily.

"Don't worry, all names have been changed to protect the anonymity of the sharers. It's understood that jobs and reputations are on the line. At least until more of the iceberg has been exposed. Once the existence of Demonai and his kind becomes common knowledge, it won't matter. So, will you be attending on Wednesday?"

"Someone should be there to protect you in case another angry spouse shows up, I guess, so, yes. And afterward, maybe you and I could go somewhere quiet, have a dessert and coffee, and just talk…? I've known you for months, and yet I don't really feel that I know you. You know?" He screwed his features into a quizzical expression. "Did that even make sense?"

Ellie laughed. "It took the words right out of my mouth, Detective Breck."

It was 10:30 p.m. The door opened on the third knock.

"Please, I know it's late, but I didn't know where else we could go."

The shelter worker standing in the lighted doorway glanced down at the little girl. No more than five or six years old, she was clutching a well-loved doll with one hand and her mother's sleeve with the other.

"You're in the right place," the worker told them. "Come in, quickly."

"We have nothing," the woman continued, tears in her voice as she stepped over the threshold. "I'm sorry. I should have packed a suitcase, but—I really thought he'd changed. Then, this evening—"

In the hallway, the shelter worker took a closer look at the woman's face. There was a fresh bruise on her cheek, and her chin was streaked with blood from a split lip.

"He just went crazy. There wasn't time for me to do more than grab Shelley and run. If he hadn't tripped over that ball and fallen on the stairs while chasing us, we wouldn't have gotten away at all."

"He tripped over a ball?" the shelter worker repeated.

"Yes. One of those ones with the LED inside to make it light up. I'm not sure whose it was. Maybe one of the neighbour kids brought it over."

"That ball seems to get around," said the shelter worker under her breath. In a normal voice, she assured the woman, "Well, you're safe here. We have a room where you and

Shelley can sleep tonight. Tomorrow we'll take care of the rest."

"It's going to be all right, Mommy," piped up the little girl. "Just like my dolly said."

The shelter worker got down on one knee, putting her face at the child's eye level. "That's your dolly? She's very pretty. And she can talk?"

"Her mouth doesn't move, but I hear her sometimes when I'm by myself."

"Shelley hasn't let that doll out of her sight since her grandmother gave it to her last Christmas," the woman explained.

"I see," said the shelter worker, still kneeling. Then, speaking to the child, she asked, "And what's your dolly's name, sweetheart?"

"Tillah. She's my sidekick."

Born and raised in Toronto, Arlene F. Marks found her storytelling muse at the age of 6, and she has been writing and sharing her imaginative tales ever since. She is also a retired educator and veteran teacher of the craft, having authored two literacy programs for the classroom, as well as *From First Word to Last: The Craft of Writing Popular Fiction*. During her life, she has worked as everything from a travel agent to a fashion consultant. However, her first love and current obsession is writing speculative fiction. She is the author of *Sic Transit Terra*, an ongoing series of sf novels set around the turn of the 25th century. *Adventures in Godhood* is her first Brain Lag release. Arlene lives with her husband on the shore of beautiful Nottawasaga Bay. She spends an inordinate amount of time following her characters around the universes in her mind, but she can be lured away from them by dark chocolate… and interesting owls to add to her collection.

www.thewritersnest.ca